"Besides, Blackwell, you should never be too busy to laugh... It's good for the soul."

"Thank you, Doctor," Violet said with exaggerated gratitude. "That is so insightful. How much do I owe you for this session?"

McCoy said, "You know, I have always appreciated your quick wit. You're fun to spar with. Even when you're being annoying and bossy."

"You mean, even when I'm doing my job?"

"Sure." He winked. "That, too."

She laughed again. Violet felt more hard feelings melting away. Was it possible that she'd read this guy all wrong?

"I should have known...since you're pretty, why wouldn't your laugh be pretty, too?"

Pretty? What...? Was he flirting with her? No, no way. He'd said it too casually, too bluntly. There was no pretense or innuendo. Just stating his opinion. He was honest, kind and genuine, and she had to admit that she was beginning to see what everyone else saw. And felt.

Also, she liked it, too.

Dear Reader,

Here we are again! Yay! Thank you to everyone who has reached out to ask when my next book will be out. I'm so thrilled that it's finally here *and* even more excited that it's once again part of a multiauthor series with my favorite writing pals. *And* that this series is another Blackwell adventure. *And* to make this experience even better for me, *A Cowgirl Finds Home* features my personal all-time favorite trope: enemies to lovers.

For me, there's nothing more fun to read than bickering that turns to banter that turns to affectionate teasing while the hero and heroine are both intrigued and mystified by what's happening. Before they ever suspect such a thing is possible, they're falling in love. Turns out, it's super fun to write, too.

I loved Violet and Garrett from the first moment I put them on the page. Hope you do, too.

Happy reading!

Carol Ross

A COWGIRL FINDS HOME

CAROL ROSS

Harlequin

HEARTWARMING

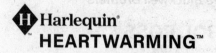
Harlequin®
HEARTWARMING™

Recycling programs for this product may not exist in your area.

ISBN-13: 978-1-335-05117-2

A Cowgirl Finds Home

Copyright © 2024 by Carol Ross

For questions and comments about the quality of this book, please contact us at CustomerService@Harlequin.com.

TM and ® are trademarks of Harlequin Enterprises ULC.

Harlequin Enterprises ULC
22 Adelaide St. West, 41st Floor
Toronto, Ontario M5H 4E3, Canada
www.Harlequin.com

Printed in Lithuania

MIX
Paper | Supporting responsible forestry
FSC® C021394

Carol Ross lives in the Pacific Northwest and is a graduate of Washington State University. When not writing, or thinking about writing, she enjoys reading, running, hiking, skiing and traveling. Carol can be contacted at carolrossauthor.com and via Facebook at Facebook.com/carolrossauthor.

Books by Carol Ross

Harlequin Heartwarming

Return of the Blackwell Brothers

The Rancher's Twins

Seasons of Alaska

Mountains Apart
A Case for Forgiveness
If Not for a Bee
A Family Like Hannah's
Bachelor Remedy
In the Doctor's Arms
Catching Mr. Right
The Secret Santa Project

The Blackwell Sisters

Montana Match

The Blackwells of Eagle Springs

Wyoming Rodeo Rescue

Visit the Author Profile page
at Harlequin.com for more titles.

Amy, Anna, Cari, Mel & Kathryn

You ladies make my writing life easier
and my real life better.

I couldn't ask for better friends or colleagues.

Thank you!

PROLOGUE

"ONE DOWN, four to go." Elias Blackwell liked the sound of his own words, as he often did. After eighty-six years, he'd earned the right to appreciate the wisdom he'd acquired, although this bank of insight and knowledge was not due solely to his age. Life had taught him a lot of hard lessons. Thankfully, Big E, as he was more commonly known, was, if not always a quick learner, then certainly a determined one. At least where his family was concerned.

It was that determination that had him embarking on this, yet another road trip, one with a specific purpose: to see his sister Denny's grandchildren, who were his great-nieces, reconciled and reunited.

"Well," Denny said, gently gliding in her rocking chair on the covered porch of her farmhouse in Eagle Springs, Wyoming. "It's no secret that I had doubts about this scheme of yours. Getting the Belles back together seemed impossible, and now it feels…" She trailed off, searching for a word. Pausing to sip her coffee, she then added, "I don't know, but it sure would be something to see my granddaughters riding together again."

Her granddaughters—J.R., Iris, Maggie, Violet and Willow—used to perform in a trick-riding troupe called the Blackwell Belles. The group was started by the girls' mother, Flora, and her late sister, Dandelion. Twelve years ago, the Belles had disbanded under adverse and unfortunate circumstances that left the family fractured. Flora was key, Big E believed, in bringing the girls back together. Luckily, she had her own motive for seeing her family mended: a Blackwell Belles reunion performance.

"Yes, it will be something special, all right," Big E agreed confidently. "We're on the way to helping it happen. You have to admit, I was right about Maggie."

Maggie was the "one down" he'd referenced earlier. He, Denny and Flora had already logged a successful visit with her. Sure, there were still some details to finalize where her performance was concerned, but he had faith it would be all sorted out in the end. They'd left a happy-for-now Maggie with her fiancé, Clem, in Clementine, Oklahoma, and then dropped off Flora at the airport. After traveling in Big E's motor home to and from Clementine, he and Denny had arrived back at Denny's ranch, the Silver Spur, a few days prior and were enjoying a well-earned bout of relaxation.

This morning, the late August sun was slowly waking, stretching graceful rays above a brushy stand of trees. The heat of the day had yet to join in, and the breeze felt fresh and balmy. Birds chirped lazily in the distance as if they, too, were enjoying the morning respite. As peaceful as it was, Big E knew he couldn't dawdle much longer. He needed to get on the road toward his next destination: Flame, Texas, a suburb outside of Dallas where Violet lived and where Flora had recently relocated, too.

Time was of the essence. In several short months, Flora and Dandelion were being inducted into the Cowgirl Hall of Fame. An honor of the highest order, as far as Big E was concerned, and one that Flora should celebrate with her daughters. Unfortunately, after the Belles' breakup, the girls had scattered like seeds on a wayward Wyoming wind. Flora wanted to make things better, but she'd waited so long—too long, maybe—to right some of the wrongs. If anyone could sympathize with her plight, it was Big E. He'd worked hard to repair relationships with his own grandchildren, all ten of them.

This would be his second go-around with a batch of Denny's grandchildren, too. The first group, right here in Eagle Springs, had been a resounding success.

All of this experience boosted his confidence,

even if this particular situation felt tougher than the last ones. He not only had to get the girls speaking to each other again, they needed to speak to their mother, too, and then all perform together. Not to mention they were in various states of preparedness where their riding skills were concerned. But J.R., Iris, Magnolia, Violet and Willow were Blackwells, and if he could help, he would.

"Isn't that what I just said?" Denny answered in the typical cranky tone she used with him.

Big E chuffed out a laugh. "Not exactly."

"Fine. All in all, it's gone remarkably well. Maggie was a tough nut. It feels like a good start."

"I'll drink to that," he said and lifted his plastic cup in a toast.

"I have to hand it to you, brother. You are a first-class meddler."

"Thank you kindly," he agreed, taking it for the compliment he believed it to be. There was a fine line between meddling and helping where family was concerned. The line, he'd learned, was rather fluid, too, depending on the circumstances and the family member in question.

Denny sipped from her cup and then added, "Maggie and Clem falling in love helped things along."

"We got lucky there," Big E said and raised his glass again. "To Maggie and Clem and bucking bulls." Maggie and Clem both worked as rodeo barrelmen. An ornery bull had brought them together, and another ornery bull had ensured they stayed together. Tough cookies, both of them, and with a love story worthy of the Blackwell family archives.

"Speaking of the latter, you don't seem overly concerned about getting that bull from Violet."

On the contrary, he *was* concerned about that. Maggie had agreed to perform in the Blackwell Belles reunion performance only if her sister Violet gave her Ferdinand, the family's pet bull. In her youth, Maggie and Ferdinand had been nearly inseparable. All of the girls adored him. Ferdinand had performed with the Belles often. But when the group broke up, Violet, instead of Maggie, had been the one to take him. From Big E's perspective, it had been a good decision, as Maggie's nomadic lifestyle had never been conducive to caring for her own livestock, especially a bull. Until now, that was. Maggie was finally ready to settle down. She and Clem were buying a ranch, getting married, making a home, becoming a family. In Maggie's mind, Ferdinand needed to be part of that.

From what he'd learned about Violet, she would not take Maggie's request lightly. She cherished that animal; she and Ferdinand had been constant companions for twelve years now. They were bonded. But Violet and Maggie were bonded, too. They were twins, for Pete's sake! He was certain that bond was stronger. In fact, he was banking on it.

Reassuring himself, he said, "What you're forgetting is that Violet and Maggie are twins."

Denny looked skyward and huffed. "How could I forget that my own grandchildren are twins?" Impatient sarcasm oozed from every word, which only made him smile. "I also gave birth to twins, Barlow and Hudson. You remember your nephews, right?" Barlow was Flora's husband and the girls' father.

"Of course I do," he said and then chuckled as she continued to scowl at him. She wouldn't be his sister if she wasn't uppity with him about something. "I didn't mean you literally forgot. I meant that I learned that sweet Violet and I have a very important trait in common."

He'd gotten to know Violet a bit, as she and Maggie had been the only two of the sisters to attend the Blackwell family reunion last month here in Eagle Springs. The fact that Violet had shown up for the gathering despite their family strife suggested that she might have regrets and longings of her own. Big E's gentle interrogation had proved this theory: Violet missed her sisters.

Denny nodded. "I hope you're right."

"I am. Violet is a Blackwell in all the important ways."

That made his sister smile, and his heart went soft with love. They'd spent many years estranged themselves. It felt good to have this sibling relationship again. It was what he wanted for the girls, too.

"I am sorry," she said, "that I have to leave you on your own with this one." Denny was going to remain here in Eagle Springs because her grandson Levi and his wife, Summer, were expecting a baby any day now.

Big E smiled gently and shook his head. "Don't you worry. It won't be the first time I've gone solo at navigating a complicated Blackwell conflict."

Denny barked out a laugh. "Is that your way of telling me you can meddle just fine on your own?"

"I won't be alone. Flora will be there. Besides, it's Violet who will be the star of this show. Violet and her sidekick Ferdinand."

CHAPTER ONE

"VIOLET!" BAILEY QUINN rasped out her name on a throaty pitch of whispered urgency, slipping into Violet Blackwell's office and gently clicking the door shut behind her. "Good, you're here."

Where else would she be, Violet silently pondered, at 8:42 a.m. on a Friday? "Hey, Bailey, what's up?" she muttered, barely sparing a glance at her friend and coworker before directing her attention back to her phone, where she was busy analyzing a text from her boss, Trent McCoy:

Cancel today's presentation.

Why would he cancel the presentation? No explanation had been given, which was why she was still staring at the screen. Waiting, assuming one would be forthcoming, or at least further instructions clueing her in on how to rearrange his day.

As executive assistant to Trent McCoy, owner and CEO of McCoy Oilfield Services, setting his schedule was not a simple task. It was a complicated time-management equation. And changing just one thing, no matter how small, never meant changing just that one thing. There was a domino effect, the repercussions of which were often colossal, and also Violet's responsibility to manage.

Trent hadn't been in the office when she'd arrived this morning, although that wasn't unusual. She was almost always the first person here, but he was usually a close second. They often used the time to pore over his schedule, prioritize and prep for whatever needed the most immediate attention that day. McCoy Oilfield Services employed hundreds of people, although most of them worked off-site at refineries, drill sites or offshore oil platforms, where they serviced machinery and equipment necessary for the extraction and refining of oil. Trent's time was in high demand, and their morning strategy sessions were essential in maintaining the extreme level of efficiency the company required.

Violet rather enjoyed these mornings, too, sipping coffee and admiring the stunning view of the East Texas skyline from his spacious office suite on the top floor of his high-rise at 331 Carbine Street in Flame, Texas, known informally as McCoy Tower. The building was the tallest in Flame, a modern metropolitan boomtown located thirty miles from Dallas, close enough to enjoy the conveniences of the big city and yet far enough to escape many of its aggravations.

She'd spent countless hours preparing for today's meeting with Hoyt-Carson Refinery, gathering the data, assembling graphics and then figuring out the complicated software in order to compile it all. No way would he cancel this presentation without a very, very good reason. She hoped he was feeling okay.

Violet looked up to discover Bailey remained by the door, where she was now peeking between the narrow gap at the edge of the window where it met the blinds. "What are you doing?"

"Shh. Watching. Hold on…" After a dramatic pause, she announced, "He's here!"

"Who are we talking about now?" Violet asked. At least once a week, she similarly entered Violet's office, usually to dish about her latest love interest or share bits of gossip. The spying suggested the former might be in play this morning. "Has your reconnaissance detected the arrival of our boss, by any chance?"

"Yes, or at least I saw him in the lobby, too. Meanwhile, I'm trying to figure out how to approach *him*. Actually, I was hoping you could help me since you probably know him better than anyone."

Violet missed the pronoun emphasis, so focused was she on the news of Trent's arrival. "Does he look okay?"

"Okay?" she scoffed. "He looks a whole lot better than that."

"Oh, good." Violet blew out a relieved sigh. "He canceled something, um, special today, so I was worried he wasn't feeling well."

"Trust me, he looks very, *very* well and…" Bailey spun around to face her. "Hold up. He canceled something *special*? Are you dating him?"

"What? No! Bailey, I didn't mean that kind of special. I meant *important*. I don't know why I said *special*." Pressing three fingers of one hand to her temple, she inhaled deeply because she did know why she'd said it; she was tired from staying up half the night putting the presentation together.

Violet revered Trent McCoy, respected him, adored him even. He was not only the best boss she'd ever had, he was the best man she knew. But solely in a father-figure sense. Even if she were interested in that way, she would never date her boss. Not to mention that Trent had recently struck up a romance with someone else.

"Okay, good, because he—"

"My mom is dating him," she revealed, saying it aloud for the first time.

"Your mom?" Bailey sounded incredulous. Moving away from the window, she dropped into the chair facing Violet's desk. "Why have you not mentioned this?"

"Yep." She answered the first question and thought about the second. Probably because she still couldn't quite believe it herself. But her mother dating her boss wasn't even the most astonishing part. No, the real shocker was that Flora claimed she was settling permanently here in Flame. Violet had never thought her rambling nomad of a mother would ever settle anywhere. A gifted equestrian, she'd spent most of her life traveling and performing. For much of it, she'd dragged her family along.

Until age twenty, Violet, along with her mother, four sisters and aunt, had been members of a trick-riding troupe called the Blackwell Belles. Her childhood was basically an indistinguishable blur of rodeos, fairs, talent shows, parties, TV appearances and various other gigs. Looking back, she had mixed feelings about the experience. Being the weak link—the "least talented," as her mother used to say—she'd been relieved when the group had disbanded.

What she regretted was the cause, and especially the aftermath, which had left her family splintered, damaged and fraught with resentments. Like so many other show-business families, the life had taken a heavy toll on her and each of her four sisters. It hadn't been easy on their dad, Barlow, either. Violet completely understood why he'd felt driven to this current extreme.

Six months ago, Flora had shown up at Violet's and informed her that Barlow had secured a legal separation and intended to file for divorce. Instead of lamenting and wasting time, Flora declared that she was ready to "start a new chapter." Initially, Violet didn't believe her. Her mom had started "new chapters" in the past and never made it past the first page or two. Violet had to admit that this time felt different. Flora had rented an apartment and gotten a job teaching riding lessons on a nearby horse ranch.

"Wow." Bailey leaned back in her chair and gave her head a little shake. "When…?"

"They've been dating for a few months."

"That's…astonishing."

"Imagine how I feel." That statement was strictly rhetorical because Violet felt great about it. Starting over would be best for both her parents. Was there a part of her that acknowledged how a relationship between her boss and her mother could be good for her, too? Yes, of course. She couldn't *not* think about that. If she could handpick a man to be her stepfather, it would be Trent McCoy. She wouldn't allow herself to imagine what might happen if it ended badly.

"I can't! I have no frame of reference. My mother is a mean-spirited frump. Your mom is gorgeous and talented and vivacious and…and…a superstar. Basically, I want to be her when I grow up."

"She hasn't grown up," Violet countered. Trent already seemed to be a good influence on her in that area.

"Precisely! How cool is that?"

Not cool at all, Violet wanted to say. Not when you were the daughter of a mother who valued fame above family and her precious horses above *anything* else, even her husband. The only surprise to her was that Barlow hadn't left years ago. Her sisters had all jumped ship when the show fell apart.

"Jealous is what I am," Bailey added.

"Why would you be jealous? Aren't you still dating Dale from Accounting?"

"What? No! Dale and I broke up last week. I told you, remember? He wanted me to go to that *culty* relationship retreat with his parents for the weekend, and I've never even met them." She jerked her thumb at the glass. "I've got my sights set on that cowboy oilman. The younger guy."

"Right." Violet nodded. But… "Wait…"

That cowboy oilman? A *younger* one? Trent was not younger than her mother, nor was he much of a cowboy, aside from his recent purchase of the "hobby ranch" where he didn't even live but where Violet was currently residing and caretaking. Which meant…

Please, no. She did not have time for this—*him*—right now.

"Bailey, are you talking about—"

A chirp from her phone alerted her that she'd finally received the long-awaited response from Trent. Hovering one finger above the screen, she hesitated because where she'd previously been looking forward to the message, now she feared it. The suspected reason behind Trent's canceling and his lateness, and Bailey's window-gazing and scattered attention span, had her on high alert. Because once she read the message, which would undoubtedly contain some outlandish request being made of her, her life would then be cast into a suspended state of upheaval for an unspecified but always too-long duration. Then again, if she was correct, she didn't have time to waste, did she? Not if she wanted to keep the impending overtime hours to a manageable level.

Heart galloping, palms sweating, she willed herself to get a grip. Her job was the one place in her life where fear was not allowed. Fear caused inaction. Fear resulted in disappointment and abandoned dreams. She forced herself to tap the screen and read:

Call Darius and Adam and make sure they're free, and then get us a tee time for 4 this afternoon. Reserve a table for 4 at Jameson for dinner tonight. I've heard they're booked way out, so you might have to call Jamie and see if he can squeeze us in. Do you know where to buy something called tibbits or tabbies or some similar name to that? Please research, and then get as much as you can.

The door to her office swung open, and Adam, head of Marketing and one of the people she was supposed to call about this impromptu round of golf, bounded inside.

"Hey, Violet, do you have a sec?"

Taking in the scene behind him, she noted how the normally industrious staff was milling around, chatting, coffee cups in hand. What should have been the familiar restrained tone of a productive morning was instead rife with animated conversation and laughter. Most were munching on what looked like… Yes, pastries. Flaky, buttery French-inspired works of culinary art, not to be confused with your everyday run-of-the-mill doughnut. Her focus veered toward a table drawn to the stack of bright pink bakery boxes where the distinctive black logo of the Fern Patisserie proved her observation. Her stomach dropped as evidence mounted. Only one person ever purchased such expensive treats for the entire office.

"Yes, Adam, I do have a sec, but I need to—"

He was bouncing on his feet like an excited child, and she didn't have a chance to ask if he was free for golf because he interrupted, "Do you know where the cornhole beanbags are?"

"Cornhole," Violet repeated flatly, conclusively.

"Woo-hoo!" Adam roared and punched the air. "Annual tournament time! Phoebe is going to need one of those giant pieces of paperboard to make a bracket. Do we still have some in the supply closet?"

Violet inhaled deeply, holding the air in her lungs while she took a mental inventory: Trent had cleared his schedule for golf, the office was all atwitter, pastries were being consumed, corn-hole was not only being played but elevated to a level of competitive juvenility normally only witnessed in middle-school PE class. She was receiving cryptic requests and being burdened with peculiar tasks. A knot of tension squeezed her chest so tightly it ached.

Her exhalation was audible, her nerves already taut. She did not need any further clues pointing to the unpleasant but obvious conclusion now before her.

Garrett McCoy was back.

GARRETT MCCOY STRODE through the maze of offices, conference rooms, hallways and workspaces that comprised McCoy Oilfield Services, greeting old friends and making new, the pastry box in his hands sweetening the task. Amazing, the goodwill a fancy French doughnut and a compliment could bank. By the time he'd finished the route, he had firm commitments for karaoke, poker night and more than enough players for the annual company-wide cornhole tournament.

While he was genuinely happy to reacquaint himself with the employees of McCoy Oilfield Services, he tried not to cringe at the sights, sounds and especially the smells bombarding his senses. Give him a freshly fertilized field or the sulfur-laced scents of an oil refinery any day over the harsh and unnatural mix of chemicals in an office building. Despite McCoy Tower's state-of-the-art heating and cooling system, the odors of pungent cleaning products, cheap cologne, flowery air fresheners and stale leftovers mingled—and lingered. His stomach rolled as he entered the break room. Silently, he decreed that microwave popcorn should be outlawed solely for the overpowering stench it left behind. Tossing the now-empty pastry box, he checked the time, decided his uncle should be settled in by now and headed for his office.

Planting a smile on his face, he paused outside the door long enough to mutter a reminder under his breath: "It's only a few weeks." And because this particular job was local, there was the bonus of spending time with Uncle Trent and his buddies Adam and Darius, who were both employees here at McCoy Oilfield's corporate base.

Knowing he was expected, he stepped inside without knocking and was surprised to find the space empty. The adjoining door stood open, though, and he could hear voices. He recognized Adam's excited tone and paused, hoping to catch the deeper tenor of his uncle. Seconds later, the outer door clicked shut, leaving only two muted female tones, one of which he recognized immediately as his uncle's perfect and perfectly annoying assistant: *Buzzkill*.

Aka *Violent Buzzkill*, aka *Bossy Blackwell*, whose given name, Violet Blackwell, seemed much too appealing for someone so utterly disagreeable. Garrett refused to use it, opting aloud for *Ms. Blackwell* or *Blackwell*, depending on the circumstances and her degree of testiness. *Buzzkill* he kept to himself.

Currently, she was droning on about something, something undoubtedly boring and pointless. As his good mood dissipated on the spot, he marveled at how the nickname had never felt so apt. The urge to attempt a quiet retreat was nearly irresistible, but the fear of being discovered kept him immobile.

Undoubtedly, she'd already been hard at work for hours upon hours. Possibly, she'd been here all night. Heck, maybe she lived here. Like one of those odd people occasionally featured on the news who clandestinely lived at their place of work for years, only to be discovered after they'd perished at their desk one night. In the morning, the staff realized there was no one to call. The personnel file then revealed all; the last known address was the Laundromat down the block, and the next of kin turned out to be the stray cat she'd fed on the fire escape outside her office. Over-the-top? Maybe, but only slightly, because from his observation and that of his friends who regularly worked with Buzzkill, the woman did nothing but work.

On a personal level, she seemed to enjoy throwing roadblocks up on any street that might possibly lead to fun and just generally making his time at McCoy difficult. Normally, he did his best to reciprocate, and often, he secretly admitted, enjoyed doing so.

But not today.

This morning, he wasn't in the mood to engage. He was exhausted from working insane hours wrangling cattle on the Wyeth Junction Ranch, where he'd most recently been employed, and then driving all night. Leaving Nikki and Remi intensified his anxiety. Added to the disappointment of falling short yet again, of even having to be here for another high-pressure job, another gig working for someone else, even if it was his uncle, had left his emotions raw. Uncle Trent was going to ask questions about him, about Nikki and about his future plans. Questions that he didn't want to answer.

He needed to resign himself to the circumstances and prepare for the long, stressful days ahead. Get his game face on. Could he slip out of here without Buzzkill hearing him? He knew his uncle's security system was state-of-the-art. Surely there weren't cameras in *his* office, though, were there? An image of Buzzkill popped into his mind, seated primly at her desk, smugly watching him right now on her monitor while he stood here like a wild-eyed doofus, not knowing what to do next. Paranoid? Possibly, but also plausible because somehow, some way, she seemed to know everything that went on around here.

He listened as the women exchanged a few more comments. Then the door opened and clicked shut again. He remained frozen. Silence settled into the space; relief seeped into him slowly. As the seconds ticked by, the only sounds were the occasional *click-click* of a mouse interspersed with a printer's *whir-hum*. Finally, like a wary cat burglar, he padded toward the far corner of the room where two cushy club chairs were arranged and where, hopefully, he could hole up out of her sight line until his uncle arrived.

He was almost there when…

"Oh!" a voice called out, startling him and dashing his clandestine dreams. "You." She clipped out the word and followed it up with a huffy sound of disgust, like *"uhhckk."*

The sound had him grinning because it was so unprofessional, so unguarded, so un-Buzzkill-like. Clearly, he'd been correct, and she hadn't expected to find him here. The best part was the look on her face, pure and unadulterated disappointment. Good, he thought, now unable to resist gleaning a speck of entertainment out of the encounter.

"Yes, me," he confirmed, fanning the fingers of one hand and planting them on his chest. "Garrett," he reminded her, even though he knew that she knew very well who he was. "Garrett McCoy. Trent's nephew."

"Yes," she returned with her own special tone

of cool condescension and a flash of disdain in her brown eyes. "I know who you are."

"Well, it's been a while," he returned casually. "Thought you might need a reminder."

"Four months is *not* that long," she fired back.

Delighted with how she'd set him up so beautifully, he said, "Four months, huh? How many days? And did you note the seconds, too, or just hours? You *knowwww*," he gushed with fake affection while planting his hands on his hips, "if you missed me that much, you could have reached out. Invited me to lunch."

She executed an expert-level eye roll. "Don't flatter yourself."

Shrugging lightly, he said, "Hey, you're the one keeping track of the time between my visits."

"It's my job."

"It's your job to keep tabs on me? My uncle is not paying you enough."

"Since I'm the one who puts you on the payroll, I can't help but be *aware* of the time it's been since you last worked a job for McCoy Oilfield Services."

"Hmm," he said, crossing his arms over his chest. "Yeah, well, I'm *aware*, too."

Frowning, she narrowed her eyes as she pinned her gaze on him, her expression a mix of disgust and curiosity. But she remained silent, undoubtedly waiting for him to counter with whatever sarcastic follow-up he had in the queue. And he couldn't blame her because what did that even mean, *he was aware*? Unfortunately, he had…nothing. He'd just spouted off nonsense. He really was off his game. More evidence of the fact that he wasn't quite prepared to spar with the wily Blackwell. As he struggled to come up with something, his gaze wandered—along with his focus.

The shape of her unsmiling mouth was both familiar and unpleasant. It dawned on him then that, in the three-plus years he'd known her, he'd never heard her laugh. He wondered what that would sound like. A rusty buzz saw, he imagined, neglected and out of practice.

She shifted from one foot to the other, drawing his attention downward. On her feet were strappy sandals, and her toenails were painted bright pink. Pink. Huh. How…pretty. As if she'd decided to add a bit of frosting to her otherwise drab, dry cake of an outfit.

The charcoal-gray skirt flowed over her hips and ended just above her knees to reveal tan, toned legs. How had he never noticed how nice her legs were? Probably because he'd never seen this much of them before. And now he couldn't help but note how her buttoned-up blush-pink blouse complemented her complexion. Weird how an outfit so clearly designed to *not* be sexy kind of was. Not that *she* was sexy. Yeesh, no! But maybe she… Did she try not to be attractive?

Or was it just that he'd always found her boring and prudish, which to him equaled unattractive?

"Of what?" she finally asked, her snappish tone reminding him of her true nature and his true feelings.

"What?" he repeated, a little dazed by the direction his thoughts had taken about a woman he didn't like. Evidently, he'd been away from the city for too long if a bit of banter and a glimpse of Blackwell's knees had him thinking...thoughts.

She huffed out a short, impatient sigh. "You said you were aware of something, too. What are you aware of?"

Unfortunately, only one word came to mind, and even more regrettable was the fact that he said it out loud.

CHAPTER TWO

"You," McCoy said, his gaze snapping back up to meet hers, dark brown eyes flickering with... Who knew with this guy? Something snarky, no doubt. Violet felt a prickle of irritation skitter up her spine.

"Me, what?" she repeated, not caring how her tone was edging into brittle territory as she braced for whatever "joke" was coming. The thing was, though, she didn't have the time or patience for Garrett McCoy's antics today. And especially not his insults.

"Yes, you. You're, um..."

"Never mind," she said, swiping one hand through the air, batting away his mumblings like an annoying pest. "You'll have to save your witty riposte for later. I'm extra busy this morning." *Which is your fault*, she silently added, knowing he was either too dense to notice or too callous to care. It didn't matter; neither excuse added anything to his appeal. "Besides, I'm sure you'd prefer to have an audience for your usual stand-up routine."

"Wow." His head tipped back as if she'd smacked him.

Uh-oh, she thought, *here it comes...* Thankfully, McCoy's visits, much like a swarm of locusts—dreaded and devastating—were also short-lived.

When his only response appeared to be a goofy, clownish grin, she amended, "I stand corrected. Apparently, you are your own best audience."

"Ha ha!" he belted out and then added, in this over-the-top tone of surprise as if he couldn't quite believe his ears, "That's *funny*!"

Gah. So annoying and so completely Garrett McCoy to be stunned that someone besides His Majesty the Cowboy Prince of McCoy Oil could crack wise. At the same time, she had to clamp down hard on the urge to enjoy the compliment, which only irritated her further.

Setting her features on distaste, she sighed and pivoted. "Whatever," she tossed over her shoulder. "I'll come back after you're gone."

"Wait! I need to ask you something."

"Fine," she said, but when she faced him again, he was looking in the direction of her feet. Thank goodness, she'd just gotten a pedicure. She followed his gaze, which then lifted, meeting hers briefly before drifting toward the windows. He was seemingly preoccupied with the view, one hand going up to his neck, adjusting his collar as if it were too tight. But it was a T-shirt, so how could it be? What was *wrong* with this guy? She waited impatiently while he scratched his neck and then scrubbed a hand across his cheek and chin.

"What is it?" she finally barked, anticipation sharpening her tone.

"Oh, uh…" Barely making eye contact, he muttered, "Is, uh, 8:30 a.m. okay for your first match?"

"My *match*?" She accompanied the baffling question with small, short shakes of her head. "What match?"

"Cornhole," he stated with a confident nod. "I took the liberty of adding you to the tournament bracket."

"Are you kidding me? That's what you wanted to talk to me about? Cornhole?" she asked, eyeing him carefully. Was he…lying? Why wouldn't he look at her? He *was* lying. *Why* was he lying?

"Yeah," he said with way, way too much conviction. "Everyone wants you to play." One shoulder went up to form an innocent shrug. But Garrett McCoy had never been innocent a day in his life. His demeanor was almost comical. If she didn't know better, she'd think he was nervous. But she did know better; this man and nervous did not commingle.

"No, they don't, it is *not* okay, and you know it. You've never asked me to play before."

"Well, I don't really *ask*. I don't have to—people sign up. Most people *want* to play. It's a great way to get to know your fellow employees, to build—"

"I know them fine," she interrupted.

"Hmm." Lips pursed, expression packed with doubt, he slowly let his head loll to one side. "Do you, though?"

"What is that supposed to mean?"

"Don't go getting all uptight on me now." He grinned, a wolfish, satisfied, baring-of-the-teeth kind of grin, which suggested he knew things that she did not. She hated it when he did that.

"Then stop being ridiculous."

"Uptight!" He popped off the word. "There it is! You know, that's your problem. You're so—"

"Yeah, I heard you the first two times," she interrupted calmly, in direct opposition to the angry pounding of her pulse. "And if *uptight* means efficient, conscientious and committed to my job, then sure, yes, I'll proudly wear that title. You should try being a little *uptight* yourself every now and then. It would certainly make my life easier, and your uncle's, too, for that matter."

Ha. Despite his relaxed posture and smirky face, she could see that got to him. There was this tightness around his jaw as he clenched his teeth. It gave him away every time.

Gaze narrowing in on her again, he nodded. "I was going to say that you are…" He trailed off with a shake of his head. "You know what? Never mind. I'm trying to help you. Or I was, but that would be pointless."

This time, she had no problem resisting the

urge to ask him to finish his thought because she knew it wouldn't be good. Instead, she dialed her expression to dubious and scoffed. "*You're* trying to help *me*? That's a good one."

"Yes! I am. I go out of my way to help people and be nice. Surely, you've noticed that about me, at least."

Not me, you don't.

"Including you," he added, like a freakish sideshow mind reader. "Occasionally, anyway. Like today."

Squinty-eyed, she peered at him. "What is this?" she asked, raising one hand and twirling a pointy finger in a circular motion at the level of his chest. "What are you up to?"

"I'm not up to anything!" The accompanying half-hearted guffaw was the opposite of convincing.

"You want me to make a fool of myself, is that it?"

"Wait. Are you scared to play?" He didn't give her a chance to respond because he went on in this condescending way that reminded her too much of her previous life and consequently made her want to slug him. "Hey, I get it. Trying new things is scary. You've probably never competed in front of a bunch of people, right? But it's okay if you're no good. You are good at a lot of other things, right? It's just for fun. Harley from Engineering plays every tournament, and I don't think he's ever won a match."

Two insults in record time. Uptight and cowardly. It would be difficult to decide which one bothered her the most. Infuriating how he always managed to home in on the insecurities she worked the hardest to hide. At least his assumption was inaccurate.

Head shaking, she looked him over. "You think I don't want to play cornhole because I'm afraid?"

"Why else?"

"I can think of about fifty reasons, but I'll just go with the first couple—it's a waste of company time and a waste of my time."

The open-mouthed, wide-eyed shock was purposely over-the-top. "Is that really what you think?"

She gave him a slow blink and an even slower response, one that she hoped sounded condescending, too. *"Yesss, I dooo..."*

"It's not, though."

With an exaggerated, staccato-style tone, she asked, "If you are playing cornhole, you are *not* working, are you?"

"In a way, yes," he answered. "If you—"

Palms up and out, she interrupted, "Stop. Is there something wrong with you? Like physically? There's a strange virus going around where people are getting dehydrated and dizzy. Two days ago, right in the middle of a marketing presentation, Edwin told everyone his dog could play the piano, and then he barked out the first few bars of 'The Entertainer' before collapsing. You seem very *Edwin* right now."

With a heavy sigh, he looked out the window for a few long seconds, then surprised her with a genuine-sounding confession: "I am a bit off this morning." He raked a hand through his dark brown hair. "Too off to do this with you anymore. Honestly, I'm exhausted. You make my brain hurt."

"Oh" was all she said, completely caught off guard. She didn't trust that he was sincere. Now *she* felt off. "I'm… Is there—"

"Violet!" Trent's booming voice coincided with the opening of his office door. "Here you are! Sorry I'm late."

A bizarre mix of relief, gratitude and disappointment flooded through her at the interruption. Had she really been about to ask if there was anything she could do? Engaging with McCoy on any sort of personal level was not a good idea. And yet she was curious. She'd never seen McCoy *off*. What could have happened in his perfectly charmed life to throw him off-balance?

"And here's my most favored kin, too!" Trent embraced him with a bear hug and a slap on the back. "Like I conjured the two people I most wanted to see this morning right here in my office."

Even though he was only slightly above average in height, with his broad shoulders and thick, muscled chest, Trent McCoy took up an inordinate amount of square footage in a room. But it was more than his size because the man's intelli-

gence, wit and natural charisma captivated whatever audience awaited inside. The star of every
show, Trent's aura just shimmered brighter than
everyone else's, as if a spotlight was perpetually
trained on him. It was a trait his nephew had inherited, she grudgingly and top-secretly admitted.
Too bad he hadn't inherited his uncle's goodness,
too. The superhero and his evil nephew.

The men made small talk, allowing her to re-
charge her wits. As usual, she couldn't help but
compare their striking physical resemblance. While
Garrett was a few inches taller and more leanly
muscled, they shared the same inky-black hair and
warmth to their complexions.

Same shape to their dark brown eyes, too, but
with a slight variation in color. Trent's were a
lighter chestnut shade of brown, and his expressive gaze contained depth, contemplation and consideration, while Garrett's darker, umber-colored
stare suggested pretty much the opposite. Not
much of substance going on up there. Too busy
brewing jokes.

If there was such a thing as a prodigal nephew,
Garrett McCoy was it. In Trent's eyes, the man
could do no wrong. At McCoy Oilfield Services,
he was nothing short of a celebrity. Literally. The
last time he'd worked a job for McCoy, he'd rolled
into town—late—on the day the job started. Most
of the staff had been gathered one floor below in
the large conference room for a required safety

training session. Seventeen minutes into the presentation, he'd arrived.

It was like a scene from an old Western where the handsome, incorrigible, gunslinging hero strolls into the saloon. The double doors swung open with a loud clang. Heads turned. Silence fell. The subsequent collective gasp was audible and followed by a rousing cheer. Ridiculous. It wasn't Violet's imagination or an exaggeration. Bailey had witnessed it, too. They'd discussed it over drinks that evening.

Everyone wanted to be his friend. Most of the single women were smitten. He pretty much had everyone eating out of his hand. Everyone except her, of course. To her, he dished out mockery and scorn with a side of cold contempt.

As always, that fact landed hard, settling right in the center of her chest. She wouldn't say it hurt exactly, but it was certainly uncomfortable. What had she ever done to deserve his dislike? Why did it bother her? Because he got what Violet wanted, the respect and adoration of their coworkers, *her* coworkers, without earning it? Maybe. Partly, she acknowledged, but she certainly didn't want to distract everyone from actually working the way that McCoy did, did she now? No, she did not. This place would fall apart if she joked her way into the office every day, handing out toys and treats. Besides, the only person she truly cared about pleasing was Trent. And the frustrating truth of the matter was that Garrett McCoy pleased Trent simply by existing.

The problem for her was that he breezed into town whenever he felt like it and then proceeded to wreak absolute havoc on her job. Her life. It was *Violet* who suffered from *his* presence. Each and every time, her world was turned upside down as Trent canceled meetings and appointments and delayed important work matters to golf or play poker or "hang out." Meanwhile, Violet scrambled around, apologizing, rescheduling, reshuffling, working late and doing whatever was necessary to hold everything together.

And, again, no one noticed! No. One. Cared.

They were all too busy trying to get a piece of Garrett McCoy.

Cornhole, *pfft*. He thought she was afraid to compete in front of people? She could juggle flaming torches, and once upon a time, she'd done so from the back of a horse. Tossing a beanbag at a piece of painted plywood was child's play compared. Her entire childhood had been about performing and bringing her A game, especially with four talented, competitive sisters, a superstar aunt and a Hollywood-style mother who demanded nothing less than perfection. It wasn't the audience that bothered her. She hadn't enjoyed it because *she* wasn't perfect, but she'd done it. She should participate in his stupid tournament—no, she should *win*, just to show him. She would—

"Violet?"

"Hmm?" Looking up, she was surprised to discover Trent now settled behind his desk. Focused on her, his expression was a mix of curiosity and eagerness. An amused-looking McCoy was watching her, too, from where he now lounged in a nearby chair, long legs stretched out, work-booted feet crossed at the ankles.

"You okay?"

"Yes! Absolutely."

"I was just asking how you did with that tee time."

"Of course, um…" With a quick shake of her head, she shifted into work mode. "One-thirty tee time."

"Ha!" Trent slapped a palm on the desktop and grinned at McCoy. "What'd I tell ya? There's nothing Violet can't do. Dinner?" he asked somewhat less enthusiastically, and she knew that he knew how much of a long shot that request had been.

"Reservation for seven o'clock," she answered, *not* beaming with pride or bothering to relay the extent of finagling that had been necessary to secure the table. Not by speaking to Jamie, the owner, as he'd suggested, but by calling the manager, Dex, who was friendly with the head bartender, Carlos, who happened to be a friend of hers.

Favors had been exchanged, including a donation basket to Dex's daughter's soccer team's fundraising dinner and the purchase of four tickets for the event. The tee time had been slightly easier to secure, as Trent was a member of the private country club where the ladies' golf pro, Julia, had a serious crush on him. All Violet had to do was mention how frustrated Trent was with the slice he'd recently developed with his driving iron and how he wished he could swing a club like Julia.

"Don't you worry," Julia had told her. "We'll squeeze him in while I'm working. I'll take a look at that swing and get him straightened out, pun intended, ha ha."

Surprisingly, the "tibbits or tabbies" he'd requested had been the most challenging. She'd had absolutely no clue. An internet search had only left her more confounded. Out of some sort of inspired desperation, she'd texted her mom, whose simple reply—You mean Tiddly, the whiskey?—had solved the mystery.

Turned out, Tiddly was one of those expensive, small-batch whiskeys popular these days. After another internet search and several calls, she'd finally found a store that both carried the drink and had it in stock. But it was, in the clerk's words, "flying off the shelf." She'd purchased their entire inventory of five bottles, shipment slated to be delivered via courier by 10:30 a.m.

"Your other request is on the way," she said cagily in case it was a gift for McCoy. Not that it mattered. With Trent, she treated everything as confidential.

He beamed, brown eyes twinkling with pleasure. "Thank you, Violet, as usual, for your miracle-working."

"No problem, boss," she replied casually, even as the compliment warmed her. From the side, she could feel McCoy's gaze boring into her. She wondered what he was thinking even as she silently willed him not to voice whatever wisecrack was cooking.

"I moved your lunch meeting to eleven at Octavius," she continued before he could ask. She didn't need to add that Octavius was also closer to the golf club. "It's with Perry, so you should easily be finished by 12:30. Your afternoon is cleared, so you can leave from there. Golf clubs are already in your car. I've rescheduled Adam's appointments, and Darius is also good to go. I'm going to finish up the paperwork that's due to Webber, so you won't need to come back to the office before dinner."

Again, all of this meant more work for Violet, as she would now be spending the bulk of her day answering Trent's calls and completing as many of his tasks as she could, in addition to her own work. The good news was that these endeavors would also take Garrett out of the office. That revelation cheered her considerably because even though the refinery maintenance job was local, it would be starting in ten days, and the hours were long. That meant she'd only have to put up with him hanging around the office for a week. With careful planning, avoiding him would be relatively simple.

"Fantastic. Thank you, Violet."

"No problem. Have fun. Don't worry about a thing," she reassured him. "I'll see you in the morning."

"Uh, no…" Trent drawled, confusion creasing his brow. "I mean, yes, but I'll see you tonight first."

"Oh. Are you and Mom stopping by the ranch?"

A year ago, Trent had purchased a property, Penny Bottom Ranch, as an investment. He'd invited Violet to live there in exchange for taking care of the house and helping with the livestock. Not only did it save her money in rent and utilities, but she no longer had to pay to board Ferdinand. The bull had worked hard for the Belles, too, and deserved to retire in style. Not to mention he was the one consistent link she still had to her twin sister, Maggie. Yes, twelve years later, Maggie was still upset with her over the situation, but what choice did she have then? Someone had to take him, someone with the means, space and time to accommodate such a large animal. Now he was her one constant loyal companion.

"Didn't your mother tell you? Or Garrett?" he asked, once again looking in that direction.

"Tell me what?" Violet followed the movement

until her gaze connected with McCoy's. As usual, his sardonic air revealed nothing. Nothing, that was, except for his apparent amusement at witnessing her discomfort.

Grinning like a goofy chimpanzee, he gave her one of those *whattaya-gonna-do* shrugs.

"About dinner!" Trent said, his enthusiasm stirring up her uneasiness. "Tonight, at Jameson. The reservation is for us."

"I'm, um, I'm s-sorry," she stuttered. "Us?"

"Yes! The four of us. Your mother, me, you *and…*" As if the emergent enthusiasm in his tone wasn't enough, he swept a hand toward his nephew, grandly introducing the utmost supreme of all dinner companions ever to grace the universe. "Garrett."

CHAPTER THREE

G<small>ARRETT GLANCED TOWARD</small> the adjoining room where Blackwell had scurried like her hair was on fire, shutting the door behind her with an audible click. He couldn't really blame her, because now that he'd put two and two together, he wasn't exactly thrilled with the circumstances either. When his uncle had invited him out to dinner to meet his "new girlfriend," he knew things were serious with this Flora person, but he'd been unaware of the family connection.

Flora was Buzzkill's mother? He tried to process this news.

Trent dated. He dated a lot. Much more than Garrett. But he rarely talked about his relationships, preferring to keep them casual. A self-proclaimed perennial bachelor, he'd never gone out of his way to introduce Garrett to anyone. With Flora, he'd done both, which was how Garrett knew this one was special. But he'd never mentioned her last name or the relationship. Then again, why would he?

"Uncle Trent, you're dating Buzz-um…" Catching himself with a fake cough into his elbow, he pointed in the general direction of Blackwell's inner sanctum. Their earlier confrontation had left him even more out of sorts than he'd already been. Maddening how superior and patronizing she could be, how she acted as if she were the only person at McCoy Oilfield Services who worked for a living. And now this, this, this… personal connection between her and his uncle?

"Her, you, you're…" He paused and then managed to form a sentence. "You are dating your assistant's mother?"

Trent frowned. "You didn't know Flora was Violet's mom?"

"No."

"Huh," he said. "I guess I assumed that you two would talk. You're always talking to her."

"What? No, I'm not. And we don't *talk*. We *interact*." That sounded weird. *Need to clarify.* "We communicate about work stuff. To be honest, I didn't really know she talked about anything else or talked to anyone else. Except for Bailey from HR, whom I suspect she's only friends with so she can keep tabs on everyone."

Brow knitted, Trent looked him over for a few long seconds before flattening his mouth into a tight line. "Really?"

"Really. The woman is…uptight." Garrett shifted in his chair, realizing that he was fidgeting under his uncle's perusal. "Uncle Trent, you have to know this. Everyone thinks so."

"Hmm. Everyone? Not me. I don't think so. Neither does her mother."

"Well, okay, maybe not everyone. But perhaps you know her better than most people who work here."

"Maybe," he conceded. "She's almost like a...a daughter, although I've never had one of those, so how could I really know? But she's the one I'd want if I could choose. Violet is the best assistant—in fact, she's the best *employee*—I've ever had. Hands down. If even ten percent of my employees worked as hard as her, I'd be a very rich man." He belted out a loud guffaw before amending, "A very richer man."

"That, I believe." The display he'd just witnessed hinted at the lengths she'd go to please her boss. Was all of that scrambling and busywork normal for an assistant? It wasn't the first time he'd wondered, but it was maybe the first time he'd cared. Okay, maybe *care* was too strong a word, but he was curious.

"You're going to love Flora."

He thought for a second and then answered diplomatically, "I'm sure I will if you do."

"I think I do, Garrett." Trent sat back in his chair, a dreamy look drifting across his face. "It's the craziest thing. I haven't known her that long, but I think I'm..." He trailed off with a shrug and

a smitten look. "For the first time in my life…
I've never felt this way before."

Wow, Garrett thought, and then said it, too,
"Wow." Because it was all he could manage to
say. His uncle was in love? This was also a first.

"Yeah, I know, and as soon as her divorce is
final, I'm going to tell her."

The statement hit him like a freight train. "Wait—
what? She's married?" Concern settled in his gut
like a cold stone. "Uncle Trent, do you think it's
wise to date the *married* mother of…" Anyone?
Garrett couldn't think of a single case where it
would be okay to date anyone who was married.
Surely, they existed, but he couldn't land on one
at the moment because this was his uncle, the man
who was like a father to him.

"Legally separated," Trent explained before adding, "It's a simple matter of dividing assets and
agreeing on terms. From what I garner, they don't
have much in the way of assets. Mostly horses,
most of which Flora insists she'll have to keep,
and that buyout probably won't be cheap. Other
than that, it should be fairly simple. I've hired her
an attorney."

No assets? And did he just imply that he was
going to help her with this "buyout"? What was
happening here?

"You've hired her an attorney? That's very generous."

"Well, she can't afford one on her own—not

the best, anyway. And Flora deserves the best, Garrett. She's glamorous and talented and smart and sophisticated. She's an exceptional woman."

"I see." But he didn't. He didn't see at all; suddenly, he had a million questions.

"Working on getting her moved to a nicer place, too. Right now, she's living in a dump of a duplex outside of town, close to Bisbee's place, where she's working, so the location is nice, but the apartment is subpar—and that's being generous. I'd like her to move out on the ranch with Violet, but she won't hear of it."

"What ranch?" he asked. Buzzkill had mentioned them stopping by "the ranch," but that hadn't meant anything to him either.

"Violet is living out at Penny Bottom Ranch—didn't I tell you that?"

"Nope." Yep, Garrett had been gone way too long, and their phone conversations had been much too brief. He was officially out of the loop. To be fair, when he was ranching, he didn't have much time or patience for his cell phone. "I didn't know you were renting the ranch out."

"I'm not. She's house-sitting. Well, livestock-sitting, I guess you'd call it. In exchange for rent, she takes care of the house and the horses and keeps an eye on the cattle. Can't wait for you to see this place! I have plans…"

Trent went on, but Garrett was too busy reeling to truly listen; his uncle had hired an attorney for his married girlfriend, whose daughter was living rent-free on his ranch. Words of warning flashed through his mind ticker-tape style—*desperate divorcée, greed, exploitation, manipulation.*

He had no idea how to address any of these concerns. It was his uncle's money, his uncle's ranch, his uncle's girlfriend and not his business. On the other hand, just because Garrett refused to accept any money from Trent didn't mean others wouldn't try to manipulate it out of him. The welfare of the animals was another cause for concern. Was Blackwell even qualified to care for a herd of cattle? Sure, she was a stellar corporate assistant, but what did she know about livestock? At some point, he was going to have to drive out there and take a look.

In the meantime, he needed to learn about Flora. Too bad he and Blackwell weren't on friendlier terms. And he'd just made things weirder with that cornhole-tournament fabrication and the ensuing *altercation*, for lack of a better word. All because she'd painted her toenails, gotten a tan and worn a skirt. He really needed to get some rest.

"Let's get the business stuff out of the way," Trent said, shifting gears. "We'll circle back to the ranch in a minute."

"Works for me," Garrett said, meaning it; he needed time to process all of this and figure out a game plan.

"First of all, I can't tell you how glad I am to have you on this job, Garrett."

"Thanks, Uncle Trent." The compliment earned a genuine smile despite the circumstances. "As usual, I appreciate you hiring me on such short notice."

One of the many great things about Trent was how he didn't feel the need to state the obvious. The fact that Garrett was here, signed on for another stint with McCoy Oilfield Services, said it all—he needed money. Trent wasn't about to rub it in how he'd warned Garrett this would happen, that he'd be back on the payroll sooner or later. But who else was going to help Nikki?

"How is your sister and the baby?" Trent asked, the question inevitable under the circumstances. Technically, Nikki was Garrett's stepsister, but he didn't think of her that way. Their parents had married when he was eight, his brother, Cade, was six and Nikki was two. The three of them had grown up as siblings; two brothers and their baby sister, whom they spoiled and adored.

Only when they were much older did they realize sibling bonds didn't always hold fast, especially without the ties of marriage. Garrett was thirteen when their parents divorced. He and Cade remained with their mom, Bree. The brothers were dismayed when Emmett, Nikki's dad, took her to live with him.

"Live" turned out to be a generous term. Emmett

rode the rodeo circuit while Nikki bounced around from one relative to the next. On his off time, he drank and gambled away what little he earned as a mediocre bull rider. When Nikki turned sixteen, she ran away and moved in with Garrett. Sure, she'd brought a bit of trouble with her, but it had been normal teenage stuff. Mostly. A couple of brushes with the law had helped get her on track.

Garrett was proud of the way she was turning things around, because it wasn't just Nikki anymore. Now she had Remi, his niece, a baby girl who needed food, diapers and a roof over her head, none of which Alex, her father, was stepping up to provide. Alex, who was also his former best friend, and not the man Garrett had always believed him to be. Disappointment didn't even begin to cover his feelings.

"She's good. They're both doing well."

"Glad to hear it. Appreciate you showing up a few days early, too, to help with orientation. Badging always goes so much smoother when you're on a job. You'll see it reflected in your paycheck."

"Badging" was a term often used for the pre-job orientation process. Oil refineries were huge compounds comprising several hundred acres. There was a lot to know. Typically, this was a two-to-three-day ordeal of lectures and training sessions on everything from equipment operation to safety protocol and evacuation procedures. The dispatch paperwork entailed filling out form after form, which for most employees felt repetitive and tedious. One of the final steps involved getting your picture identification card or "badge," the item that granted access to refinery property.

For a group of highly skilled men and women who thrived in a fast-paced work environment involving heavy equipment, specialized machinery, welding and other challenging tasks, the mountain of paperwork was hands down the most unpopular. Over the years, Garrett had developed some creative ways of team building that not only made the ordeal more tolerable but also allowed employees to get to know each other before the long, physically taxing hours of the job officially began, the cornhole tournament being one of the more popular examples. In his experience, people who were friendly with each other worked better together.

"I appreciate that."

"Someone, probably from HR, will be helping you. I'm just not sure who yet. We are woefully short of employees these days, not to mention qualified team leaders."

"No problem," Garrett said. "We'll figure it out. I can work with anyone. You know that."

Trent leaned forward, threaded his fingers and placed his forearms on the desktop. Catching Garrett's gaze, he held it, his own expression grave. "I hope you mean that, son."

"Of course I do," he answered, hoping he did, because he could see his uncle was about to reveal something he wouldn't like.

Trent sighed. "I hired Alex Bauer for this job, too. Before I hired you. He'll be foreman, and because I hired him first and he's clocked more oilfield hours than you, he'll be the senior employee."

Garrett hoped his uncle couldn't see the pulse of anger pounding in his temple. With Nikki and Remi already on his mind, the mention of Alex's name was enough to make his blood boil. So much history, and so much bad blood between him and his former best friend.

"Uncle Trent, I don't think I can—"

Trent raised a hand to stop him. "I know you don't want to work with him, and I don't blame you. And I know I said I wouldn't hire him again after things went south with him and Nikki. But, if you think about it, your paths will barely cross. You're in charge of different crews, assigned to different parts of the plant. He'll just make any final logistical decisions regarding the overall operations. Look at it this way—it'll save you a pile of paperwork."

Garrett knew that where Alex was concerned, none of that would matter. He'd go out of his way to make Garrett's life difficult and then cover his tracks. He was good at that. Look at what he'd done to Nikki. But what choice did he have? He needed the payday. In a bitter twist of irony, it was Alex's daughter who needed it most.

When he'd learned Nikki was pregnant, Alex had ghosted her, refusing to speak to her or even acknowledge his paternity. When he hadn't shown up for Remi's arrival in the world, Nikki refused to put his name on the birth certificate. Garrett's ongoing pleas to pursue legal action regarding child support were met with stubborn refusal.

"How's the ranching proposition?"

Garrett knew this was Trent's way of asking, without words, how the property search was going.

"Getting closer," Garrett said, which was true only in the most literal sense. His savings account had roughly two hundred dollars more than it'd had the last time he'd worked a job for McCoy Oilfield Services. They both knew that if he wasn't supporting Nikki and Remi, he'd already have a ranch of his own. It was difficult to make dreams come true when someone else's reality kept rearing its ugly head. Well, in this case, the head was pretty dang cute. He adored his niece, and he'd continue to support her in any way he could, even if that meant working with Alex.

"How close?"

"Maybe two years," Garrett said, knowing in his gut that was optimistic. Two more years before he could afford his own place, and even then, it would take years to build it to what he wanted.

Trent brought the tips of his fingers together,

forming a steeple beneath his chin, and then nodded his head thoughtfully. "How would you like to get a whole lot closer, a whole lot faster?"

"Uncle Trent, I can't take—"

Trent waved him off. "I'm not offering you money, Garrett. Well, not in the sense that you're thinking I am."

Garrett couldn't help but chuckle. This was a game they played. His uncle offered him a loan; he refused. After a certain, unspecified amount of time, they did it all over again. It was no secret that Trent's dream was for Garrett to take over McCoy Oilfield Services one day. Garrett's dream was to own his own ranch. Trent couldn't understand why Garrett would choose a lifestyle over financial security and kept trying to steer him toward the light.

"You're the only family I have that I can count on, son. You know that."

"I feel the same way, Uncle Trent, which is why I can't accept money from you." Garrett knew what it was like to be the family member everyone came to when they needed something. He refused to have that kind of relationship with the only person in his family who didn't ask *him* for anything.

"I understand that, and I respect you for it. I always have, but this is different. This is an opportunity, an investment of your time and skills."

With a setup like that, he couldn't help but feel flattered—and intrigued. "I'm listening."

"It's also…"

Trent paused, looking uncertain, nervous even. A sense of foreboding settled over Garrett, because his uncle was rarely either of those things. Something was up. Was this the circling back to Flora Blackwell that he'd mentioned?

"Uncle Trent, what is it? It's also what?"

"A favor, Garrett. I need a favor."

VIOLET PAUSED OUTSIDE the door of the currently commandeered conference room and felt anger heat her blood. A sign on the door read Stop! Tournament in Play. Intermittent *thumps* could be heard, followed by triumphant cheers and disappointed groans.

"Give me a break," she muttered under her breath.

Exasperating how these people could so easily abandon their jobs. The tournament hadn't even started yet. This was company time! Granted, many of them were refinery employees like McCoy who weren't technically on the clock yet. But they certainly could be using this time to study the new safety regulations or review the changes to their health insurance plans. And judging from the fact that many, *many* of the office staff were currently not at their desks, there was plenty of graft going on, too.

Still, Violet hesitated. Maybe it could wait? She knew the interruption wouldn't be popular. But it had to be done. The stack of new per diem forms and the thick policy booklets she held were a heavy reminder. Each employee absolutely had to fill out the new form before they could be paid their increased stipend. She'd advocated this increase on their behalf. They'd thank her later, right? Yes, of course they would. Or not. It didn't matter because it had been the right thing to do.

Ultimately, that was what propelled her forward through the double doors. A surge of nervous adrenaline accompanied the shove, causing the heavy doors to clang loudly when they met their respective walls.

All action halted.

"Dang it!" someone shouted.

"Ha!" Darius declared. "Game over. Stick a fork in Howie! He's *doooone.*"

"Come on!" Howie Renfield gestured toward Violet. "She broke the rules by entering the field of play while a throw is in motion. Do-over." He scowled at her. "Could you have shoved those doors any harder, by the way? I expected a herd of buffalo to come charging through."

A chorus of chuckles and snickers prompted Violet to look around the room, now cordoned into three long cornhole rows or courts or lanes, or whatever you called them. Every head was turned in her direction, smirks dominating the sea of faces.

"Sorry," she said flatly, not sorry at all. "I have the new per diem forms and the—"

"Seriously? You interrupted us for more *homework*?"

Groans and grumbling broke out.

"Do you sit around inventing new ways to torment us?" a different voice asked from deeper in the crowd. Laughter followed.

"Yeah, what's next? A test on how to buckle our seat belts?"

"Hey, now!" McCoy stepped forward. "I'm sure Ms. Blackwell would only interrupt for a matter of utmost importance. Right?" Catching her gaze, he seemed intent on holding it, but she didn't see the warning until it was too late. He added, "These people have already filled out mounds of paperwork. We all know we're facing *days* of orientation and training, and we're—"

"Playing," she interrupted. "Yes, I can see that. But no one is going to get—"

A buzzing sound broke out, breaking her concentration. Soon, the entire room sounded like a swarm of bees. Puzzled but careful not to react, she looked around.

"Hey!" Garrett held up a hand. "Hey, guys, let's not, huh?"

"Give it up, McCoy," another voice called out.

"It's only a matter of time before she hears the nickname you gave her."

Nickname? A sick feeling churned her stomach. Violet didn't dare respond or even acknowledge that she'd heard the comment. Undoubtedly, Bailey would have heard this nickname by now. She could ask her, although she wasn't sure she even wanted to know.

Stepping forward, she placed the bundle on the long side table that was normally reserved for a coffee maker, cups and the requisite assortment of beverage condiments but now held spare beanbags, tournament brackets, bottles of water and a basket of protein bars. Protein bars, seriously? She resisted the urge to roll her eyes.

"I'll just leave these here. Questions can be answered via the book or by emailing me. After you fill them out, you can return them to—"

"It's Buzzkill." It was a gleeful Howie who filled her in. "Violent Buzzkill, to be exact. Get it? Instead of Violet Blackwell. You know, because you kill the mood everywhere you go?"

CHAPTER FOUR

CONSTRUCTED OF AN eclectic mix of new and upcycled materials, Jameson Steakhouse was almost as famous for the modern building it was housed in as it was for its superbly grilled Texas beef. Constructed on a bluff above the scenic Claro River, innovative architecture and creative interior design melded beautifully in the structure. High ceilings were supported with thick, industrial-sized steel beams where exposed pipes and braids of thick cable crossed the span. The warehouse effect was softened by the addition of tall, pastel-colorful stained-glass windows, weathered antique furniture and vines of luscious greenery. Steampunk decor tied it all together.

Violet adored everything about the place and normally spent several minutes appreciating the meld of old and new. This evening, however, she didn't waste even five seconds looking at any of it. She hurried into the crowded foyer and headed straight through toward the bar. While everything about the restaurant felt upscale, the bar, Jamie's, emitted a more laid-back vibe. The casual atmosphere, ice-cold craft beer on tap and a peaceful view of the river valley, all without a loud party crowd, equaled, in her opinion, decompression perfection. Checking her watch revealed that she was twenty minutes early. Perfect. Just enough time to unwind with a drink before this unpleasant dinner put the final touches on a day filled with unpleasantness.

Come to think of it, that should be McCoy's middle name, Unpleasant. If he could dole out nicknames, then so could she.

As anticipated, after the busy day, there'd been no time left to run home and change before dinner. Last week, she'd dropped clothes at the dry cleaner down the block, and thankfully there'd been a dress in the mix suitable for the occasion. She kept basic toiletries at the office, so she'd changed and freshened up there. After a quick call to her neighbors, Jorge and Rebekah, asking them to check on Ferdinand and the rest of the crew, she'd been good to go. Seriously, sometimes it felt like she lived there!

Carlos, the bartender, spotted her almost as soon as she entered the room. He raised a hand in greeting and then pointed, asking without words if she wanted a seat. She nodded, and he waved her over to an empty stool at the end of the bar. Perfect. So focused was she on navigating through the crowd to reach the spot that she didn't even bother checking out the space around it. All she cared about was the fact that she'd finally have a few minutes of peace.

"Hey, Carlos," she said, settling on the seat. "Thanks so much. I'm beat."

"Anything for you, my friend. The usual?"

"Yes, please," she answered, with what was possibly her first genuine smile of the day.

"Will your lady friends be joining you this evening? Do you want me to snag a table?"

Jamie's was the usual Friday night stopover for her, Bailey and a few other friends. Even though Vago was the chosen hangout for most employees, with the Tex-Mex cantina and bar conveniently located on the ground floor of McCoy Tower, Violet found the place too loud, especially the Friday night karaoke.

Through their own Friday night ritual, they'd become acquainted with Carlos, but Violet had secured a special place in his heart when she'd scored an "impossible to get" birthday cake from the trendiest bakery in town for his daughter Lucy's quinceañera.

"No. Actually, I'm meeting my mom and some, um…friends for dinner."

"Ah, very nice. In that case, may I recommend the peppered flank steak," he said. "It's the best Graciela has ever made."

Graciela was Carlos's wife and head chef at Jameson. They'd been married for twelve years, had four kids and, by all appearances, were devoted to each other. Their marriage was both an inspiration and a heartache to Violet. She hadn't had much luck with relationships, although she'd recently had a couple of dates with a guy, and things were going well. Funny, smart and good-looking, at this point, there wasn't anything about him not to like, although she feared that he'd bolt when she inevitably chose work over him one too many times. But maybe, since he worked in the industry, too, he'd understand.

"Yes, thank you. Tell her and Lucy that I said hello."

"You got it," he promised with a wink before heading off to tend to fellow customers at the other end of the bar. She sipped her drink and, bracing herself, did a final check of her phone. Relieved to find nothing pressing from work, she tucked it inside her bag and tried to relax.

That was when a deep, low voice crooned from the stool next to her, "So that means we *are* still friends?" She didn't need to turn her head to know the comment came from McCoy. Seriously? Could this day get any worse? Apparently, it could, because the voice continued, "I can't tell you what a relief that is. I need to—"

"We are not friends, and you know it," she interrupted. "I would never be friends with someone like you. You are a mean-spirited, disrespectful, unprofessional, low-life slacker of a human being. Even so, that was low, even for you. I did not take you for the kind of person who would name-call and backstab. Before today's incident, I respected you for the way you spoke your mind, even if I disagreed with the content. I should have known better. So, let's just get through this dinner, and then we can go our separate ways and never speak again."

For once, the man seemed to have no snappy comeback. She took his silence for acquiescence and sipped her drink.

"I deserve all of that and then some." He shifted on his seat, and Violet could feel him looking at her. She refused to return the favor or acknowledge him in any way. He went on, "I am really, *truly* sorry about this Buzzkill thing. I actually got here early tonight, hoping I could apologize before dinner. I gave you that nickname a long time ago, but I never meant…"

"For me to hear about it?"

"I never meant for *anyone* to hear it except Adam and Darius. It was after my last job here, the one for Peachtree Oil. Do you remember? We were understaffed and barely managed to finish on time, even after working overtime every day for three weeks. But we did it, and on that last day, a bunch of us oilfield guys were out celebrating. We were downstairs at Vago drinking some beer, and you came charging in like you do—like you did today—with your stacks of papers, all pushy and demanding. The last thing any of us wanted to do was more work. I could hear the grumbling from the guys, so I blurted out the joke to them. I do that sometimes. It's my coping mechanism.

"Unfortunately, it was at your expense. It was thoughtless and stupid. Apparently, unbeknownst to me, Hank and Josh overheard and ran with it. It was a total jerk move, and I regret it. Again, my fault, although I admit to referring to you that way sometimes, but only inside my own head."

Huh. It was a good apology. She wouldn't have guessed he had it in him. Earlier, right after the incident, she'd briefly fantasized about slashing his tires or spiking his coffee with a laxative, but the feeling was short-lived. Revenge would just add fuel to the fire. Besides, she wasn't naive. She knew what people thought about her. But she had a job to do. Why couldn't they see that?

She attempted a calming breath, but the effort only resulted in a whiff of deliciousness. *Just great.* Didn't he have enough going for him? McCoy had to smell good, too? Like pine trees and dried cherries, with hints of leather and saddle oil. The man was a cowboy who worked part-time in oil refineries. Logic dictated that he should stink like cow pies and rotten eggs.

She heaved a breath and exhaled, trying to eradicate all the nicely scented particles, reached for her drink and downed about half the contents.

"Hey, now. You might want to whoa up a bit

there. Something tells me we're going to need our wits about us tonight."

"Whoa up?" She repeated the phrase before firmly planting her glass on the bar.

"Yeah, you know—*whoa*—like a horse?"

"I know what *whoa* means." Swiveling her stool, she finally faced him. "You're not actually suggesting that I slow my alcohol consumption, are you?"

"What?" His eyes went wide as he realized how his words had sounded. "No!"

Violet wished she had her phone in hand so she could snap a photo, because the look on his face was priceless.

"Hey, I was just—"

"You were just what?" she prompted. "Insulting me and then telling me what to do?"

"I am so sorry. I was joking. I didn't mean to offend you again. Please, don't—"

"Calm down," she said, turning to face the bar again. "*I* was joking."

"*You* were joking," he repeated, a mixture of disbelief and relief tuning the words.

A young couple, hands entwined, eased up to the bar, and Garrett moved over to the stool next to Violet, graciously offering up his seat for the lovebirds.

"Yeah, just a little payback."

"Huh," he said. "Wow. I had visions of getting sent to HR for a time-out." Head gently shaking, he let out a chuckle.

Wow was right. Violet felt her heart sink. Did she really come across as *that* uptight? So uptight that she'd send him to HR for something like that? Buzzkill. Yeah, that pretty much answered both questions, didn't it? She wanted to correct him, to tell him that she could be fun, too. Make it clear that her work persona and her real-life persona were completely different. But thankfully, she also realized how pathetic that sounded. Like her sister J.R. often said, if you had to point something out about yourself, it probably wasn't true; you just *wished* it was true.

That thought snapped her out of it because J.R. would also ask her why she cared what he thought. She *didn't* care what Garrett McCoy thought about her. Okay, so she cared a little, but only because he was Trent's nephew. Yes, she was confident in her position as his most valuable employee, but also careful. Experience had shown her how tight the bonds of family could be. Not *her* family, of course, but the irritant currently lounging on the stool next to her consistently provided all the proof she needed.

Taking his time, he sipped his beer before gently placing it on a nearby coaster. "So…" he droned, brushing his hands together and looking exactly like the eager miscreant that she knew him to be, "if your mom and my uncle get married, that would make us what? Like stepcousins?"

"Married?" she repeated sharply, turning her

head to look at him. Correction, to scowl at him so she could properly refute the suggestion. "But…" But then her gaze met his, and another *Wow* snagged the words in her throat. Different this time, though, as she realized she'd never been this close to him before. Not like this, with their faces only inches apart and no easy way for her to get some distance.

She'd thought smelling him was disconcerting. But looking felt unsettling, too, because she couldn't help but notice how his brown eyes were every bit as dark in color but so much…warmer than she'd believed. The thick lashes framing them were even blacker than his hair, if that was even possible. Soft lines fanned out from the outside edges of his eyes, attractive ones. Caused by a combination of sun and laughter, she imagined, and the wistful, fleeting thought occurred to her that she could use more of both of those things in her life.

Maybe she was too uptight? But no, she wasn't *uptight*, was she? She was just very…what? Focused? Driven? Determined? She didn't know how to be those things and "fun" at the same time. If she allowed herself to be fun, then everything would fall apart, just like it had all those years ago with the Belles. For a long time after the breakup, she'd been so lost and so…poor. There'd been very little fun in getting to the point where she was now: able to take care of herself, emotionally and financially. And she wasn't about to do anything to mess that up.

"Yes, married." He answered her quasi-question after it became apparent that she wasn't going to add anything. "Are you honestly telling me this possibility hasn't occurred to you?"

"No, it has not." She did sound kind of edgy, didn't she? Did she always sound like that? Shifting her tone, she asked, "What gave you this absurd notion?"

"Why else would they have invited the two of us out for dinner like this?"

"Because we're their family, and a dinner invitation is a nice way to spend time together and express affection?"

Shrugging, he threw up his hands, opened his mouth and closed it again, all in conjunction with a dramatic slow-motion head-shaking. The man should have been an actor.

"Are you serious with this?" he asked.

"Yes! They've only been dating a few months! My parents aren't even divorced yet."

"Uncle Trent says it's a legal separation."

"Yeah, so?" She barked out the confirmation, irrationally resenting how he knew this about her parents, her family, her life. She could only imagine his satisfaction at learning the extent of her family's dysfunction. Or maybe *malfunction* was a better word, because could you be dysfunctional if you didn't even function as a unit at all?

"He's hired an attorney for your mom."

A knot of tension tightened her chest. Understandable, she immediately reassured herself. Even though she believed divorce was best for both her parents, no one *wanted* to see their parents part ways. Further disintegration of the already fractured Blackwell family was imminent, but that didn't mean she was excited about it.

"I assume from your silence that you were not aware?"

"No," she admitted.

"How does that make you feel?"

"How does that make me *feel*?" she repeated derisively. "You don't actually believe I'm going to chat with you about my feelings and my family issues."

"It's my family, too, though, isn't it?" he returned, seemingly unfazed by either her mocking tone or the content.

Silently, grudgingly, she acknowledged that he had a point. Trent had no children of his own, and she knew that Garrett was his favorite relative. She was now officially cranky at the turn of this conversation. She decided she hated when he made sense even more than when he made jokes.

Her answer was a sigh of resignation.

He misread the sound and continued to sell his argument. "You need to look at it from my perspective."

"What perspective is that?"

"The one where my uncle gets his heart broken when the woman he loves reconciles with her husband. I'm not sure if you've noticed, but my uncle is head over heels for your mother."

Violet stared back at him, surprise and fear colliding inside her at that insightful and terrible thought. The surprise part was solely due to the concern and caring the statement revealed. She hadn't realized he was capable of such deep emotion. The fear, well, the fear was more primal and contributed to the earlier notion of the family she once knew fracturing for good. But, she reminded herself, fractures weren't always bad. Sometimes when a thing broke apart, you were left with multiple pieces of something good, right? Like with minerals and rocks and, and, and... Bones? Okay, maybe not so much. Earthquakes could be productive in breaking... Or not. Whatever. She'd puzzle out some excellent examples later when she could think more rationally.

"You're jumping the gun here a bit. It's just dinner." She hated how unsure she sounded.

"Dinner with an announcement," he said with a grin.

"That's pure speculation. There will be no announcement."

"Oh, there's going to be an announcement, all right."

"No, there's not."

"Do you want to make a bet?"

"Yes!"

"Sweet." He leaned back and slapped his palms on the bar. "What do you want to bet?"

She shrugged a shoulder. "Eight million dollars?"

His face erupted with a grin. "I respect that kind of confidence, but I can't in good conscience let you lose that kind of cash. How about this—I win, you play in the cornhole tournament."

"Fine. If I win, you never say the word *cornhole* in my presence again, and if you do, I get to light your hair on fire."

Head shaking, he busted out laughing. "Have you ever bet on anything before? That's not really the way it works, but…" He broke off to chuckle again. "But, okay, you're on. I'll even supply the matches."

"Great," she answered, and why did she suddenly feel like smiling?

"Okay, so I bet Uncle Trent and your mother make an announcement tonight. You bet that no announcement will be forthcoming. Correct?"

Holding up one finger and feeling very clever, she amended, "I bet that they will not be announcing anything of substance this evening whilst the four of us are dining together."

"Whilst?" he teased. "Have we suddenly been transported back in time to the fourteenth century?"

"Vocabulary is important. Distinctions can be subtle."

"Indeed, fine maiden, so 'tis." He lifted a hand, signaling to Carlos. "Barkeep, another round of mead for myself-*eth* and the lady fair. Is that a word, *myself-eth*? Me-self? Me-self-eth-ish?"

Rolling her eyes, she let out an exaggerated sigh. "Just so you know, I'm fond of those strike-anywhere matches. In fact, I'm going to add that to my bet—I get to light the match on your teeth."

"Done!" Still grinning, he thanked Carlos for the drinks as they were delivered. Lifting his glass, he said, "Now, since we're going to be related, I think we should get to know each other better."

"We are not going to be related," she returned, all urge to smile and/or laugh snuffed like a hotly burning candlewick, because he was right about one thing: this whole dinner did feel off. Why hadn't she seen it earlier? She'd briefly wondered about it, considered calling her mom, but then brushed it off because she'd had bigger fish to fry. Like a company to help run.

"How about hobbies? What do you like to do when you're not scurrying around on my uncle's behalf?" The fingers of his left hand fluttered toward her along the top of the bar.

"Scurrying?" she repeated, genuine annoyance flaring inside her. "That's what you think my job entails?"

"Uh…" he said, his eyes going wide with concern. "I don't think I meant that the way you interpreted it. I just see you working hard, and… Am I going to end up visiting HR after all? Maybe you're right—let's not talk. It's becoming pretty clear that polite, constructive conversation between us is difficult, if not impossible, so let's just call it good. Enjoy the evening, and let this bet of ours play out."

"No!" she cried. "See? You always do this—you say things to try and upset me and then act surprised when I react."

"I wasn't trying to upset you," he returned calmly.

"You're saying you didn't mean to compare me to a spider or a mouse?"

"Of course not. If anything, I'd go with one of those superefficient AI robots that are all over the news these days. You are tireless, efficient, organized and professional. Never let your emotions get in the way. That's…admirable."

Violet felt her cheeks go hot, anger mixing with humiliation and disappointment. An uptight robot. She knew that was what he thought, what he'd always thought, so why did it bother her extra tonight?

"Excuse me, Ms. Blackwell? Mr. McCoy?"

Swiveling on her stool, Violet discovered the question had come from a young man outfitted in the signature black and white of Jameson employees.

"Yes, hi," she answered.

"Good evening. I'm Brian, your host tonight here at Jameson. The other Mr. McCoy and Ms. Blackwell from your party have arrived, and your table is ready. I'll send your drinks over if you'd like to follow me?"

"Thank you, Brian," Violet parroted, adding, "You have no idea just how much we'd like that."

"Not me," Garrett said. "I'm having a good time. I could stay right here all night."

"That's nice, sir. I'm happy to hear it, and I bet your girlfriend is, too."

Brian smiled eagerly at her, and for some inexplicable reason, she couldn't bring herself to kill yet another buzz. "I'm not his girlfriend, but that would be a nice compliment, if I were. I just meant that I'm hungry and looking very forward to dinner. The food here is always amazing."

"That's wonderful to hear."

McCoy grinned at Brian. "And I'm looking forward to the bet I'm about to win."

"That, too!" Violet stretched out a hand toward him and mimicked the sound and action of striking a match.

McCoy laughed hard, and the look of appreciation he gave her felt way better than she was comfortable with.

Then he peered thoughtfully at the young man. "Brian, can I ask you a question?"

"Certainly, sir."

"What comes to mind when I say the word *scurry*?"

Violet followed the men as they cheerfully discussed the nimbleness of rodents and arachnids. She shook her head and found herself fighting a smile. What was wrong with her? In mere minutes, the man had managed to drum up more emotions than she normally experienced in a month: anger, frustration, annoyance, sadness, confusion and, yes, there were even short spells of comic relief.

Feeling this much was exhausting.

This night could not be over soon enough. All she had to do was get through this dinner, and, with any luck, she would barely even have to think about Garrett McCoy anymore, much less see his annoyingly handsome face, smell his annoyingly delicious cologne or hear his annoyingly funny jokes.

CHAPTER FIVE

"So," Uncle Trent said approximately halfway through the entrée. "Can I have everyone's attention for a minute? I have an announcement."

Blackwell dropped her fork. It clattered so loudly on her plate that Garrett feared she'd broken the dish. Fellow diners at nearby tables quieted and looked in their direction. The expression on her face was priceless. He couldn't have requested a better setup.

"Oopsie-daisy!" Trent exclaimed. "You all right there, Violet?"

"Honey, are you okay?" Flora asked simultaneously.

"Yes! Um, sorry," she muttered, retrieving the offending utensil with two fingers. "Fork slipped. Got a bit of butter on there or…something."

"Or something, all right," Garrett agreed.

When she looked up, he caught her eye and grinned.

She glared and shook her head.

He grinned more and nodded.

"Would you like me to get you another fork?"

he asked in a loud, overly solicitous tone as she made a show of wiping the handle with her napkin. "Before my uncle makes his *announcement*."

"No, thank you," she answered too sweetly through a teeth-clenching that she tried to pass off as a smile.

"Are you sure?" he asked as she continued to polish. "Looks like you're about to rub the silver right off that one."

"Quite." She gently lowered the fork onto the edge of her plate.

"Okay, then," Flora said, curious gaze bouncing between him and her daughter. After settling intently on Violet for a few seconds, she looked at Trent. "Trent?" She beamed at him, looking every bit like a woman prepped and expecting a proposal. "You were saying something about good news?"

"Hold on a sec," Trent said, flagging down their server. "Hey, Brian, can we get those drinks now?"

"Sounds like this *announcement* has some *substance* to it?" Garrett said, smiling against the glare coming from his opponent.

"Absolutely!" Brian answered, stopping before their table, his smile a bright beacon of enthusiasm. "I suspected it might be time, so Monica is actually on her way out with them right now." He gestured toward the woman carrying a tray of crystal tumblers. "Ah, here she is."

"Thanks so much." Trent gushed his appreciation. "Your timing is perfect, as usual."

"My pleasure, sir."

Monica rounded the table, efficiently depositing a drink of amber liquid before each of them.

To the others at the table, Brian said, "Enjoy this joyous occasion, everyone. You're very fortunate, as Trent has impeccable taste."

"*Wh-wha*-what occasion?" Blackwell stuttered. Like an orphan from bygone days ready to mutiny for her meal, she now held her fork fisted in one hand, knife in the other, as if gearing up to bang them on the tabletop.

"Taste this!" Flora said after sipping the amber liquid in her glass.

Keeping his attention fixed on a wide-eyed Blackwell, Garrett took a slow drink.

"Well?" Flora asked.

Blackwell blinked, the long and slow curtain-draw blink of the blindsided.

"What do you think?"

"'Tis delightful," Garrett declared.

"That's lovely, Garrett," Flora said.

"Well, vocabulary is important *whilst* one is imbibing in such celebratory fashion," he said earnestly to Flora.

She giggled and looked at Trent. While they made eyes at each other, Garrett winked at Blackwell.

"Well said!" Flora agreed. "It's called Tiddly.

Trent has decided to invest in a company called Redfern, which makes this handcrafted whiskey. It's going to be a huge success." She picked up her glass again and lifted it high. "Go ahead," she urged Blackwell, who still hadn't touched her glass. "Taste it, sweetheart."

This time, the entire table acquiesced.

"Whiskey," Blackwell said with a breath of relief. "It is delicious!" The smile she directed at Trent was electric, and Garrett couldn't help but appreciate how different she looked when she wasn't being bossy and contrary. "Congratulations!" What made it even more perfect was how she made eye contact with Garrett when she added, "I have to say, this is better than the announcement I was expecting!" Raising her glass in a toast, she said, "Here's hoping my mom's prediction is spot-on."

Garrett raised his glass. "Cheers. To new ventures and honor among friends."

That was when the light bulb came on. He watched as she absorbed the consequences of her epic loss.

"No way! This doesn't count. Are you kidding me?" she said, glaring at him.

"Violet!" Flora cried in the clipped tone of a disapproving mother. "What in the world?"

"Sorry, Mom. Um, I just meant are you kidding me with how amazing this stuff is? Just, just, just..."

"Un-*match*ed?" Garrett supplied, carefully enunciating the key word.

"Unmatched?" Flora repeated.

"Unmatched in terms of sheer deliciousness. Well-balanced, smooth, yet robust."

"I *wish* I had some matches right now," Blackwell muttered, her eyes pinned on him and shooting fire. "Because I would not hesitate to use them."

"You would use matches?" Flora frowned at her daughter. "That doesn't even make sense. Violet, is something wrong with you? You've been acting funny all evening."

"No! Yes, matches, Mom." Blackwell struggled to explain her way out of the corner she'd talked herself into. "To light the candle here in the middle of the table to celebrate the, um, news."

"Announcement of substance," Garrett amended, even though he couldn't help but feel mad respect for her ad-libbing skills.

They all sipped while Garrett inconspicuously mimed a beanbag lob across the table. Blackwell ignored him.

"Thank you, everyone," Trent said, executing a thorough perusal of his dinner mates, his gaze pausing on Violet and then lingering on Garrett, no doubt wondering what he was up to. His uncle was used to his shenanigans. "I'm excited about it, too. It was your mother's idea, Violet." He went on to explain how the investment had come about when Flora had received a bottle as a gift from a parent of one of her equestrian students.

"Oh, Trent," Flora gushed. "You are sweet to give me any credit. This is your deal. All I did was introduce you and Spence."

Garrett watched as Blackwell relaxed into a conversation about whiskey and his uncle's investment. She was good at this, he thought, asking the right questions without smothering Trent with too much praise. He sat back and waited because he knew what was coming. That was not the announcement he'd been anticipating.

"On that note," Trent said after they'd exhausted the topic, "I think you'll be even more pleased to learn the rest of our news."

Blackwell did the blink again, and this time Garrett didn't bother to smother his chuckle. Smiling at her with glee, he said, "*Another* announcement."

"Actually, this one concerns both Flora and me and you, too, Violet. And you, Garrett, but of course, you already know about it."

Blackwell squinted in his direction. "You already knew something?"

"Well, actually, Violet," Trent said as he and Flora exchanged adoring smiles, "you're the only one who doesn't. I had to ask Garrett first. But your mother and I are so excited about this. We're hoping for a very positive outcome."

"Mom?" Blackwell ventured. "Can I talk to you privately?"

Flora frowned. "Of course, honey. Later, after Trent tells you the news."

"Okay," she squeaked, now staring down at the table. Poor thing looked pale. He was beginning to feel sorry for her.

Uncle Trent said, "Garrett has agreed to stay on the ranch, share the place with you."

Brow knitted in confusion, she looked up at Trent and mumbled, "He…" She gave her head a quick shake. "What?"

"Yep, isn't that great? Garrett is going to help your mother with a horse. I'll let her tell you all about that part."

"Trent bought me a horse, Violet. Can you believe it?"

"Did he, now? That's so generous."

Was it Garrett's imagination, or was there a hint of disapproval in her response?

"Yes, and she's gorgeous! I knew from the second I saw her that she was a performer. The kind that would have been perfect for you back in the day."

"Mmm-hmm."

"I wanted her, but as you know, I don't have a place or the money to board another horse right now. Trent offered to keep her at Penny Bottom Ranch with you. But when I told him how Cadence needed to be ridden and worked with, he suggested that Garrett might be able to help with that."

Trent interjected, "You know Garrett is a rancher,

right?" At her feeble nod, he went on, "He's excellent with horses, too. Gifted, like your mother. And he's going to advise me about the cattle herd and make some improvements around the place. I think it'll be a real help to you, Violet."

"I see," she said, and Garrett had to give her credit for keeping her composure. "When is this happening?"

"Tomorrow."

"Tomorrow?" Her voice went up, but she quickly dialed it down. "Um, I don't know if I can…"

"Don't worry. I've already asked Heather to prepare the guest suite." Heather was Trent's housekeeper. "As you know, and as I was telling Garrett earlier today, the house is big, and there's plenty of room. Of course, you'll share the kitchen, living area and all that, but he'll have his own wing."

"Plenty of room," Blackwell repeated, reaching for her water goblet and then draining the contents.

"We're going to be roommates," Garrett said to her, unable to contain his grin. "That'll be fun, huh? Like family, almost."

The look in her eyes reminded him of a scared cat, weary, nervous and a little wild. Her tone matched her expression as she started rambling. "I think *roommate* is an overstatement. *Neighbors* is more like it. As your uncle said, the house is huge. You'll have your space, and I'll have mine.

You'll have an entire wing. We'll rarely even see each other."

He knew very well that her proclamation was nothing more than a wish. He wasn't thrilled about the living arrangement either, but he'd agreed to his uncle's request to stay at Penny Bottom for several reasons. One was, plain and simple, the livestock. He was curious about this horse that Flora wanted help with and concerned about the welfare of the cattle on the ranch. Also, staying there would save him a ton of money.

But the main reason was so that he could find out more about the woman who had stolen his uncle's heart and who may or may not have her hand on his wallet. He had no idea how much the horse had cost, but from the look of Flora's clothes, bag and hair, it wasn't cheap. His first impression suggested a person with a fondness for expensive things.

Garrett was officially committed to discovering if Flora Blackwell was a gold digger, and was her daughter in on it.

"Garrett, I can't tell you how much this means to me," Flora said, snagging his attention. "When Trent told me about your experience with horses and that you'd be willing to help with Cadence, I'll admit I made a few phone calls."

"Checked my résumé, did you?" he responded and admitted to himself that her actions induced a measure of respect on his part. He wouldn't let just anyone in on the training of one of his horses either. Nor would he accept an offhand claim of "experience with horses" without vetting the individual himself.

"We have a few acquaintances in common." As she went on to name them, he felt good about the fact that many were horse people whom he respected and admired. It was also clear that the woman knew about horses herself. Surprising because he hadn't pegged her daughter for a horse person.

Speaking of, he grinned at Blackwell. "Maybe we can go riding? Uncle Trent says there are some nice trails along the creek."

Flora answered for her, smiling sadly, "Oh, no, my Violet doesn't ride anymore. There was a time when she showed real promise, but unfortunately, that particular gift did not pan out."

"Why is there a bull trotting down the driveway?" McCoy asked the question the next afternoon while scaling the porch stairs two at a time.

"Because he escaped," Violet calmly explained from the porch on the bench where she sat, putting on her hiking boots. It figured that the man would choose the worst possible timing to "move in."

"Escaped from where?"

"Did you shut the gate when you came in?" she asked, ignoring his question to ask her own. She did not have time for his questions or commentary.

"Of course," he answered calmly. "It was shut when I got here."

Relief coursed through her. *Leave it the way you found it*, that was ranching etiquette, but unfortunately, disaster was often only the slim width of a fence away. People came and went, and while most of them were conscientious, livestock could be both curious and opportunistic, and a carelessly unlatched gate presented endless possibilities for mischief or worse. And this particular bull was downright clever.

"What's the plan?"

"To go get him." Standing, she adjusted the worn leather cross-body bag on her hip. She couldn't resist asking, "Did he look okay?"

McCoy frowned and nodded. "Physically, yes. He's not lame or anything. A little agitated, maybe. Do you want me to get the trailer hooked up to my pickup? Uncle Trent told me there's one here."

Already hurrying toward the steps, she tossed the answer over her shoulder as she quickly descended. "No, thank you."

He caught up with her at the edge of the yard. "Where are you going?"

"Barn," she answered simply, hoping he'd go inside the house, get settled and leave her alone with this task—and then leave her alone forever. When he continued in step beside her, she said, "Your room is all clean and pretty. Make yourself at home."

"What's in the barn?"

Despite her best efforts to keep her stress at bay, she heard herself puff out a little sigh. "Horses, tack, hay—you know, the usual. I thought you were a rancher."

Ignoring her sarcasm, he walked with her all the way to the barn, then followed her inside. "Are you going to saddle up a horse? Can I help?"

"No." She answered both questions, opened the door to one of the tack rooms, stepped inside, wrapped her hands around the handlebars of her mountain bike and then wheeled it out.

He followed. She hitched her leg over and sat on the seat. For the first time, in all her dealings with him, he looked dumbfounded.

"Blackwell, you can't… You're going to herd a two-thousand-pound bull on a mountain bike? Do you even know if he's dangerous? Is there something else going on with you?"

She fired off a series of quick responses. "Yes, but he's closer to twenty-three hundred pounds. Yes, I do know that he's not dangerous. And no, period." With that, she pedaled off.

"Wait! Blackwell, you *cannot* go after a bull on a bicycle!"

HEART RACING IN time with the pounding of Henna's hooves on the hard-packed dirt, Garrett tried to calculate how far the bull could have gotten in the time that had passed since he'd first spotted the animal.

Taking into account the conversation with Blackwell and the minutes he'd spent rounding up gear and saddling the horse, it had been… More than long enough for her to get maimed, or worse, by an agitated bull.

"Exasperating, stubborn, reckless Blackwell," he muttered under his breath, urging the sleek mare into a gallop. What in the world was she thinking? Racing away on a mountain bike to round up a bull! Proof, as far as he was concerned, that he'd made the right decision in agreeing to stay here at Penny Bottom Ranch. Clearly, she needed help. Uncle Trent's ranch needed help. He suspected that Uncle Trent needed help, too, in untangling himself from the greedy clutches of Mother Blackwell.

Confident he'd find them quickly, he channeled fear into action and put his skills to work. This was what he loved, what he lived for. He was a rancher to his core.

Unlike the storybook beginnings of the kid who grew up following generations of ranchers before him, Garrett had stumbled into it. Before his death, his dad had been an oilfield worker, like his brother, Trent. His mom was a dental hygienist. At fifteen, he'd needed a summer job, and his best friend, Alex, had gotten him one on his family's ranch. Garrett had never even been on a horse, but he immediately took to it, and cattle and everything about ranching. By the end of the summer, he was hooked.

He rode the entire distance of the long driveway before accepting that neither woman nor bull was in sight. He spotted the open gate through which the animal had likely escaped, but once outside of that pasture, there were several unfenced areas where the animal could have wandered or veered into other fields. Acres and acres of land, which Garrett hadn't yet had time to familiarize himself with. For all he knew, the bull could make it all the way to the main road. Even in livestock-aware Texas, cars and bulls were a bad combination.

Despite what the movies suggested, tracking a single animal across hard-packed dirt was difficult. A mountain bike's tires should be easier to spot, but the sheer amount of tread marks in the dirt told him that Blackwell biked here a lot. The unhelpful thought also occurred to him that it explained the toned condition of her legs. There was no way to tell today's tire marks from yesterday's, or last week's, for that matter.

Slowing the horse to a walk, he studied the ground, hoping for the telltale sign of fresh manure and trying to think like a bull. Several long minutes later, Henna neighed and pulled her head to the west.

VIOLET GAMBLED THAT Ferdinand would not be at the end of the driveway. Instead, she veered west toward the neighbor's property through an empty field. And that was where she found him, standing by the fence that cut through a stand of pine and juniper trees. The vegetation along here remained lush due to the sprawling, meandering waters of Penny Bottom Creek.

During the warmer months, the oasis provided both water and shade for the cattle. To prevent overgrazing, the livestock were rotated around the property, allowing the grass to grow in the vacant areas. Right now, they were grazing in a different location while this patch blossomed to its full potential.

"Hey, buddy," she said, bailing off the bike.

Ferdinand lifted his head and bawled a happy greeting.

She joined him by the fence where he stood. "Where were you headed?" she asked, reaching out a hand and scratching his neck.

Shifting his massive bulk, he seemed to gaze north, which happened to be Maggie's current direction. Violet felt a pang deep in her heart. She knew the animal couldn't possibly know this, and she knew he couldn't understand her, and yet Ferdinand was the smartest bull she'd ever seen. She was pretty sure he was the smartest bull on the planet. He was also a sweetheart, a goof and a bit of a show-off. Understandable, as he'd had Maggie for a teacher.

"I miss her, too," she said. "One of these days,

she'll come around." She sighed, desperately hoping the words were true. Ferdinand brayed a deep, almost mournful sound and gently nudged her with his muzzle. She scratched his neck as they contemplated this possibility together.

The distinctive clip-clop of a horse's gallop interrupted their musings. Turning toward the sound, she spotted McCoy atop Henna and heading their way. No surprise that he'd managed to choose the fastest horse in the herd. Watching them, she observed that the man rode with as much skill as he did everything else. Flora would definitely approve.

Unlike her disapproval of Violet.

There was a time when she showed real promise, but unfortunately, that particular gift did not pan out.

Ouch. After all these years, why did those words still sting? There had been a time in her life when she'd enjoyed riding. Before she'd realized she wasn't good at it—not good enough, anyway. Even with Aunt Dandy's patient encouragement and extra help, she couldn't quite get to the level of her fellow Belles.

She knew when McCoy spotted them because he slowed Henna's pace to a trot and then a walk before ultimately halting before them.

"Huh," he said, taking in the scene. "Well." He reached a hand around to the back of his neck and scratched. "This is not what I expected."

"Let me guess," she said flatly. "Did your vision

involve me splayed out on the ground with a bull standing on my chest, snorting, all red-eyed and slobbery with smoke shooting out of his nostrils?"

He stared at her for a few long seconds before shaking his head. "No on the smoke," he finally admitted, mouth curling at the corners as it wrestled with a smile.

"I knew it," she said, and despite the fact that he'd ignored her request, she had to grin at his honesty. "I did tell you that I didn't need help."

"You did. I'm..." He lifted a helpless shoulder, seemingly at a loss for words. She couldn't help but feel a smidgen of satisfaction at that observation, rare gem that it was.

She patted the bull. "This is Ferdinand. He wouldn't hurt a fly."

"Blackwell, I know that it appears that way. But bulls are unpredictable, and they can be extremely dangerous."

"Not this one. He's a kitten."

He ground out a frustrated groan. "This isn't like on TV. *Any* bull can act in ways that you don't expect. Now, I'm going to head back to the ranch and get the trailer hooked up to my pickup. I'd like you to come with me. I'll drop you off and then come back and load him."

"Not this one," she repeated. If they were going to be working together, he would have to quit talking to her like she was eight years old. But, generally speaking, he was correct in that bulls could be dangerous and unpredictable, and she understood that he was worried, which was sort of nice. So, for now, she'd let it pass.

"How could you possibly know that?"

"Because…"

"Because what?" he repeated, shifting impatiently in the saddle.

"Because Ferdinand and I grew up together."

CHAPTER SIX

SHE *GREW UP* with a bull. What did that even mean?

Garrett peered at Blackwell and tried to make sense of the statement. "How did you…? You mean, like the *Jungle Book* story with the wolves, but you were raised by a herd of cattle?" he joked, because, surely, she wasn't serious.

The bull snorted, and Garrett tried not to notice how it sounded as if it were mocking him. The animal was massive, muscular and well toned. His blond coat was short and sleek except for a fringe of thicker fur above his forehead that hung like shaggy bangs over the base of his long, curled horns. Wide-set, deep brown eyes and a lighter-toned nose gave him an expressive face and an almost friendly appearance. If he'd been anxious earlier, it was no longer evident.

"Sort of." She shrugged. "More like Ferdinand is Mowgli and lived with us humans. We got him when he was a calf."

"Who is *we*?"

"My family. We're... We *were* the Blackwell Belles."

"Uh..." he drawled. "Who consists of this family you speak of? And what is a Blackwell bell?"

"My mom, my aunt, me and my four sisters. The Blackwell Belles is, *was*, the name of our trick-riding troupe."

"So, *belle* as in 'belle of the ball,' not a cowbell or a bell that you ring?"

"Correct."

"But your mom said you couldn't ride."

"If you think about it, that's not exactly what she said."

He silently replayed the conversation. "No, I guess not. She said you didn't ride *anymore*."

"Right. Because I'm not a *gifted* rider," she clarified. "Everyone in my family is amazingly good at riding—except for me." She brushed off this bombshell with a breezy wave of her hand. "Yeah, so all of that is irrelevant. The point is that Ferdinand was an orphan, and we adopted him. Maggie and I were only eight years old at the time. She doted on him."

"Maggie is one of your Belle sisters?"

"Yes, my twin."

"You have a twin." Garrett was reeling. He'd known her for nearly three years and suddenly realized how little he actually knew about her. For the first time, right before his eyes, Blackwell was becoming a three-dimensional human.

"I know." She grinned.

"Her name is Maggie?"

"Yes. Well, technically, it's Magnolia. We're not identical."

"Violet and Magnolia and mom Flora. That's cute."

"You think so? My other sisters are Jasmine Rose, Iris and Willow. Our aunt was Dandelion, but she died. And now Mom has a dog named Zinnia, who she calls Zinni." Delivering this news, she winced slightly and commented, "Now it seems a little campy, right?"

"Is Willow a flower?"

"Kind of. Most willows are dioecious, so they produce catkins, which are sometimes referred to as incomplete flowers, a term I don't care for because there is nothing *incomplete* about my sister Willow."

"Wow. That's really…interesting."

Tilting her head, she said, "If you think that's interesting, you'd need popcorn for some of the stories I could tell you." She retrieved her bike from where it lay on the ground. As she wheeled it by, Garrett bit back a warning about how the action might spook the bull. Ferdinand now seemed chill to the point of Zen.

"Do you know how he got out?"

"The neighbor kids rode through on horses this morning. They like to cut through the pasture he's in and ride along the creek. They know to shut the gate, but the latch is a little wonky, and I noticed it was open. I'll take care of it."

Leaning the bike against the fence, she stepped close to the bull again and flattened one hand on his shoulder. "I'll walk with him, get him settled and come back for my bike. We'll see you at the house," she told Garrett in a dismissive but not unfriendly tone.

"Are you sure?"

"Yes, one hundred percent. We'll be fine, won't we, buddy?"

The animal lowered his head, pressed his nose close to her arm, then lifted his head again. Garrett told himself that what he'd just witnessed was not a nod and then watched as Blackwell scratched between his ears and around his eyes. With a final pat to his neck, she and her bovine brother ambled off, side by side, in the general direction of the barn.

BY THE TIME she returned to the house, the sun was in Violet's eyes, but she could see well enough to notice the man on her porch. Why was there a man on her porch? Alex had mentioned stopping by, but he'd texted earlier to say he was still out of town. Probably, it was Adam or Darius or one of McCoy's other partners in mayhem already showing up to further disrupt her peace.

Veering to the left, she intended to sneak around to the back door when a deep, distinctive voice called out, "Howdy there, Ms. Violet! Where ya headed?"

She froze in her tracks, because although she hadn't known that voice for very long, she remembered it well. But no, it couldn't be, could it? Her great-uncle Elias Blackwell lived in Montana, and she'd only just seen him last month at the family reunion in Eagle Springs, Wyoming.

Violet stopped and lifted a hand to shade her eyes, which confirmed her suspicion. "Big E?"

"Yes, ma'am."

"Hi."

"Hi, yourself. You need to get yourself a hat, kid. A cowgirl needs a hat."

Despite her surprise and confusion, she felt herself smiling. "We've been over this. I'm not a cowgirl."

"Sure you are! You're just a little rusty. A good saddle would help, too."

Violet stiffened at this comment, the ache in her heart as raw as the day she'd watched Iris load Aunt Dandy's saddle in her car. In an instant, she'd lost another sister, her precious saddle and any remaining notion that she'd ever live up to Belle standards. Did Big E somehow know about her saddle? She wouldn't put it past him. The man was sharp as a tack and nosy as a cat.

Lifting one hand, Big E made a scooping motion. "Get on up here and sit with us." No one would accuse Elias Blackwell of being jovial, but he had a charmingly folksy way about him that made it difficult to refuse. Charisma, she decided, as she felt herself gliding toward the porch. It wasn't until she got closer and saw movement off to the other side of him that she registered the word he'd used, *us*.

There was something familiar about the gesture.

Maggie? Hope bloomed inside her, fast and bright. Now that Maggie and Clem were together and her sister was finally happy, Violet had been thinking more and more that her feelings would soften, and she'd come around. If not for Violet, then certainly for Ferdinand.

Then the figure waved, and her mom's tiny terrier, Zinni, let out a bark from where she sat on her lap. Violet's hopes crash-landed into the hard Texas dirt. How had she never noticed how similar Maggie and their mother were in the way they moved and spoke? Probably because most everything about their personalities was different. Maggie was unpretentious and genuine while Flora was…not so much.

"Mom, what are you doing here? Is Trent with you?"

"No, Violet, he's not." Flora sat back in her chair while Zinni settled in for a nap. "Big E and I are here to talk to you. Don't worry. Nothing is wrong."

Despite the assurance, her boots felt heavy on her

feet as she climbed the porch stairs. Big E stood, and she noticed the empty chair between them, seemingly positioned just for her. Before she could claim it, he removed his hat, stepped forward and held out his arms. Tall and broad with a set of strong shoulders, her great-uncle looked every inch the cattle rancher in his denim jeans and short-sleeved, pearl-buttoned shirt.

His hug felt so natural, unhurried and heart-felt. As Violet returned the embrace, she felt an unexpected welling of affection and longing. Tears sprang to her eyes. *Family.* It'd been so long since she'd felt accepted on that simple connection alone.

"It's good to see you again, kid," he said, letting go and stepping back, but his blue eyes held on, and Violet knew he meant the words.

"You, too," she said, quickly blinking the tears away. She cast an assessing look in her mother's direction. "Mom didn't mention you were coming to town."

Flora gave her an apologetic shrug, but Violet could see she was anything but repentant. "I wasn't sure *exactly* when he'd be arriving," she said unconvincingly. "He's traveling in his motor home. You know, the one I returned in with Grandma, Maggie and Albert after the reunion."

After the reunion last month, Violet had flown home while Flora had traveled hundreds of miles in the RV with Big E, Grandma Denny, Maggie and Clem, whose given name was Albert. She'd heard the story multiple times now about how the trip had resulted in Mom and Maggie "patching things up." She'd believe it when she saw it. Because how could Maggie forgive their mother but not forgive her?

Violet asked Big E, "How long are you staying?"

"As long as it takes."

"As long as what takes?" Violet asked, suspecting the answer and already shaking her head slowly from side to side.

Flora answered, "As long as it takes us to convince you to perform with your sisters and me in the Belles' reunion performance."

"Oh, well, in that case, welcome to Texas, Big E. I hope you like it, because you're going to be here forever."

Flora scoffed and huffed like a steam engine. To Big E, she said, "Didn't I tell you she could be dramatic?"

Violet wanted to laugh at the irony of her mother's theatrics.

Big E did chuckle and then winked at her. Clearly, he got it, and she adored him all the more for it. Undoubtedly, the man had Flora's number. RV traveling was close quarters, to say the least, and plenty of time to get the full measure of Flora Blackwell, including her contradictions and complexities.

"Violet, the least you can do is hear us out. Your

uncle came a long, long way. Grandma Denny was going to come, too. That's how important we *all* feel this is. But your cousin Levi and his wife just had a baby. You remember his wife, Summer, right? The incredibly talented equestrian."

"Of course, Mom." Once her mother got started on Summer and her eventing skills, they'd be here all night. "In that case, I'm all ears."

She wanted to laugh as she looked from her mother to her great-uncle and back again, taking in their reactions. As she suspected, they'd both been prepared to talk her into listening before trying to convince her to participate in their scheme. Experience had taught her that it was easier not to argue. Instead, she'd listen and then do what she wanted anyway. There was a time when doing what was best for "the show" might have swayed Violet, but those days were long gone.

For the last twelve years, she and her mom had maintained a relationship with the understanding that they did not discuss the Belles, particularly the breakup. Nor did Flora get to tell Violet what to do anymore. The days of Violet being Flora's errand girl had ended along with the show. In the last few years, and especially since her parents' estrangement, their relationship had shifted to the point where Violet often felt more like the adult. She knew this dynamic wasn't particularly healthy either, but it was better than it used to be.

Big E, a man adept at pivoting, got on with

it. "The National Cowgirl Hall of Fame is a big deal."

"I am aware of that. I'm very excited for Mom and Aunt Dandelion to be inducted, and I'll be there for the ceremony. I told you that at the reunion."

"On horseback?" Big E asked with a grin that was impossible to resist.

"Funny, Uncle. No, my riding days are over."

"We have other news, too," Flora said, fidgeting a bit in her seat. "News that just might convince you to perform."

"Yeah?" Violet said, barely keeping her skepticism at bay. "Let's hear it. Just so you know, there are no amount of sparkles that will tempt me." Flora used to insist that their outfits were bejeweled to the max. She and Iris used to joke about how, in Flora's mind, sequins and fire could fix anything.

Jeez, she missed Iris. She missed all her sisters, the sibling bond they'd shared as kids, the wild experiences, the camaraderie, the…fun. In ironic opposition to Violet, her twin sister, Maggie, would never have a life where fun wasn't a key component—at least the Maggie she used to know.

"Can you stop being difficult for one minute? Honestly, Violet, even your twin has agreed to perform, and if anyone has a reason to hesitate, it's Maggie."

"Maggie has agreed to perform?" she asked, openly skeptical now.

"Yes. Well, there are conditions."

"Now the truth comes out."

"Violet! You—"

"All Maggie wants is the bull," Big E interjected. "She says she'll participate if you give her Ferdinand."

Violet absorbed the words and tried to rally. Despite her disappointment, she felt a welling of pride for her sister. *Well done, Maggie, negotiating the terms of your performance.* Maggie had finally stood up to Flora. For years, she'd wanted to tell her sister to do that very thing, but how could you gift someone else the courage to do what they needed to do when you couldn't? Standing up to their mother now, however, was not her problem.

"Good for Maggie," Violet said. "But I'm not Maggie, am I? And I'm not interested."

Big E tried a different tack. "As you are aware, your grandma Denny has been ill, and she's had time to think about the past and the future. She's realized a few hard truths, and the bottom line is that all she wants is for you girls to reconcile. I'd like to see that, too, and so would your parents."

Violet found it difficult to believe that Flora truly wanted her family back together. That would entail her owning up to years of bad behavior. Apologies would have to be meted out sincerely and with heartfelt contrition, conditions she was certain her mother could not meet. In fact, had she apologized to Maggie?

"Did Maggie say anything about—"

"Hello there, Garrett!" Flora interrupted with a tone oozing sugary sweetness. "Nice to see you again."

"Hi, Flora," he said.

Violet swiveled in her chair to discover McCoy standing on the porch, one hand on the rail as if he'd just climbed the stairs.

"Nice job on that gate adjustment," he said to her as he walked toward them. "The reminder was a good idea, too." She'd tightened the mechanism and added a Please Make Sure the Latch Is Closed sign.

"Thanks, um…" she answered, distracted by his presence and the fact that he was holding a… "Is that a chicken? Why are you holding a chicken? What are you doing with her?"

"Oh, yeah." He looked down as if just realizing the bird was nestled in the curve of his elbow. "This is Mrs. Specklesbrock."

"Excuse me?"

"It's a long story, but yes, she's a chicken, and I'm going to put her in the coop."

"What coop?"

"The one I brought with me. Needs a few adjustments. I'm going to get some tools out of my pickup."

"You want me to take her?" Big E held out his hands. "She's a good-looking hen. I'm partial to banties myself."

"I'd appreciate it," Garrett said, somehow managing to seamlessly pass the chicken off and introduce himself with a handshake as if it was something he did every day. "Garrett McCoy."

"Elias Blackwell, but most folks call me Big E. I'm Violet's great-uncle." The chicken released a mellow cluck and settled on the big man's lap. Excited at the possibility of making a new friend, Zinni wiggled and emitted a gurgling noise. The dog made the strangest sounds. Violet wasn't sure if her repertoire even included a conventional-sounding bark.

"Nice to meet you, Big E."

Could this get any weirder? Violet wondered while the two men made small talk, the chicken clucked and the dog chittered and snorted in response.

"It's warm out here. Can I get you guys something to drink?" McCoy asked after a few minutes, annoying Violet both by his presumptuous behavior and his good manners. The first because it signified that he was good and truly living here now, and the second because his courtesy made her look bad. "We have… I don't know what we have. I just got here myself."

Violet forced a smile and rattled off the beverage choices. "Lemonade, sweet tea, diet soda, water, milk."

"I'll take a glass of that sweet tea," Big E said.

"Lemonade sounds nice," Flora answered, making Violet feel worse because, clearly, they were both thirsty. What was she thinking, making her mother and elderly uncle sit out in this heat without a cold beverage? McCoy left her...discombobulated. When did she get to make him look bad? She took a second to fantasize about what that might look like. She didn't want to get him fired or anything but—

"Coming right up," he said, turning and then strolling inside like he owned the place.

The door had barely shut behind him when Flora asked, "How are you two getting along?"

"Mom, seriously? He just got here."

Big E's curious perusal felt like a spotlight. "You kids make a handsome couple. Moving in together, huh?"

"No! I mean, yes, but we're not a couple," she explained as her cheeks went inexplicably hot. "He's my boss's nephew, and he's moving in here to help with Mom's new horse and the ranch. It wasn't my idea."

"Huh. Whose idea was it?"

"Trent's," she said, not wanting to talk about this. She wanted to talk about Maggie. What was her sister thinking? How was she feeling about performing again? Why didn't she just ask Violet for Ferdinand? Did she now have a place to keep him? Violet would not let him go unless Maggie had suitable accommodations and a lifestyle that was conducive to caring for him, which meant Maggie needed to be there! Ferdinand was getting old, and he needed special attention. Violet knew she'd spoiled him, but he was used to both a morning and an evening chat, treats and regular grooming.

"Trent is Violet's boss," Flora explained in a tone that sounded rather prim and maybe a tad uncomfortable.

Hmm. Could it be that her mother hadn't divulged the entire truth of her marital discord to her uncle?

"Trent is also Mom's boyfriend," Violet volunteered and could see from Flora's expression that she'd guessed correctly.

Big E's deeply furrowed brow seemed to confirm that this was news to him, too. "I see. What about Barlow?"

Yeah, Mom, what about Dad? What about me? And my sisters? You want to explain how this show that you romanticize and so badly want to resurrect is what ruined our family in the first place?

Instead, Violet pushed to her feet and hitched a thumb toward the house. "I'm going to go help with those drinks."

Flora could handle Big E's interrogation about Barlow on her own. Maybe that would teach her to stop ambushing people. Violet had made it very clear that she wasn't interested in participating in any Blackwell Belles reunion performance. They didn't need her, never had. When the group disbanded, she was done. She hadn't ridden a horse since.

Once inside, she realized she'd jumped out of the frying pan and into the fire, so to speak. She had no choice but to join McCoy in the kitchen.

"Hey, roomie," he called from his spot near the sink, where he was busy slicing a lemon. Four ice-filled glasses were at the ready, and a pitcher of lemonade stood nearby, along with a bowl of what looked like water.

She pointed at the bowl. "Is that…?"

"Water for that, um, unusual little dog. It is a dog, right?"

"Yes." She couldn't help it—she wanted to laugh even as something inside her softened. Her mom was going to lose her mind at the thoughtful gesture.

"What's wrong with its voice box?"

"I don't know. It's very disconcerting, though, right?"

"That's putting it mildly. There's like an entire soundstage inside of this tiny little creature. It's wild. You wanna grab the tea? I don't know if your uncle wants lemon, so I'll just put some slices in this little bowl here. Found it in the cupboard. Hope that's okay?"

"Mi casa es su casa," Violet said dryly, heading across the kitchen to retrieve the jug of tea she'd brewed that morning. "Or, in this case, I guess I should say *su tio's casa es su casa*? Or… something like that."

"Close." He chuckled. "Technically, it would be *la casa de tu tio es tu casa*," he corrected in perfectly accented Spanish.

"Of *course* you speak Spanish," she muttered.

"No choice in the matter. Grandmother on my dad's side is from Mexico. My *abuela* insisted we learn, and I've lived in Texas my entire life."

"That's nice. I'm trying to learn." Back by his side, she asked, "What are you having?"

"Tea," he answered, and she began to pour the liquid into the glasses. "I'd be happy to help with your Spanish. And don't mock me, but I like lemon in my tea."

"Why would I mock you for that? I like it, too."

For some unfathomable reason, that made him smile. She wanted to ask why and then reminded herself that she was not interested in making small talk, or getting to know him better, or taking Spanish lessons. She was certain he wasn't either. He never had been before, so why would things change now just because they were roommates?

She was about to make this clear to him when he asked, "Did you get injured?"

"What? When? Just now, with Ferdinand?"

"No. I mean, is that why you don't ride? I over-heard part of the conversation outside. Were you injured?"

"Oh. No, my sister was injured."

Setting the pitcher down, she inhaled a deep breath. After ten years, the horrifying memory of Maggie and Willow's accident still hit her with surprising force. She absolutely did not want to think about it right now. As nice as it was to see her great-uncle again, she was not happy with her mother for springing this on her. It had been a very long day—two days—and she just wanted them out of there so she could decompress.

"So, you don't ride because your sister was injured?"

"Not exactly. Sort of." Flustered, she picked up two of the glasses and turned to leave. "It's complicated. The accident was, um… It changed a lot of things for me—for all of us."

"Wait," McCoy said, and for some reason, she did.

"What happened? Was she thrown from her horse?"

"No, she was shot with an arrow."

CHAPTER SEVEN

"This is the tack room, which you've already seen." Inside the barn, Blackwell opened a door and swept an arm inward. Garrett had, but quickly, and now he took inventory of saddles, bridles, stirrups, blankets, reins, ropes and other assorted gear hanging neatly on the wall.

Big E and Flora had taken their time sipping drinks and visiting before they departed. Even though the conversation hadn't been rife with substance, the dynamics had piqued Garrett's curiosity. As he'd already noted at dinner, the mother-daughter relationship felt off-kilter, and he'd picked up on hints of discord among the sisters. Huge red Flora flags, as far as he was concerned. Not to mention the bombshell about her sister getting shot with an arrow. Who was this woman?

"How long has your mom been living here in Flame?" Garrett asked as Blackwell continued his brief tour of the ranch.

"About six months," she answered, marching toward the stables. "Your uncle has five horses here. Mom's addition will make six. I always bring them in at night, feed them, administer meds and turn them out in the morning. A sheet hanging over there by the door lists how much of what everyone gets, including their supplements and etcetera."

"Where did she live before that? Where did you live when you were growing up?"

"Ha. Nowhere. Everywhere." She added a shrug. "I think my parents have lived in every state west of the Mississippi. But usually not for more than a few months, six at the most. She's probably on track to break a record here in Texas for the most time spent in one place."

"So, she continued to perform after your family's show broke up?"

Blackwell exited the barn through a side door. He followed. Reaching up, she dipped the sunglasses down from her head onto her nose. Bummer because he liked watching her eyes when she talked. How had he never noticed what a unique shade of gold-brown they were? There was much to be discovered swirling around in there, information he needed, along with emotions he wouldn't have guessed she possessed. He was familiar with the angry sparks and the flat glow of contempt but not so much the rest.

"Yep. Flora went solo with performing. She gave riding lessons and did some training on the side. She's very talented. I know she comes across as kind of high-maintenance, and she is to a degree. But it's mostly an act. I mean, it's for her act—her image. End of the day, it's all about her horses, the tricks specifically."

"Interesting."

"I'm glad you think so. From my perspective, it's a lot. *She's* a lot, and for some reason, I'm the one she comes to when things go bad."

"Because you're nice?"

"I don't know about that. I am the one who will tolerate her. Maybe because I wasn't as critical to the success of the show, I was able to develop a different relationship with her. Back then, I think she felt sorry for me. But she also relied on me to take care of things for her. More and more as I got older, and especially after our aunt died, I took over many of the business aspects—arranging her schedule, booking events, handling the details."

"So, your first job was as your mom's executive assistant?"

She opened her mouth and closed it again before landing on a crooked half grin. *Cute.*

"I guess so," she finally answered, letting herself relax into a smile that felt genuine. Garrett decided he liked making her smile, so much so that he was tempted to end the discussion right here at this happy place. The visit with her mother and great-uncle had obviously, if not upset her, thrown her off-balance. He wanted to change the direction of the conversation to more personal, less stress-inducing details. Like what did she like to do when she wasn't working? Did she ever just chill? What was the last show she binge-watched? What book was on her nightstand?

"Your uncle is a *way* better boss," she commented wryly.

The comment sobered him, reminding him of his mission. There was too much good stuff coming out about Flora, details he needed to know if he was going to rescue his uncle.

He refocused, asking, "What happened with your sister?"

Turning away from him, she pointed. "The cattle are currently in that field. Your uncle probably told you he hired a part-time wrangler, the neighbor Jorge, who moves the herd. His wife, Rebekah, helps me out sometimes, too. Their kids are the ones who like to ride down by the creek. Have you seen the creek yet?"

"He did mention Jorge and gave me his number. I'll be in touch with him in the next couple of days to discuss all of that. No, I haven't seen the creek, except here and there from a distance when I was searching for you and your bull."

"It's pretty amazing. You likely already guessed that the ranch is named for the creek, Penny Bottom. But the creek was named that because, in places, the bottom is copper-colored, and it shimmers like pennies."

"Sounds nice. I'll be sure to ride down there and check it out."

"There's a great swimming hole about a quarter mile upstream from the old silo. You can't miss it because the previous owners built a dock and stuff."

"I'll keep that in mind," he said, biting his lip to keep from inviting her for a swim. He had enough of a distraction seeing her dressed all casual like she was now in shorts and a tank top. At work, she always looked über-professional.

Garrett thought she was going to ignore his question, which would be understandable. He was delving into her personal life, her family, and it wasn't as if they were friends. Although, getting to know her like this had him thinking they could be friends, or could have been. It also had him wondering how they'd gotten off on the wrong foot in the first place.

Surprising him, she stopped at the fence, rested her forearms on the top rung and leaned into it. Then she turned and looked at him, and Garrett could feel her gaze on him, analyzing, assessing, wondering.

"Why in the world would you want to hear about this?"

Why indeed. He couldn't tell her the truth: *I don't trust your mother, so I want to learn about her and discover her intentions with my uncle.* He could also add: *I'm not sure I trust you either.*

But his gut was telling him he could, that whatever Flora was up to didn't involve her. But he'd let that kind of instinctive gut-trust guide him in the past. With Alex, in particular, and he wasn't about to make that mistake again.

Moving slowly, he joined her. Letting his gaze float around, he set his tone to lighthearted. "Seriously? Where do I begin?" Thumb first, he began ticking off reasons on one hand. "I show up here and find a bull on the loose, only to discover his name is Ferdinand, and he is your pet. Meanwhile, back at the ranch, Great-Uncle Big E and Mom surprise you with a visit, whereupon I learn that your mom and her sister are being inducted into the National Cowgirl Hall of Fame. Kind of a big deal to a cowboy like me."

Switching hands, he went on, "You are estranged from your sisters, including your twin. The relationship among some, if not all, of your sisters is not great. All of this centers around your family's trick-riding show, in which you participated from childhood until age twenty. You were a trick rider, but now you don't ride. At all. But your twin is a rodeo clown who wants Ferdinand back. I'm running out of fingers." He threw up his hands. "This is reality-show stuff. Who wouldn't be curious?"

She stared out at the field where Ferdinand was grazing with two horses. The bull lazily lifted his head and looked in their direction.

Garrett let some seconds tick by, thinking about how to convince her. "I'll make a deal with you."

"Sure," she answered sarcastically. "Yeah, like the sketchy bet you tricked me into at dinner? No, thanks."

He chuckled. "I'm not going to hold you to that. I was just messing with you. But for the record, I didn't know about the whiskey, so there would have been an announcement regardless."

"Right." She added, "I'm going to let you remind me, and the entire office, for the rest of my life that I lost a bet and didn't pay up? No, I'll play in your silly tournament."

"I tell you what. You tell me what happened with your sister, and I'll release you from your debt."

Inhaling deeply, she appeared to think it over. Finally, she nodded, sighed and said, "Fine. Where do I start?"

"How about the show? What was that like? I'm imagining the Partridge Family on horseback."

"Hardly. It was fun when we were small. But as we got older, the show, the performances— our acts—" she paused to add air quotes "—were never good enough for Flora. After Aunt Dandy died, my mom poured everything she had into the performances. It was like an obsession. The tricks got more and more difficult and dangerous.

"Maggie and Willow had this act where Willow shot arrows through rings that Maggie held like this." She stretched both arms out straight from her sides. "While she stood on Ferdinand's back, and he trotted around the ring, and Willow was on horseback, too."

"What?" As a cowboy, Garrett was no stranger to riding, even in risky conditions, but this sounded downright irresponsible. He felt a little queasy just thinking about the danger involved in a number like that. "You were like Hollywood stunt people."

"Pretty much. Did I mention the rings were on fire?"

"No." A tingle of dread had the hair standing up on the back of his neck. "Horses do not like fire."

"No, they do not. I can attest to that, but that's why Flora liked using it so much." She closed her eyes and shook her head with disgust. "During our last show, things went horribly wrong, and Willow shot Maggie in the arm."

"That's…awful. How old were they? How bad was it?"

"Willow is the youngest. She was eighteen. Maggie and I were twenty. It was pretty bad. Maggie went to the hospital and had to have her arm sewn back together. She's lucky to have the use of it. The scar still bothers her."

"Wow."

"The worst part was that Flora wanted Maggie to take all the blame."

"Are you kidding me? Why?"

"My sister Willow is the most like Flora in that she's very, very talented and gifted with horses. She's also beautiful, composed and just a natural performer. *And* she's ambitious like Flora. So, as you can probably imagine, Flora spent a disproportionate amount of time and energy on training and teaching Willow. She had aspirations for her that were grand and maybe even admirable but also unrealistic. It was also a lot of pressure to put on a teenager.

"Bottom line, she was worried about Willow developing performance anxiety. She thought if Willow believed it was Maggie's fault, then it wouldn't mess with her head as much. But all her scheming achieved was to damage them both. And..." She paused as if thinking about her words. "And the rest of us, too, to varying degrees.

"By the time of the accident, so much had already happened. As I mentioned, we'd lost Aunt Dandy, who was a counterbalance for us girls, a more loving, reasonable and stable influence. I see now that Flora was grieving her sister when she went off the rails. She pushed us harder and harder, became even more critical, demanded perfection. She and my dad grew apart. And then the accident...

"It was terrifying. Things blew up. Little quarrels became big ones. We all wanted to quit— some of us more than others. So we did. That was it. The end of the Blackwell Belles and the end of the Blackwells, or at least our branch was irretrievably broken. My family was forever damaged right along with Maggie's arm and poor Willow's psyche."

"What about your other sisters? Jasmine Rose and Iris, was it?"

"Yeah, Jasmine Rose is the oldest but goes by J.R. She was already looking for a way out. She'd, um… Let's just say she'd outgrown her signature act. Flora had her and Ferdinand in lace and frills, and if you knew J.R.…. Well, it's a miracle she didn't jump ship long before that day.

"And Iris… Looking back, I see her as indispensable. She could do it all, fill just about any role that needed filling. She did it without complaint but never got the credit she deserved. As much as she tried, as perfect as she rode, it was never enough to be the spotlight act. Flora was hard on us all in different ways."

As if he knew what was being discussed, Ferdinand ambled up to the fence until he stood in front of Blackwell. Garrett couldn't help but smile at the bull's complete lack of respect for personal space. Slowly, he raised his massive head, nudging her with his nose. "Even you, huh, Ferdinand?" With one hand, she reached out and scratched his forehead. The other she used to push up her sunglasses.

That was when Garrett saw the tears.

A mix of sympathy and guilt welled inside him. The reason behind his sympathy wasn't difficult to discern and something he leaned into. The guilt was more complicated. Yes, in a sense, he was lying to her, using her to get information, and that was uncomfortable. But necessary, he assured himself.

But there was another layer to the guilt— disappointment in himself because he'd never *seen* her before. He'd known her for nearly three years, argued with her, mocked her, teased her, silently cursed her, but never taken the time to get to know her.

Now he felt protective and… There were other fuzzy feelings he couldn't quite land on—respect, for sure, and affection. He wanted to hug her. What would she do, he asked himself, if he wrapped his arms around her? What would happen if he pressed his nose into her silky, sun-kissed brown hair? She smelled good, he already knew, like peaches and vanilla.

After a quick swipe of her tears, she sniffled once, inhaled deeply and then exhaled with a loud *whooshing* sound. "Sheesh. I'm sorry. I'm very tired. I get weepy when I'm tired, and this reunion performance is dredging up so many memories and… And that was probably quite a bit more than you wanted to know about my screwed-up family, huh, McCoy?" She gave Ferdinand a final, gentle pat, pushed away from the fence and then brushed her hands together as if to rid them of the remnants of this conversation.

Garrett was trying not to judge, but he couldn't help it—he was thinking the worst of Flora Blackwell. And making plans to extricate his uncle from her perfectly manicured clutches. Even if it turned out she wasn't after his money, the woman was destructive, a tornado that wreaked havoc on everyone in her path.

"Hungry?" she asked, sealing the topic change.

"Uh, yes, actually, I am."

"You like calzones?"

"Sure."

"Good. I don't cook, but I can turn on the oven. This Italian place on my route home makes the most amazing take-and-bake. I've got two calzones in the fridge."

IF SOMEONE HAD taken Violet aside a few days earlier and told her she'd be sharing her family drama over calzones with Garrett McCoy, she would have laughed and laughed and laughed. Even harder than she was laughing right now at his story about when he and his younger brother, Cade, were kids and they got into trouble for spray-painting the neighbor's goats.

"We tried to deny it for about five minutes, but Mom found the empty paint cans in the garage."

"It never occurred to you criminal geniuses to hide the evidence?"

"It wouldn't have mattered. We both had paint all over our hands. Cade had it in his hair. We were not good delinquents."

"That is so funny."

Smiling, he leaned back in his chair and gave her a once-over. Violet couldn't shake the feeling that he was seeing something for the first time.

"You have a great laugh," he told her.

"Thank you. But that was a funny story. Now I want to meet your brother."

"You'd like him. He'd like you, too."

His eyes were fixed on her, his gaze traveling over her face. The intensity made her feel funny, analyzed maybe, but in a good way. Heat flooded through her. Her neck felt hot and she hoped he couldn't see any color there.

His voice was soft as he said, "I've never heard you laugh before."

"Really? Is that true?" She winced. "That's kinda sad."

"Maybe…" he agreed with a thoughtful tip of his head. "Is it just me, or do you laugh with other people?"

"Um…"

"I knew it." He grinned at her. "Me."

"Don't take it personally. Everyone else thinks you're funny."

"Everyone else?"

"Yeah, everyone at work."

"But you've never wanted to laugh at me? Never found my *antics* funny."

The emphasis he put on the word had her grinning all over again. Crinkling her nose, she took a sip of lemonade and then said, "Your antics have driven me nothing but crazy for three years, and you know it."

Why did she suddenly like how his eyes twinkled when he smiled? "I appreciate how honest you are," he said.

"Honesty is important to me."

He nodded and looked away for a few seconds, fiddling with his napkin. Then he met her gaze again and said, "I'm sorry. You know, for giving you such a hard time."

She snuffled with laughter. "No, you're not."

"I am! For certain things, anyway. Things we can discuss at some later date. But to be fair, your…"

"Uptight ways?"

Both hands came up, palms out, in a gesture of self-defense. "You said it, not me, so we'll go with it. Your uptight ways always seemed designed to, you know…"

"Kill your buzz?" she supplied.

Now it was her turn to enjoy his laugh. Interesting how the once too-familiar sound used to grate on her nerves.

"You're good," he said. "Witty."

Wiping her fingertips with a paper towel, she

confessed, "I don't laugh at work much. I'm way, way too busy. Or maybe, if I'm being completely truthful here, it's that it doesn't feel very professional to me."

"Hmm."

"What is that, hmm?"

"Professional? Who cares about that? McCoy is oilfield work, not a court of law. Levity is... stress relieving, and your job is stressful. I can see that. And, I don't know, this might not be an official corporate-sanctioned strategy, but I've always found that things run smoother at work for me when I'm friendly with my coworkers, especially where the refinery jobs are concerned. Camaraderie strengthens a team, and when you're doing the kind of dangerous work we do in the refineries, you need to be a team."

Violet understood the concept. But her job was different from his. She couldn't be friends with her coworkers. She didn't work *with* them the way that he did; she needed results *from* them. It felt like too much to explain.

He saved her from having to formulate a response. "Besides, Blackwell, you should never be too busy to laugh. It's good for the soul. It takes the rough edges off just about any sharp emotion."

"Thank you, Doctor," she said with exaggerated gratitude. "That is so insightful. How much do I owe you for this session?"

Through another smile, he said, "You know, I

have always appreciated your smart mouth. You're fun to spar with, even when you're busting my chops. Even when you are being annoying and bossy."

"You mean, even when I'm doing my job."

"Sure." He winked. "That, too."

She laughed again.

"Ugh," he said. "Honestly, that sound is so much better than I imagined."

Violet felt more of her hard feelings melting away. Was it possible that she'd read this guy all wrong?

"You imagined my laugh?" she asked doubtfully.

"Yeah, and I'm going to be honest. It wasn't pretty."

"What did it sound like?"

"Like a… Let me see…" Then he made this awful, grinding, grating noise that set her off all over again.

"Stop," she said when she could breathe. "That's horrible."

"I should have known better, though, because you're pretty, so why wouldn't your laugh be pretty, too?"

Pretty? What the…? Was he flirting with her? No, no way. He said it too casually, too bluntly. There was no pretense or innuendo. Just stating his opinion. He was honest, kind and genuine, and she had to admit that she was beginning to see what everyone else saw. And felt. Because she liked it, too. Who wouldn't like a compliment from him?

Lowering her chin, she tucked it onto one lifted shoulder, then gave him a playful blink and delivered a simple "Thank you."

"I also like how you didn't deny that you're pretty. It's annoying when women do that."

"Flora would disown me if I failed to graciously accept a compliment. She did do some things right."

"You know what I'm going to do?" Shifting in his chair, he leaned forward until his face was inches from hers.

Violet's entire body went hot. It was like the space where all of those negative feelings had dwelled was draining away, only to be filled with new emotions, sweet, wonderful, but also kind of scary emotions. The kind of emotions that had her *liking* him. And sweet buttered biscuits! She really hoped he couldn't see what he did to her, because her pulse was racing at an embarrassingly high rate of speed.

Calm down, Violet. There was a difference between liking the guy and *liking* the guy. She needed to keep the former from morphing into the latter. This was Garrett McCoy, charmer, playboy and perennial heartbreaker. Who was now staring at her again.

"What?" she prodded.

"I..." He drew out the word and pointed at himself. "Am going to make you..." He turned the finger on her, extending the drama, before declaring, "Laugh at work."

"Pfft," she said, brushing off the vow with a toss of her napkin.

"Pfft?" he repeated. "You think I can't do it?"

"In three years, McCoy," she teased, "all you've done at work is irritate me. A cute story over calzones and lemonade does not equate to letting my guard down and risking my hard-earned professional reputation at my place of work."

Grinning like the Cheshire cat, he leaned back again. "Challenge accepted."

CHAPTER EIGHT

"VIOLET WILL BE helping you with badging." The announcement came from Trent on Tuesday morning mere minutes following Garrett's arrival, after he'd taken a seat but before his coffee had cooled enough to drink. Thankfully, Blackwell had graciously brewed enough at home that he'd already had one cup.

He glanced over, and judging by the open laptop, tablet, files and stacks of papers surrounding her, she'd already accomplished more than anyone else in the entire office. At this early hour, she'd probably accomplished more than everyone put together. Her bland expression revealed nothing regarding her feelings about this assignment. She was good at not reacting, he already knew this about her, but he'd also learned it could be a giveaway. The less she showed, the more she felt. Did she want to work with him? He wanted her to want to.

"As you are both aware, we are short-handed. We don't have time to bring in someone new and familiarize them with the process before this job starts."

"Understood," Garrett said.

"Happy to help," she agreed.

"I appreciate it," Trent said, and the accompanying nod suggested he'd anticipated their acquiescence. Not surprising, Garrett thought, because did they really have a choice? Especially Blackwell. He couldn't help but consider how much extra work this would be for her.

Years of ranching ensured that Garrett was an early riser, but he'd logged another restless night. This one had nothing to do with his financial situation, his stepsister's dilemma or his uncle's potential plight, and everything to do with his new living arrangements, specifically his new roommate. He'd spent the remainder of the weekend getting to know the ranch's routine and her.

On Sunday, Flora's horse arrived, and Violet helped him get the mare settled in. He'd saddled the horse and taken her for a long ride to the neighbor's house. He had to give Flora credit; the horse was exceptional. From Garrett's assessment, she'd been well trained and then neglected. Not abused-neglected, just unridden and left to her own devices for far too long. All she needed was TLC and some practice, both of which he was happy to bestow.

Jorge was friendly, funny, easygoing and seemed relieved to have Garrett lighten his responsibilities.

Even though Trent was paying him, he had plenty on his own ranch to keep him busy. All things considered, he appeared to be the perfect neighbor. Garrett looked forward to getting to know him better.

Sunday evening, Garrett offered to cook but made no promises about "complexity of flavor" and "melding of the senses" or whatever other gibberish she may have heard on the cooking channel. She laughed and assured him it would be better than the can of soup she was going to suggest.

He grilled chicken and made buttermilk biscuits. She made a salad. For dessert, he surprised her with vanilla ice cream and fresh strawberry topping. From her reaction, you would have thought a celebrity chef had arrived and cooked a five-course meal. How nice to spend time with a woman who enjoyed the simple pleasures in life like he did.

With Monday being a holiday, the office was closed. Garrett spent the day finishing the chicken coop, getting to know the rest of the horses and further familiarizing himself with the ranch property. Violet helped him with all of it, swinging a hammer, hauling hay, mucking stalls and just generally getting her hands dirty. They visited Ferdinand, and she told him more stories of her life as a Belle.

That evening, they'd pooled their cooking skills,

making sandwiches with the leftover chicken. They'd laughed and talked and watched a few episodes of a mystery thriller by one of their mutually favorite authors. He'd been delighted to learn she liked to read. He couldn't remember a single detail about the show because he'd been too busy trying not to look at her and thinking about how much fun the weekend had been.

They'd gone to bed early, but he'd only tossed and turned. By early morning, exhaustion had finally knocked him out, and he'd overslept. Not by much, but after showering and answering a call from Cade, Violet had already left. He'd had to tamp down his disappointment at not seeing her. The coffee in the pot was barely warm, so he knew he'd missed her by a while.

Ready to conquer his new ranch responsibilities, he'd headed straight to the barn, only to discover the chores were done and the horses had been let out to pasture. She'd even fed the chickens. Back inside the house, he'd poured a cup of coffee and spotted the note leaning against a porcelain sugar dish. The last couple of mornings, he'd scooped the sugar out of a bag he'd found in the cupboard.

In typical Violet fashion, he fondly mused, she'd even streamlined his coffee experience. The note read:

Coffee is fresh. Fed and watered Mrs. Specklesbrock & Co. She made the rounds with me. Cute! Check your phone! See you at the office. ps: Has anyone ever told you that you're a good listener?

For the signature, she'd drawn a tiny heart and written the letter *V.* Grinning goofily, he studied the note, the signature particularly, and irrationally hoped she didn't sign that way for everyone. The familiarity felt intimate, special. He folded the paper and tucked it in his shirt pocket, the left front one, right next to his heart.

A quick check of his phone revealed a photo of the chicken standing on Ferdinand's back. That bull was something else. She'd added: This chicken is no chicken! Mrs. Specklesbrock is a trick rider! Maybe Flora will let her take my place?

"You all settled in out at the ranch?" Uncle Trent asked him, pulling him back into the present.

"Pretty much."

"I assume you've divvied up the chores?"

"We're working on it," Garrett answered for them both.

"Excellent!" Trent flattened both hands on the desktop in his signature *this-meeting-is-over* gesture. "You two are going to slay this orientation process. You're a perfect team. Violet knows the technical stuff, and you have an excellent rapport with the workers. I'll let you out the details. I have a meeting and need to run."

"Yes, you do," Violet agreed. She'd already stacked her papers, bundled her tablet and supplies, closed her laptop and stood. With the kind of efficiency honed through years of practice, she gathered it all into a giant mound. The amount of paper, gadgets and trappings was almost comical.

"Can I help?" Garrett offered.

"Nope," she confirmed. "I have a system." A paper fluttered to the floor, and then another. Garrett retrieved the wayward offenders, as well as a stray pen, and handed it all back to her.

"Not a perfect one, obviously," she joked. "Thank you."

He stowed his phone—the only item he'd brought to the meeting—into his back pocket, followed her into her office and closed the door behind him.

After plugging in her computer, she set about restacking the paperwork and arranging the gear she'd hauled over from his uncle's office. While she worked, he studied the roomy space with fresh eyes. He'd never noticed that her office was almost as large as his uncle's. Probably because there was more stuff. Organized clutter, he'd call it. Behind her desk, running along the wall, stood a large printer. Next to that was an even larger cart stacked with reams of paper. *A lot* of paper. *Violet and her paper*, he thought, which now made him smile. There was also a cabinet, some sort of projector, an easel and various other *business-y* equipment.

Near the windows was a cozy arrangement of comfy-looking leather furniture: a sofa, two chairs, end tables, a lamp and a TV, which he was certain she'd never watched during business hours. A kitchen nook took up one corner where there was a sink, small fridge and microwave. Across the room, a door stood partially opened, and he could see the vanity inside. Nice. She deserved her own bathroom. Truthfully, she deserved more than that.

"Why don't you have these morning meetings in here?"

"Hmm?" she asked, now unplugging a cord. Scowling, she fiddled with some buttons on the docking station, then plugged in the cord again.

"You're the one who has all this paperwork and tablets and stuff, so why doesn't Uncle Trent meet you in here? Why doesn't *everyone* come in here instead of you running all over the place?"

"This is my *job*," she said in a tone that he would describe as a cross between horror and amusement. "Your uncle is the owner and CEO of a multimillion-dollar company. He doesn't have time to be— What was it? Oh, yes, *skittering* around from office to office."

"Scurrying," he corrected. "But you do?" he asked, because he was beginning to seriously question some things. Things about her, about his uncle and her role at McCoy. She did everything around here, things that couldn't possibly be in her job description. Who helped her out?

Ignoring the question, she said, "Before we start on the orientation schedule, I want to tell you my idea. I think we should start on Wednesday. We usually cram it all into two days, but it never works well. There's always stuff that's left incomplete, which, as you've pointed out, forces me to seek people out and—" she paused to tip her head thoughtfully "—contributes to my unpopularity.

"But if we spread the process out to three and a half days, maybe people will be less grumpy. Here's why—I can install software that will allow the forms to be filled out in sections. They can log in and work on a section, save what they've done, log off and come back to it later. There will be a learning curve getting registered and setting up passwords, but if you're here to help, and make jokes and keep things light, I think we can make it fly. Bailey will help, too. She's great with technology.

"That way, people can work on this stuff and then go to a training session or a safety briefing, play their cornhole matches or go get a bite to eat. We'll keep it open until noon on Saturday for anyone arriving at the last minute or whatever. Of course, there are those who will want to get it all done as quickly as possible. That works, too.

The point is, now they have options. I thought we'd bring in some food, too. That way, it will feel like less of a chore. Ideally, anyway. What do you think?"

"I think it's brilliant."

"Yeah?" She beamed at him.

"Yes. It's almost like you're trying to be popular now."

"Never! It's all about efficiency, McCoy," she said, but in a playful tone and with a spark of what looked like pride in her eyes. He wanted to believe he had a little something to do with that light, too. "Efficiency is my goal. Speaking of, if you have any ideas on how to get your refinery crew to turn in those new per diem forms, that would be great. Oh, wait! I can add that as an online option. You're right—I am brilliant," she joked.

"I looked at that form, by the way. That's a significant rate increase."

"Right? I am so happy that it got pushed through before this job. That will make a huge difference for people."

"It didn't *get* pushed through—*you* pushed it through. I asked Adam. People have no idea how much you do around here. Do you know that? I don't even think my uncle realizes how valuable you are, and he calls you the best employee he's ever had. I am not kidding. He said that right to my face. He might as well just come out and ask me why I can't be more like you. How do you think that makes me feel?"

Smothering her laugh made her smile look as bright as the sun. And so incredibly beautiful.

"I almost got you, didn't I?" he teased.

"No," she lied. "That wasn't funny. Besides, in order to claim your victory, other people need to hear my laugh."

"Hmm, I see. I'm glad you mentioned this important detail. So, it's like that old saying about the tree falling in the forest. If a woman laughs in the office and there's no one around to hear it, did she really laugh at all?"

"Exactly! The laughter must be heard."

"Fine," he agreed with a laugh and an easy shrug. "Efficiency is your goal, laughter is mine. Thank you for the coffee this morning."

"Oh, sure," she said, meeting his gaze. "I'm not as heartless as you seem to believe if you think I'd only make coffee for myself. I left a sugar bowl out for you, too. Did you find it?"

"I did," he answered, holding her gaze and thinking.

Thinking that she'd not only noted how he liked his coffee but also that she'd gone out of her incredibly busy way for him to make sure he had it the way he liked it. The realization hit him in the sweetest way, like a soft, warm squeeze to the heart. Then she'd performed the ranch chores, and *then* arrived at the office and put in hours of work before single-handedly streamlining the dreaded and tedious orientation process.

She was right about one thing: Violet Blackwell was so, so, *sooo not* the woman he'd believed her to be. Heartless? Not a chance. Once upon a time, he might have answered yes. But now he wanted, he *needed*, to correct each and every misassumption he'd made about her over the last three years. And the ones others had made, too.

He was, he realized, starting to— No, he *did* care about her. Instead of questioning how his opinion had changed so quickly, he simply accepted that it had. And now pondered what he wanted to do about it. That wasn't true; he knew what he wanted to do.

"Thank you for feeding the girls, too," he said, moving closer to her.

"How could I refuse when they were all running around being feisty and adorable?"

"I know the feeling." When he was close, he stopped and let his gaze wander again, purposely lingering on her lips. "It is very, *very* difficult to resist feisty and adorable."

Her eyes were locked on to his now, and she looked wary and flattered and maybe a little confused. Garrett couldn't blame her. His heart felt like a mass of gathering thunder in his chest. He knew what he felt, knew what he was doing. What he didn't know was if she felt it, too. This...pull. He'd never felt an attraction this strong—irresistible, in fact—and he told himself that he was stepping closer just to see if he was right. He didn't stop until he was in her space.

Not too close, though, because he didn't want her backing away. But close enough that he was satisfied, because, thank the lucky stars, she was flushed and breathing a little heavy. And there it was, a little spot on her neck where the pulse was pounding fast and hard. All the evidence he needed, but what to do about it? He fixated on the area for a few long seconds, wishing, wanting to kiss her. His focus shifted to her mouth. One more step and a dip of his head, and his lips would taste hers. Wait. What was he doing? This was probably too fast, especially for her. Methodical, disciplined, responsible Blackwell. He needed to be careful.

But when he looked up, intending to angle away and make a joke, her gaze collided with his, and he couldn't move, much less think of anything even remotely humorous, because she didn't look like any of those adjectives. She looked…intense, captivated, attracted.

Then they spoke at the same time.

"Violet."

"Garrett."

Several hushed seconds passed, awareness crackling between them as they each heard their name from the other's lips for the first time.

"Violet," he repeated, louder this time, cementing the sound and acknowledging the shift between them.

She let out a husky rush of nervous laughter. "I wasn't sure you knew my name."

"Oh, I know your name." He focused on her lips. "Violet," he repeated and thought, no more Blackwell, no more Ms. Blackwell or Bossy Blackwell, and definitely no more Buzzkill. Just Violet. All Violet.

My Violet.

I tiny-heart you, too, Violet.

"What…" she whispered, her breathing fast and shallow. "Is…" She shook her head.

"Happening?" he supplied, finishing her thought.

Nodding slowly, she reached out with both hands and grasped the front of his shirt. Relief shot through him at the gesture, the encouragement, because he'd never been so sure of anything in his life. And yet he still couldn't move. Someone had glued his feet to the floor. What if he kissed her and ruined this…whatever this was before it even had a chance to begin? He knew her well enough to know that she didn't do anything carelessly. The woman didn't even laugh at work. She would not take an office kiss lightly.

That was when his heart attempted to jump out of his rib cage because she took the step that closed the distance between them. Awareness rushed through him. He didn't have to worry about kissing her because she was going to kiss him.

Or at least she was going to meet him half-way. She flattened her hands on his chest and looked up.

"Garrett?" she whispered.

"Yes, Violet," he answered as she slid her hands up to his shoulders and urged him closer. Their mouths were a hair's breadth apart when a loud knock sounded on the door.

STARTLED, VIOLET FLINCHED and took a step back. The door opened.

"Hey, cutie," a smiling Alex Bauer said from the doorway. Arms outstretched, he announced, "I'm back! You busy?"

"Cutie?" Garrett muttered softly, scowling toward the door.

"Alex!" she said with way more enthusiasm than she felt. Disappointment was washing over her like a cold, drenching wave. She struggled to regain her senses. "Hi. Come in."

"Bauer?" Garrett said. "Are you kidding me?" He ground out the question while scrubbing one hand across his mouth.

Even though they hadn't kissed, Violet wanted to reach up and touch her lips, too, to capture the sensation, the longing. Ugh. They'd been so close to kissing. She'd *wanted* to kiss him. Her cheeks heated as she owned that fact, and, given one more millisecond, she would have.

"Hey, old friend," Alex said, strolling toward

them. "Long time no see. How've you been? Still wrangling cows?"

Of course they knew each other. Alex had done oilfield work for most of his adult life. His skills were legendary. Undoubtedly, they'd worked together in the past. Probably, they were friends. Garrett was friends with everyone.

Or not, Violet realized, as the two men stared each other down.

"Do not call me friend," Garrett stated in a hard, flat tone, confirming her observation. The tightness in his face, the tension in his body, felt almost menacing. "I am not your friend."

To his credit, Alex held his ground. Violet read his reaction as equal parts wariness and exasperation, with maybe a touch of amusement. Garrett seemed tense to the point of anger.

Seriously? What were the chances of her having dated the one guy he didn't like? And why in the world would these two not get along? Violet had barely given Alex a thought the last few days, but now she acknowledged how similar the two men were in their easygoing dispositions. Physically, the differences between them were like day and night. Not nearly as tall as Garrett, Alex was broader in the shoulders with thickly muscled arms and great pecs. This morning, he looked extra handsome with his short blond hair freshly cut and his gold-red beard trimmed close.

In his snug T-shirt, shorts and sneakers, he could easily pass for a boxer or a personal trainer.

Garrett, on the other hand, was all cowboy. Tall and lean with work-hardened muscles, his thick, black hair was an untrimmed, attractive mess, and he had a two-day scruff of whiskers. He'd donned his signature outfit of broken-in denim jeans with a short-sleeved, button-up shirt. Today, he wore it unbuttoned, and Violet could see the logo of one of her favorite country bands printed on the T-shirt beneath.

Alex sighed and shook his head. "Whatever, man. I've said my piece. You need to talk to Nikki."

Nikki? Who was Nikki?

"How long have you two been dating?" Garrett asked her.

Alex answered, "A while."

Twice! Violet wanted to shout it out. They'd only gone out two times! Sure, they'd been friendly for a while, but that was it. What was happening here?

Garrett nodded, his face a cold, hard slab of chiseled stone.

"Violet," he said, turning toward her but not meeting her eyes. "Thanks again for clarifying this matter. Text me when you're ready to work on the schedule. I'll be around."

CHAPTER NINE

ALEX SHUT THE door behind Garrett and faced Violet. "Sorry if I, uh, interrupted something. You know what? No, that's not true. I hope I did interrupt." He grinned and hitched a thumb toward the door. "He seemed annoyed, didn't he?"

"Without a doubt," she agreed. "You two obviously know each other."

"Yep, we do. I've known Garrett since the first grade. Are you guys…?" Alex made a motion with his hands. "Dating?"

"Not exactly, but, um…"

"I see." He crossed his arms over his chest and eyed her thoughtfully. "I thought you didn't like him."

"I don't!" Her cheeks went hot. "I mean, I didn't… But then he moved in with me, and now…"

"Excuse me?" Alex said, cupping one hand to his ear. "It sounded like you said he moved in with you."

"I did, but not like that." Her cheeks heated

with embarrassment. "I don't even know where to begin."

"How 'bout at the part just before he moved in? Violet, I've only been gone a week. I texted you. I like you, and I thought you were into me."

"Okay, Alex…"

She explained about the ranch and Flora's horse and how they'd been assigned to head up orientation. She followed it up with, "He's different than I thought. Alex, I'm sorry. I didn't plan this. Like you said, I didn't even like him a few days ago. It's all happening very fast. To tell you the truth, I'm not even sure what's happening exactly."

Alex studied her, uncharacteristically silent. Finally, he said, "Garrett is a good man, the best man I know. You two… I can see it. You could be great together."

Violet smiled. "Is this your way of breaking things off with me?"

"Let's call it being proactive."

"Thank you for being so cool about this."

He nodded. "I'm not going to lie, Violet. Part of the reason I gravitated toward you initially was because you didn't like him. But you turned out to be different than I thought, too. Better. I'm not sure Garrett deserves you."

"Thank you, Alex. That's incredibly sweet."

"Just promise me one thing. Don't believe everything he says about me. The problem is that *he* believes it, and I don't know how to get him to see the truth without breaking confidences. All I'm going to say to you is that Nikki is... The situation is not what it appears to be."

Who was Nikki? Violet desperately wanted to ask, but it seemed as if she should already know. Maybe Garrett should be the one to tell her?

"I don't know how much Garrett told you, but he and I used to be best friends."

"He hasn't mentioned that. We haven't talked about you. I didn't..." She didn't want to say that it hadn't seemed important. "He didn't know about you and me. That we've...dated."

Alex nodded. "As far as I'm concerned, he'll always be my best friend." Then he smiled and said, "Don't tell him I said that either."

VIOLET TOOK A rare lunch break, one that didn't involve eating at her desk, and invited Bailey to Vago. She hadn't seen Garrett since Alex had interrupted them, nor had she texted him. Yet. Because she couldn't stop thinking about things. Shockingly, it wasn't the almost-kiss that had her preoccupied. No, that wasn't true. The incident was foremost on her mind, but she had no idea how to proceed.

Meanwhile, word had gotten out about the new orientation procedure. Garrett was right; it had made her, if not quite popular, then at least less unpopular. That, along with other comments, had her pondering something and needing Bailey's advice.

They'd just ordered drinks when a foursome of oilfield workers ambled in their direction. When the man in front reached their booth, he halted.

"Hey, Violet," he said. "Sorry to interrupt, but did you get my per diem form? I emailed it."

"No problem. Yes, I did, Roy. Thanks."

"Great. The new rate is way cool, by the way, and I heard you were responsible, so thank you."

"I'm glad I could help," she said.

"Ditto from me, Violet." A tall, burly man with red hair and a matching beard took a few seconds to cast an engaging smile at each of them. "Enjoy your lunch, ladies."

Violet said, "Thanks, Logan. You, too."

Bailey, who was facing the direction they headed, watched them walk away. When they were safely out of earshot, she let out a low whistle. "Oh, man, that redheaded guy is hot. You know him?"

"Logan?" Violet grinned at her now-nodding boy-crazy friend. "Yeah, he's a good guy. And he's got mad skills. He's one of the best crane operators in the industry. So glad we snagged him for this job before Blankenship hired him. He basically does the work of two or three people."

This morning, she'd assigned Logan to Garrett's crew, knowing how much smoother it would make the job go for him.

"You mean, *you* snagged him, right?" Bailey said.

"Well, yes, it was my idea to recruit him, and I sent the email offering him a raise."

"Lucky for me, then, because he is easy on the eyes. Maybe you can introduce us?"

"I should have thought to introduce you just now. Bailey, I'm sorry."

"No problem. I'm sure there will be other opportunities."

"Right." She sighed. "This just proves that I am officially distracted. Can I ask you a question?"

Alerted to the subject change, Bailey looked her over. "We'll circle back around to what, or who, has you so distracted. But the fact that you're asking me if you can ask me a question tells me one of two things. Either a, you already know the answer and want confirmation, or b, you've had some sort of revelation."

"It might be both."

"Intrigued." Bailey sat up a little straighter and folded her hands on the table. "I'm ready to give you an honest answer to whatever the inquiry is that has you so distracted."

One of the things that Violet liked best about her relationship with Bailey was their honesty pact. They'd been hired at McCoy around the same time and become friends within days. At a company lunch, Bailey had gotten a smear of barbecue sauce on the tip of her nose. Violet had taken her aside, let her know and followed up with the comment, "I'd want someone to tell me."

"Me, too," a grateful Bailey had agreed. "Absolutely. I'll be your someone if you be mine." They'd been tight ever since.

Violet asked, "Do you think it's bad that the employees don't like me?"

Thoughtful expression in place, Bailey swirled a chip in the bowl of queso on the table between them. After consuming the chip, she said, "From an HR perspective, it's not a problem. No one *complains* about you being mean or anything."

"You don't need to sugarcoat this, Bailey. I know my reputation. I know my nickname."

"What nickname?"

"Buzzkill."

"Ouch." Bailey winced. "I have not heard that one, Violet! I would have told you, and I would have done my best to put a stop to it. Although, it does show a good deal more creativity than Bossy Blackwell. Do you want to file a complaint?"

"No. You shouldn't have to stick up for me, though. That's my point. I'm beginning to think that in my quest for excellence, I've overdone it. Meaning maybe I've expected too much of other people. Just because I'm a workaholic doesn't mean everyone else has to be, too."

"Okay." Bailey peered at her carefully as if choosing her words. "From a friend-slash-coworker perspective, if you've now decided that you care what people think about you, you would, in fact, attract more bees with honey than vinegar."

Violet did care. She'd always cared; she just cared about her job more. She had to. In order to excel, you had to be committed. You had to be… perfect. If being a Belle had taught her nothing else, it was that.

"Isn't that saying supposed to be about flies, not bees?"

"Yes, but I can't very well call my fellow employees flies, now can I? That sounds insulting. Bees work very hard and are supercool, while flies are…kind of gross. Yes, I know they're useful, too, but it works better with bees."

"Good point."

"It's not so much that people don't like you. They just don't *know* you. Where is this coming from all of a sudden?"

Violet tried to explain without revealing *everything*. She started with dinner and her bet with Garrett, explained about his move to the ranch and the weekend they'd spent together. She wrapped it up by confessing how drastically her opinion of him had changed.

"Holy moly," Bailey said when she'd finished. "I can't believe you get to live with the hot cowboy oilman. I already knew he was a good guy, but that's pretty nice of him to help out in addition to his regular job."

Violet agreed. "I think he told everyone about

the per diem increase. That's why Roy was thanking me. And Trent put us in charge of badging." She outlined the new procedure they were going to try.

"Yeah, I heard some scuttlebutt about that. People are pleased. Well done, you."

"Thank you. I mean, it's not like I invented it. It's just something we've never tried before. As I was saying, I think I sometimes overestimate other people's enthusiasm for my goals." Chuckling, she dipped a chip in salsa.

Bailey pointed at her. "See? This is a thing you do as well. Humility is great and all, but you always downplay your contributions and successes. It's like you think you don't deserve kudos. You're the only one who thinks you're not good enough, Violet. No one in this place even approaches your productivity, your work ethic, your stamina or your brainpower, with the possible exception of our boss. But even he doesn't appreciate you like he should."

"I don't know about all of that, but I do feel like I might get more work out of people if they liked me better. It seems to work for Garrett."

"It does indeed."

"Can you help me?"

"Aw," Bailey said, reaching out and patting her hand. "My little flower wants to be popular."

Violet chuckled and rolled her eyes. "Something I've never been in my entire life. How do I do that?"

"Remember back to your middle-school days? What was the one thing guaranteed to elevate a girl's social standing?"

"I hope the answer doesn't entail making a video and posting it on social media."

"Ha! No, that's not the kind of popularity that lasts. I'm talking about a social event where you forge relationships and acquire friends."

"I'm lost."

"Violet, are you kidding me?"

"Bailey, are you forgetting who you're talking to here? In my world, what guaranteed *popularity* was the ability to do a handstand on the back of a galloping horse."

"Right." Bailey laughed and smacked the heel of her hand on her forehead. "Sorry. How could I forget how weird your childhood was? Fortunately, there are no dangerous tricks required."

"Okay…?"

"A party!"

"You… You want me to throw a party?"

"How's my girl?" Garrett cooed into the phone. He'd commandeered a quiet corner in the downstairs lobby of McCoy Tower. He'd been over to the refinery, checking on the status of some equipment, but wasn't quite ready for the possibility of running into Violet and Alex.

A giggling Remi thrust her chubby arms into the air.

"She misses you," Nikki told him, holding the phone away so it panned her face. There were bluish half circles beneath her hazel eyes, and her skin looked waxy and pale. Single motherhood, nursing school and working part-time were draining her dry, another black mark for Alex. But even exhausted and with her blond hair unwashed and crookedly secured with a hair tie, his stepsister was still a beauty. "She points and yells when we walk by your bedroom."

That made him smile. "I miss her right back. Are you sleeping any better?"

"Sometimes." Smiling wearily, she pulled one shoulder up into a helpless shrug. "I try to nap when she does. How long will you be gone?"

"Not sure yet. The job starts Wednesday and is scheduled for three weeks. I'll do my best to stay on schedule, but you know how it goes. There are so many moving pieces on one of these jobs, elements I can't control."

"Cade stopped by yesterday," Nikki said. "Brought us some groceries and diapers. Supersweet. I don't know how I'm ever going to repay you guys."

He made a mental note to text his brother a thank-you. Cade was busy, too, and lived fifty miles from Garrett's place, where Nikki and Remi were currently staying.

"We're family," he said. "There is no need to repay anything."

"We'll see," she said, nibbling on her bottom lip the way she did when anxiety took hold. "I'll find a way. It may not be money, at least not right away, but I'll figure something out."

"How's school?" he asked, changing the subject.

"Good!" she said. "I like all my classes. My friend Betsy and I have managed to coordinate our schedules again so we can trade babysitting and both have time to study."

Nikki had just started year three of four toward her goal of becoming a registered nurse. A tough road made tougher with the birth of Remi, but she was on the home stretch. Garrett was proud of her. She'd overcome many obstacles in her life.

With a fistful of Cheerios, Remi twisted her wrist back and forth and let out a squeal, his cue to perform "Itsy-Bitsy Spider." Happily acquiescing, he recited the nursery rhyme with accompanying hand gestures while the baby garbled along in her special version of gibberish. Without fail, the waterspout brought out a belly laugh, even without him there to tickle said belly. Adorable.

Laughing along with her, he felt his heart swell with love. It was still difficult for him to wrap his head around the fact that something that had gone so wrong could have produced such a miracle. The going wrong being Nikki and Alex's relationship, not that there'd been much of one. Alex was a full-time oilfield worker, meaning he was gone more than he wasn't, and he knew long-distance romances were tough. But he hadn't even tried. How could he voluntarily miss out on this, on fatherhood? What had happened to the friend he'd once thought of as a brother?

He thought about the earlier encounter with Alex and considered his comment about Garrett needing to talk to Nikki. It wasn't the first time his former best friend had suggested there was more to the unpleasant story of their turbulent ending. Didn't matter. Because, at the end of the day, he'd abandoned his child, and what kind of man did that?

And now he was dating Violet? The idea of Alex and Violet together made him want to punch something.

"Just a sec," Nikki told him. "I'm going to release her into the wild." That was what she called it now that Remi was crawling. Leaning back onto the sofa cushions, she blew a relieved breath. "Okay, she's happy with a chew toy. How are things going so far? How's your uncle?"

"Busy. I have more responsibility this time around. Uncle Trent is good. The company is short-staffed, so I'm helping as much as possible. I'm staying out at his ranch property to get some stuff sorted."

"Of *course* you are," she said wryly. "Garrett

saves the day! Again. Garrett saves everyone. But who saves Garrett?"

"Would you stop? I don't need saving." In their family, he was the one everyone leaned on. His mom, Cade, Nikki and even his ex-stepdad, Nikki's dad, Emmett—they all came to Garrett when they needed help, advice and money. "Speaking of work, I wanted to let you know that Alex has been hired for this job, too. I'm going to be seeing him around."

Nikki looked away for a few seconds before saying, "I'm sorry. I know you hate him."

"I hate what he did to you and Remi."

"It's not…" She sighed. "I wish you could separate what happened with Alex and me from your friendship with him. You two were best friends since first grade, and I hate myself for destroying that."

"It's not your fault. Are you sure you don't want to hire an attorney and make him pay child support? Uncle Trent would loan me the money." He thought about Flora's impending alleged divorce. "Heck, he probably even has an attorney on retainer that could help."

"No! Please, Garrett, no! Can you *please* just drop this?"

"Nikki, I've never asked you this, but I need you to tell me what happened."

"What? Why?" she cried. "It doesn't matter. I don't need him. Remi doesn't need him. He doesn't want us, Garrett. I know that's difficult for you to

accept, but it's the truth. And I know I'm impos-
ing on you—again—but I promise once I'm done
with school, I will get on my feet and I'll—"

"Nikki, stop. You could never impose on me.
You're my sister. It's not that. But I feel like you
should know… Alex is dating someone."

That news seemed to shake her. The phone swept
up and away before refocusing again. "Who?"

"Does it matter?"

"Maybe. Who is it?"

"Someone here at McCoy."

"A name, Garrett. I need a name."

Garrett couldn't think of a reason not to tell
her, and so he did. "Uncle Trent's assistant, Violet Blackwell. They are not a good match, by the
way. She is way too good for him."

"Too good, huh?" Her face came close to the
screen, all squinty-eyed and stiff-lipped as if trying to see him better, to analyze him. "What is
this woman to you?"

"She's, um… A friend." *Friend.* He suddenly
hated that word. But until he could convince Violet
to break it off with Alex, that was all she would be.

"Hmm. A friend, huh?"

"Well, there's a little more to it than that. There
was… It's complicated."

"Yeah?" she asked, eyebrows taking an eager
trip upward. "Do you *like* her? It's been a long time
since you liked anyone."

For some reason, Garrett couldn't bring himself

to admit the truth. Losing Violet now that he'd finally found her was painful enough. Losing her to Alex was unthinkable. Instead, he told Nikki part of the truth.

"Her mom, Flora, is dating Uncle Trent. I'm worried about her intentions. She's not exactly rich. Uncle Trent is… And he's helping her with some stuff."

"Ohhh…" she drawled and flopped back against the cushion. "You think this Flora woman is a gold digger after Uncle Trent's money?"

"I don't know what to think. I'm just investigating at this point."

"I see. And her daughter, this Violet, is how you're going about that. Clever, as usual, brother, and a little devious." Nikki sat back and smiled. "And right up my alley."

CHAPTER TEN

WE'RE NOT IN a relationship.

We've only gone out two times.

We've never even kissed, not like you and I almost did.

I don't even want to kiss him. I want to kiss you.

Can I have a do-over?

These were just some of the thoughts running through Violet's mind that afternoon as she worked in the large conference room, setting up computer stations for the orientation. She wanted to have the technology available for those workers who wanted it, as well as a paper option for the surprising number of people who preferred the old-school method. Those people were secretly close to her heart.

Luckily, the task didn't require a ton of brain energy, because all she could think about was the fact that she hadn't seen or heard from Garrett all day. As each hour passed, the episode kept evolving in her memory. The way he'd left her office had her afraid she'd ruined something before it even had a chance to begin. She certainly would have told him about Alex, but the situation sneaked up on her. Never in a gazillion years would she have imagined she'd be almost kissing Garrett McCoy at that exact moment. Or at any other moment. Ever. She was certain he'd say the same.

So…

Maybe she'd made more out of it than it had been? Maybe *she'd* been all caught up in her feelings, and *he* was happy about the interruption. How embarrassing. Butterflies swarmed in her stomach.

What had happened between Garrett and Alex? It had to be big if they'd once been best friends. This Nikki seemed to have played a role. A love triangle seemed likely.

Regardless, she had no idea what to say to Garrett.

Now they had to do this badging together, and it was going to be so…

"Ugh," she muttered aloud. "Awkward."

"Which part?"

Just the sound of his voice made her stomach flip. Turning quickly, she discovered he was close, only one long table length away. She hadn't even heard him enter the room.

"Garrett, hi."

"Hello, Violet," he said, and her spirits plummeted because he sounded so much like the old Garrett, the one who didn't like her. She wanted to scream all of the things she'd been thinking at once. But what if he'd come to his senses and regretted it? The whole episode felt like a dream now.

When she didn't respond, he asked again, "Which part was awkward? The part where your boyfriend almost caught us kissing or the part where I almost punched him?"

"You almost punched him?"

"Every time I see the guy, I want to punch him."

"So, the punching desire isn't due to the fact that he and I, um…"

"You and he, what?" Garrett prompted.

"Nothing!" The words rushed out of her. "He's not my boyfriend. We've only gone out twice. I have no idea where that 'cutie' comment came from. We are nowhere near the nickname stage."

"Hmm." It was subtle, but Violet thought she could see his body relax as a thoughtful look flickered across his face. "Does he know that?"

"He does now."

"Yeah? You sure about that?"

"Yes!"

"What did you tell him?"

"I told him I—" She couldn't tell him what she'd told Alex without revealing feelings. "I, um…I plead the Fifth."

But the way he was looking at her now made her think maybe some revealing of feelings would be okay. "You don't want to incriminate yourself?"

"Mmm-hmm."

"About what, Violet?" He moved toward her, and her brain scrambled. "Did you commit a crime?"

"Um… No, but…"

This time, he didn't stop until he was right in front of her, toe to toe, so close that she could feel the heat radiating from his body. Hope gathered inside her. Every breath she took was now laced with his delicious scent, which made it even more difficult to think.

"But, what? What is it that you don't want to tell me?"

She liked the deep, low tenor of his voice. The way his eyes were traveling over her made her skin tingle. She looked up into his dark brown eyes, the ones that she'd once foolishly concluded were void of any deep feelings. How could she have ever believed that? Because they were brimming with heat and affection. She cursed herself for missing out on this, on him, for so long.

"I don't want to tell you how much I wish he hadn't interrupted us."

"I see." His lips curved at the corners in a satisfied half smile. "Well, that's even better than I hoped for. Why wouldn't you want to tell me that?"

Still a little nervous, it mixed with a lot of anticipation and left her trembling. She shook her head. "That's enough true confessions from me, for now, I think. Why do you smell so good?"

"Violet?"

"Yes, Garrett?"

"Do you really want to change the subject, or do you want to try kissing me again and see if it goes better this time?"

The breath caught in her throat as her stomach did this delightful sort of dip and dive. "Mark me down for the second option, but what if someone—"

"I locked the door behind me."

"That's…" The gesture meant so much more to her than the obvious intention of giving them privacy. It meant he'd had hope before she'd confessed her feelings. He wanted this, too.

"In that case…" Reaching up, she placed one hand on his shoulder, the other on his chest.

"Violet." He whispered her name just before his mouth met hers. One hand slipped around the back of her neck, and the other went low on her back.

She moved her hands to his shoulders, fingers gripping tight, and it was a good thing, because she'd never been kissed like this before. She was pretty sure that if she weren't holding on, she'd melt right to the floor. His touch felt hot, but his mouth was soft, and the way he moved with such skilled confidence confirmed for her that he was all in.

"Enough," he finally said, pulling away to look at her. She studied him, too, and his look felt smoldering. She hoped she was reading it right. He confirmed it with a whispered, "Maybe not quite…"

He kissed her again. Slower this time, at first, but it intensified quickly, leaving her lightheaded. This time, when he broke off the embrace, he touched his forehead to hers and took a few seconds to catch his breath before glancing toward the door. "Let's, uh, keep it there for now. I think I heard someone trying to get in, and I know you would be mortified to get caught kissing at work."

Would she? She didn't know at this point. She could barely think. But she appreciated his consideration.

"Violet." He took her hand, squeezing gently. "Will you go out with me? I know that sounds weird, considering we already live together, but I want to do this right."

This. The word landed on her heart. Do *this* right? Oh, heavens, yes, she most definitely wanted to do this right, whatever this was shaping up to be.

"Yes, of course, I'd love to go out with you."

"Today? After work?"

"I would like that, but I don't know what time I can get out of here."

"You'll be done by four."

"Garrett, there's no way I can leave early. I don't have a lot of freedom where my schedule is concerned. My life revolves around your uncle's. Even with the two of us setting up here, it's going to take us until five, at least. After that, I still have my regular work to do, and your uncle has a late conference call."

"Mmm-hmm," he agreed, but his nonchalance said he wasn't convinced. "Yes, that freedom thing is a problem for you, isn't it? Have you ever noticed how everyone else in this office asks for help when tackling monumental tasks, including my uncle?" When she started to respond, to tell him her job was different, he held up a finger to stop her. "Let me finish, please. Now, I understand that you aren't the boss, but everyone works together sometimes, Violet. We're supposed to be like one big team, right?"

She shrugged noncommittally because she wasn't sure this applied to her.

He went on, "I have a plan. If it doesn't work, that's fine. We'll make a new plan. We'll go out on a different day, but let me try, okay?"

She wanted to argue, tell him everything she had to do and list all the reasons why this wouldn't work. Inevitably, this became a problem when she dated. All her relationships ended because she worked too much.

But he looked so confident, so hopeful, that she couldn't bear to break this news to him. Instead, she nodded and said, "Okay."

GARRETT RECRUITED ADAM and Darius, who arrived within minutes, and apparently Bailey, too, who showed up soon after with tall cups of iced sweet tea for everyone. As a result, everything went exponentially faster than Violet had anticipated.

When they were almost done, Garrett shooed her off to get started on her normal duties.

When she returned to her office, she discovered that Rhea, the receptionist, had answered her calls and dealt with most of them, which left her with only a handful to return. Skyler, the new wunderkind from Accounting, had completed the spreadsheet they'd been working on, and Trent was in his office on the conference call for which she'd planned to attend and take notes. Instead, Rhea informed her that their coworker Caleb had volunteered to take notes so that Trent was able to facilitate the call earlier.

"Don't worry, Vi," Rhea told her. "I will type up the notes for you to take a look at tomorrow."

Huh. Once inside her office, it took her a total of twelve minutes to return three calls and another four minutes to place another. The latter of which to Maple Boss Barbecue had her feeling triumphant because it meant the party that Bailey suggested she host might actually be a possibility. Perhaps not in quite the manner she'd imagined, but Violet thought this was going to be even better. Pulling up Trent's calendar, she fired off three emails, made a few more calls and, while waiting for responses to her messages, rescheduled his haircut, and… Done.

She checked the time. Hmm.

For another full minute, she sat at her desk gazing absently around, not quite believing that she had nothing pressing left to do, when her phone chimed with a text. Ha! She knew this kind of tranquility couldn't last. There were always some last-minute details that needed her attention.

The message was from Garrett: You must be about finished by now, huh? Get going! Get outta here! You have a date. When you get home, change into something cool and casual. We'll be outside, so grab sunglasses. I'll meet you on the porch.

Grinning, Violet replied: All right! Okay! I'm going...

ps: Well done, McCoy.

She felt heads turn when she walked out of her office and announced to Rhea that she was leaving for the day. But, for the first time in her tenure at McCoy Oilfield Services, she did not care.

Trent's door was slightly ajar. She pointed and asked Rhea, "Is the conference call over?"

"Yep. Caleb just left."

Perfect. Just enough time to launch her plan.

In keeping with their idea to implement Operation Friendly Flower—Bailey had insisted on naming their project—Violet stepped inside and forged ahead. "Hey, boss, can I talk to you for a minute?"

"Sure," he said, waving her inside. "I need to talk to you, too."

She sat in her usual chair. "Do you want to go first?"

"Yes, because my question is personal and will only take a second, and I assume you're here to talk business."

"I am," she said, adding a silent, *Mostly*.

"What is your mother's favorite color?"

"Oh." Not a question she'd expected. This was probably a fun fact a daughter should know about her mother. Thinking quickly about Flora's clothes, costume choices and the leather bag she used to cart Zinni around, she answered, "Blue, I think."

"Perfect! That's what I guessed."

Yeah, me, too, she confirmed silently.

"You're up," he said, and she couldn't help the rush of relief that washed through her at such a simple inquiry. She still hadn't gotten used to discussing her mother with her boss.

"As you are aware, it's been a couple of years since the company has hosted a party for the employees."

"Darius and Adam were just discussing that on the golf course. You have some ideas?"

"I do. Instead of the dinner we've done the last couple of years, I was thinking we could reinstate the picnic with a twist. We could have a barbecue and host it out at Penny Bottom Ranch. Beautiful scenery, space to mingle, plenty of parking. We'll have mounds of good food, games, maybe even a band or a DJ?"

"And a dance floor."

"Sure! Bailey and I were at a wedding reception recently where they hired this DJ husband-and-wife team. The woman led all these fun line dances and taught people dance steps. The DJ made jokes and had a music trivia contest."

"Your mother would love that."

"She sure would," Violet agreed, resigning herself to the fact that Flora would be attending her company party. "Getting one of those guys with the traveling smokers would be fun."

"Like Maple Boss!"

"Exactly." Violet smiled as he threw out the name of his favorite barbecue place, which she'd just reserved. In a massive stroke of luck, they'd had a cancellation, and she'd snagged the open date. "I say we do it soon. Let's give people something to look forward to. I believe you have a free Saturday toward the end of the month."

Trent examined his desktop calendar, which Violet knew very well was blank on said day, as she'd just rescheduled his life to make it so.

"Perfect. The turnaround crews will still be in town. Can you put a party together that quickly?"

"I can." It would take some world-class maneuvering, but that was where she excelled.

Slapping one hand on his desk, a move he executed when he was particularly excited about something, he declared, "Let's do it! Spare no expense," he said. "I'd like this to be the party of the year. It's been too long since we showed our employees how much we value them."

She knew he didn't mean that expense directive in the literal sense, but his enthusiasm would bode well for her ulterior goal: planning the event and using the opportunity to show her coworkers that she had a fun side, too.

"I'm on it," she assured him. "And I agree."

CHAPTER ELEVEN

UPON RETURNING TO the ranch, Violet hadn't wasted any time. Trying not to overthink Garrett's instructions, she changed into a pair of shorts and a tank top. She grabbed a loose-fitting, long-sleeved blouse that could serve as both protection from the sun and as a light jacket. The ranch's ATV was parked nearby, a four-wheel-drive vehicle with room for two passengers to ride side by side.

Trent had purchased the vehicle for the ranch, knowing she didn't ride. "A lazy person's horse," her mother liked to call it, while Violet preferred the term "horse upgrade," a term she mainly used to irritate her mom.

Garrett strolled over from where he'd been waiting in the shade of the porch. Looking at him was such a joy, it was difficult not to stare. Even in shorts, a faded T-shirt that fit snug across his shoulders, sneakers and a baseball cap, he looked like a cowboy, an off-duty one, but still, there was something about the way he moved that somehow screamed rugged toughness and graceful competence all at once. She'd never dated anyone who appealed to her in so many ways.

"What's in there?" She pointed toward the cargo space at the rear of the vehicle, loaded with an ice chest and a large duffel.

"You'll see. Come on." He waved her over, and she climbed into the passenger side. "Hop in. Buckle up."

"Is there anything else I need to bring?" she asked after following instructions. "All I have is sunglasses, a shirt and lip balm."

"Perfect. I have everything else, I think. I hope." Garrett lingered by her side, fiddled with her seat belt and then leaned in close. "Thank you," he said.

"For what?"

"For agreeing to this. I know it was probably physically painful for you to leave work early."

She laughed. *Not for this, it wasn't, not for you.* "Well, you made it difficult to refuse. I'm starting to—"

"Starting to what?"

Doubt my life strategy, she'd been about to say but didn't know if she was ready to admit that. She had some more thinking and experimenting to do on the subject.

She changed course and went with, "I'm starting to relax already. Thank you for this. I'm having fun, and we haven't even left the driveway."

"Good. Me, too." He smiled and then gave her

a quick kiss. Violet decided this was already the best first date she'd ever had.

"WHAT DO YOU know about the history of this place?" Garrett asked after he'd parked the ATV.

During his weekend scouting, he'd ridden here to scope out the creek and had officially fallen in love. Penny Bottom Creek itself was spectacular, the water a vision of crystalline tranquility. The meandering stream sported banks rife with vegetation, and tall trees lined both sides. There wasn't even a hint of overgrazing, and he'd made a point to call Jorge and compliment him on the livestock rotation strategy.

Large rocks protruded here and there, helping to form nice deep pools in the creek, providing convenient perches from which to cast a fishing line or soak up the sun. In shallow areas, you could see the creek bed beneath the water, consisting of tiny smooth pebbles of multiple colors that did indeed shimmer with the color and brilliance of copper coins.

"Rebekah told me the original homestead was built there." She pointed to where the remnants of a small log cabin could be seen. "They wanted to be close to the creek because it was supposed to be good luck. People used to come down here and throw pennies in the water. According to her and Jorge and their kids, you can still find them along the bottom. Back then, the creek would flood every spring, so sometime in the 1930s, family members built a new house where the barn is now.

"Then the previous owners purchased this place as well as the adjoining property. They tore down *that* house and built the barn where it is now. They built a new house, the one where we're living, which has since been remodeled. But they loved the creek, too, so later, their kids constructed all this stuff so the entire family could come down here and enjoy the water."

The "stuff" she referred to was a small rustic-style cabin with a sign on the door that read Pool House. The rectangular structure consisted of three rooms. The largest open area contained a solid wooden table with six chairs, a living room that currently held no furniture and a "dry" kitchen. Another smaller room appeared to be a changing room, as it contained a bench and a mirror. Hooks of varying heights lined the wall. The third room was a bathroom with a solar shower and a compostable toilet.

Outside the entrance, a wooden walkway lined the perimeter. At one end, if you continued left, there was a gazebo with a picnic table. To the right, an adjacent deck stretched along the creek for about fifteen feet alongside a large, deep pool. A bridge over the creek led to a huge rock on the other side, where a wooden ladder had been constructed up to the top. A sign there labeled it Diving Board.

"It is the coolest place," Garrett commented after they'd finished discussing the features at length.

"Isn't it?"

"Do you know if my uncle has plans to move here to the ranch?" Garrett asked the question and felt a yearning so strong it was almost painful.

He couldn't afford a place like this, but this was what he'd choose if he could. This was the property he'd design for himself if such a thing were possible. Since he couldn't have it, he was happy his uncle did and hoped he didn't have plans to sell anytime soon. There were times when images sneaked in uninvited, snapshots of what his life would look like if he hadn't had to help his mom and Cade, too, after his dad died and his mom again after her second divorce. She'd decided to go back to college while he'd helped put Cade through school. And now here he was supporting Nikki again, and Remi, too.

"He hasn't said. All he's ever told me is that it's an investment property."

Garrett shook off the pointless what-ifs and thwarted the encroaching melancholy. He was good at that, and adept at living in the moment, and right now, being with Violet, he knew this particular moment was about to get even better.

"Have you been swimming here before?"

"Nope. I keep meaning to but never seem to get around to it. I've ridden out here on my bike many times, poked around a bit. But now that I'm here and looking at that water, I don't know why I haven't. I love to swim."

"Good. Me, too. Let's go." He'd harbored a fear that she'd been here with Alex. Not that it would have stopped him, but he was gratified not to have to compete with the memory of anyone.

"You didn't tell me to bring a suit."

"I packed one for you."

"You packed me a swimsuit?" she asked skeptically. "Why didn't you just tell me to bring one?"

"Well, here's where things got tricky. I wanted to surprise you, but I didn't want you to feel pressured in case you didn't want to swim. I had concerns it might not be an acceptable first-date activity, even though we already know each other a bit. But I also didn't want to rifle through your things, so I had Bailey run out and buy you one." He handed her a bag. "I hope that's okay."

"What was your plan if I didn't want to swim?"

"A picnic. Do you want to just do that instead? I get it if you're feeling weird about swimming on a first date."

"No, it's not that. I'm going to be honest here— Bailey and I don't always have the same taste in clothing."

He nodded and said with faux sincerity, "Oh, I get that, too. That's why I asked her to get one with the least amount of fabric possible. That's okay, right?"

She busted out laughing and took the bag. They went inside, where Violet headed into the bathroom to change while Garrett headed into the other room. A check of his phone revealed a text from Nikki.

"Hey, Violet," he called to her. "I have to make a quick call. I'll meet you outside."

"Sounds good," she answered.

Miraculously, he managed to keep the conversation brief. Nikki couldn't get the printer to work, but his first solution did the trick. She told him about how much Remi enjoyed their Mommy and Me music class, and he could tell she wanted to visit, but he let her go.

Still, by the time he went outside, Violet was nowhere to be seen. Glancing around, he had a vision of her getting cold feet and heading back to the house. He even checked his phone for a text.

"Hey," a voice called. "Up here."

He looked up to find that she'd climbed to the top of the rock and now stood on the diving board.

"What are you doing?"

"I thought we were going swimming. Or wait— are you one of those ease-into-the-water type of people who take twenty minutes to get their knees wet?"

"*You* are going to jump from there?"

"You sound surprised."

"Well, Buzzkill," he teased, "you don't exactly strike me as the jump-off-a-rock-into-the-water type of—" The rest of the statement was drowned by the sound of the splash, which also managed to douse him with water.

She came up smiling, and the look on her face, the pure joy in her laugh, had his heart expanding nicely inside his chest. Too many emotions to contain.

"Yeah?" she said. "How 'bout now?"

Garrett dived from the dock. Staying under, he swam toward her. He briefly considered giving her ankle a tug, thought better of it and circled around her before finally surfacing a few feet in front of her.

"I thought for sure you were going to try and pull a shark on me."

Chuckling, he pressed a thumb to one finger and held it up. "I was this close. You almost got it."

"No, I was ready to piranha you."

"Piranha me?"

"When someone tries to shark you, you piranha them. You put the heel of one hand on their forehead, and with your other hand, you go like this and make little pinches on the back of their neck." Lifting one hand out of the water, she used her thumb and fingers to mimic the chomping action, which made him laugh.

He sighed dramatically. "I cannot tell you how scared I am of getting piranha-ed."

"Yeah, well, you should be. It's terrifying. The move was designed to make you think twice about shark-ing someone."

Laughing, he wondered how this woman had been right in front of his face for so long. He was… enchanted. At that second, if given the chance, he'd stay right here with her forever.

"What is it about a good swimming hole that takes you right back to childhood?"

"Totally," she agreed with a chuckle. "There was this ranch in Idaho where we stayed one summer. It was on a river, and there was this cool rope swing that hung from a limb out over the water. You know, the kind where you stand on the bank, let go and then swing out until you're ready to drop? So much fun. We hung out there every spare minute. If we weren't riding, or practicing, or doing chores, we were there." Then she tipped back, straightened her legs and stretched out her arms to float.

"My sister, Nikki, would love it here," Garrett said, paddling closer and turning over to float by her side. "The first few years she lived with us, our house was on a lake. Cade and I couldn't keep her away from the water. I was so scared she'd find her way down there alone and drown that I enrolled her in swim lessons. Every summer, Cade and I took turns taking her."

Sister! Nikki was his sister. That explained a

lot, but not everything. "So, what's the deal with her?"

"What do you mean?"

"Trent doesn't talk about her. I didn't even know you had a sister until after you moved in."

"Oh, right. Trent doesn't know her that well. Technically, she's my stepsister, but Cade and I don't acknowledge the 'step.' Trent is my dad's brother. My parents were divorced when I was five and Cade was three. My mom married Emmett, and he had Nikki."

"But you still saw your dad after the divorce?"

"Yes, until he died a few years later. Cade and I still spent time with Uncle Trent. Even after Dad died, Uncle Trent kept us in his life."

"I'm so sorry about losing your dad, especially so young."

"Thanks. It was rough. He was a good guy and a great dad. He and Trent were close. Trent tried to pay my mom the child support he'd paid, but she wouldn't take it." Garrett explained how he'd started working odd jobs at thirteen and kept at it until he got hired at his first ranch. Cade had followed in his footsteps work-wise, although he wasn't a rancher. After graduating from college with a wildlife biology degree, he now worked as a game warden.

"So, how does Alex fit into all of this?"

"Alex's family owns the ranch where I got my

first ranching job. He is my ex–best friend and the father of Nikki's baby."

"What happened to make you not friends?"

"Synopsis version, he got my sister pregnant and then left her." He told her briefly about Nikki's childhood and struggles as a teen and a young adult.

"So, you took her in when she was sixteen?"

"Yep. She had no one else. Her mom died when she was a baby."

"Wow. I'm…"

"Surprised?"

"Yes, but also impressed that you would take that on. I'm also sorry for your sister and for you."

"Me?"

"Well, you've been left with the repercussions, too, haven't you? Not just financial but emotional. I don't want to get into it all, but that's a lot of responsibility to take on at that age."

"Yes, but I—" He stopped short of saying he didn't mind. Because that wasn't exactly true, was it? Being here, at Penny Bottom Ranch, getting a taste of what it would be like to have his own place, was making him fully aware of his sacrifices. Nikki's calls and texts were also a constant reminder.

Which made him angry with Alex. If he would step up and do the right thing, Garrett wouldn't have to. The truth wasn't easy to swallow, but something about Violet and being here with her in this magical place made him want to be honest. She was so open with him, which made him feel guilty and increased his desire to somehow make it up to her. He knew that didn't make sense. The right thing to do would be to reveal his suspicions about Flora. But what would that do to their blossoming relationship? Nothing good, that was for sure. He couldn't risk it. He might not be able to reveal his overarching plan, but he could be truthful about himself.

He wanted his fears about Flora to prove unfounded, but it wasn't looking good. The woman kept earning one bad mark after another. He could only hope that once he told Violet the truth, if it came to that, she'd have fallen in love with him the way he was falling for her, and none of it would matter. The very idea of her finding out left him terrified.

So instead, he said, "I have. I love my sister and my niece, but it's been a challenge, for sure."

CHAPTER TWELVE

VIOLET GRIPPED THE beanbag and tried to decide how to play this out. They were supposed to be warming up and "getting a feel for the boards," but she didn't want to tip her hand before the match started, so instead, she nonchalantly watched her opponent, filing away useful information about his technique.

"Logan, can you excuse me for one second?" she asked the crane operator, who happened to be her first challenger.

"Sure."

She caught Bailey's eye and waved her over. "I just need to ask my friend a quick question."

"Who? Bailey?"

"Excuse me?"

"Bailey, from HR. She's your friend, right?"

Violet threw him a curious smile. "Yes, she is. Why?"

"Do you, uh, know if she's single?"

Ah. *Perfect.* "Yes, Logan, in fact, she is."

"Hey," she said to Bailey, who'd jogged over. She looked extra gorgeous with her long blond hair in a thick, loose braid. Wispy tendrils framed her delicate features. Like most other participants, she'd dressed down. Unlike some of the more serious and a few self-declared contenders, she wasn't wearing workout clothes. She'd opted for denim jeans and a bright blue T-shirt. On the front was a cartoon dachshund wearing boxing gloves, with the words *doxie moxie* inscribed below.

"Hi, friend. What's up? What are you doing in here?"

"We'll get to that in a sec." Violet swept a hand toward Logan. "Bailey, this is Logan."

"Nice to meet you, Logan. I've seen you around."

Logan grinned, his pretty green eyes flashing with appreciation. "I've seen you, too."

"Logan operates those huge cranes in the refinery. You know, the ones you told me the other day that you'd like to see up close?"

"Mmm-hmm," Bailey agreed with a brilliant smile, even though she'd never said any such thing.

"Yeah?" Logan said eagerly and then dialed it back a notch. "They are pretty cool. The tall one can lift twenty thousand pounds. I could show you sometime?"

"Awesome!" Violet gushed. "Bailey, since you work in HR, you probably know the procedure for making that happen, huh?"

"I am very familiar with the visitor's policy."

"Great. Maybe you two can get together after our match and discuss it?"

"Sure, yeah," Logan said quickly. "Works for me."

"I'd like that, too," Bailey said with a smile. "Thank you, Logan."

"Perfect." Violet held up a finger in a *just-a-sec* gesture. "Logan, I'll be right back." Lightly gripping Bailey's arm, she led her to the side.

Bailey whispered, "Nicely done, wing-woman. Is that why you called me over here?"

"You're welcome," she said, feeling pretty pleased herself. Her potential shellacking of Logan would go over so much better if he were looking forward to a date with Bailey. Not to mention his distraction could only help her, too. "No, I called you over here to ask you this question—would it be better for me to win this tournament or lose? You know, from a fellow employee's perspective?"

"Wait, wait…" Bailey shook her head. "Violet, you are playing in the cornhole tournament?"

"Yes."

"Why?" It was a good question. Bailey knew how she felt about the tournament. She complained relentlessly about it every year.

"Long story, but you know how I lost a bet with Garrett where I agreed to play in the tournament? He tried to release me from my debt, but a bet is a bet. But now that I'm here, I see a different opportunity, one in keeping with Operation Friendly

Flower. There's a lot of teasing and camaraderie, people getting to know each other. I know we didn't discuss this specifically, but spontaneity seems in order here."

"Yes, that's the point. From an HR perspective, it's genius. Garrett uses this as a form of team building. He organizes all sorts of activities for the oilfield personnel before a job starts so they can get to know each other. Working that closely together, under those dangerous conditions, it's helpful to have that connection."

"Right," Violet said, the statement filling her with a combination of admiration and guilt. At almost every turn, she'd underestimated the man.

"I get that now, and I'm officially on board. But I'm not sure how my *performance* would best go over. What do you think?"

"Your *performance*? Violet, are you telling me you truly believe you can win this tournament?"

"Yes."

Bailey took her gently by the shoulders and stared into her eyes. "You can beat Adam and Garrett, and heck, even Darius? Darius has been champion three years in a row."

"I can beat them all. I don't care who I have to play or who's the reigning champion. What I care about is what it will do to my likability if I win. Or do you think it would be better to lose gracefully? I could ham it up and act like I don't know how to throw a beanbag."

"No!" Bailey said. "Don't do that." Nibbling thoughtfully on her lip, she said, "You're sure you want to do this?"

"Yes. People are already talking about the party, and that's great. But that's easy, and it's not really letting people get to know *me*. I mean, everyone loves a party."

"Mmm-hmm. True. You know what *else* everyone loves?"

"What?"

Bailey's grin was electric as she answered her own question and Violet's in one fell swoop. "A winner, Violet. Everyone loves a winner."

PLEASED BY HER first tournament victory, which she'd won handily, Violet strolled into her office. The thick, bright pink ribbon caught her eye the second she entered the room. She studied the object it was tied to and tried to make sense of what she was seeing. Taller than waist height with three shelves, it was square in shape, maybe two feet by two feet, with four wheels mounted on the bottom. It was…some sort of cart?

She walked closer and discovered there was an envelope on top with her name written in black Sharpie. She plucked it off, tore the paper seal, removed the note and read:

Dear Violet, I present to you your cart, Blanche.

He'd drawn a tiny heart and written the letter *G*.

Violet smiled. She got it, both the purpose and the reference.

Carte blanche. Freedom. Affection rushed through her, leaving her a little giddy. A happy giggle followed as she fully appreciated his cleverness. Best. Gift. Ever.

Crossing the room, she removed her phone from her bag to send him a text. A knock on the door stopped her. Hoping for Garrett and an in-person thank-you, she called out, "Come in."

"Hey," Flora said, opening the door and giving her an almost shy smile. "I would ask if you're busy, but I already know the answer to that because you're always busy. But can I come in? I need to talk to you."

"Hi, Mom. Sure, of course."

Flora walked in, Zinni-in-a-bag over her shoulder.

"I was just going to make a pot of coffee. Would you like a cup? You can let her out."

"Yes, please, I could use a coffee." She knelt, freed the dog and then paused, eyes narrowing as she spotted the cart. Practically leaping to her feet, she stood, planted her hands on her hips and then walked forward. In front of the cart, she stopped and pointed. "What in the world is this?"

"Oh." Violet dialed her tone to casual and tried not to cringe. She really, *really* did not want her mom to spoil this gesture for her. Like the time when she was a teenager and her boyfriend brought her a bouquet of flowers. Flora had lectured her about how a man's gift to a woman he was courting symbolized how well they were paying attention. This boy, she informed him, had taken the easy, *obvious* way out.

"Just a gift from Garrett."

Flora was nodding and frowning, but then she shocked Violet by exclaiming, "I get it! Because you're always hauling stuff back and forth from here to Trent's office—and all over this dang building, for that matter. Now you can stack your papers, files, tablets and whatever else on this little beauty."

She patted the cart, and the smile she gave Violet was radiant. "You know what this is? This is the office version of a wheelbarrow. Not like that cheesy boy who brought you the bouquet of violets that time. Do you remember him? What was his name, Cody or Bobby or Tubby? Violets for violet, how original." She added jazz hands. That was how much the incident had disappointed her.

"Tubby, really? No one is named Tubby, Mom. His name was Brodie, and he was my boyfriend."

"Well, who can remember a name like that? That's why I love my girls' names so much. They're unforgettable." Then she stepped closer and laid a hand on Violet's shoulder. "Violet, honey, this is the most thoughtful gift ever. Like next-level on the gift scale."

There was a scale? Certainly, in Flora's world there was. Still, Violet had to agree it was special. "I know."

"I am so impressed."

"Me, too."

"You know that man is in love with you, right? Has he told you?"

"Mom, no!" Violet protested even as she absorbed the possibility and acknowledged how desperately she wanted it to be true. "We... We haven't even known each other for very long."

Flora gave her a slow blink. "You don't think three years is a long time?"

"I mean, we haven't been dating for very long."

"But you've *known* each other. Trent says you two have always gravitated toward one another. He thought you were already friends." She waved a breezy hand. Zinni snorted out a piglike snuffle that sounded like a confirmation. "Doesn't matter. I could tell that night when we were out to dinner at Jameson when you were acting so strangely that he *liked* you. Believe it or not, my own daughter is more difficult to read than a stranger."

"You could tell he liked me? We were fighting."

"Fighting, *pfft*. That bantering you two do reminds me of your father and me. Back in the day before the bickering turned... Real." She sounded almost sad when she added, "Trent and I don't do that, though. He treats me like a queen."

"You are a queen, Mom," Violet reminded her gently. As a teen, her mother had been crowned rodeo queen. Growing up, she'd once jokingly told her daughters that she'd decided she preferred the title "Queen" to "Mom," the latter of which only reminded everyone how old she was. When J.R. then took to calling her "Queen Mother," Flora dropped the idea.

"Thank you, honey." Flora smiled, but it didn't quite reach her eyes. Despite her own issues with Flora, her mom was a person, a woman, and a sensitive one at that, despite how she tried to hide it. Violet knew the breakup of her marriage was way more difficult than she let on.

In typical Flora fashion, she shook off the creeping melancholy and focused on the issue at hand. "Violet, I know you don't like hearing advice from me anymore, and I try not to give it to you because you really do seem to have your life together. Mostly. Your professional life, anyway. Definitely not your love life, though. And on—"

"Mom, please," she interrupted, tipping her head and squeezing her eyes shut. "We have an agreement, remember? And I don't—"

"Violet," she interrupted right back. "We have— had—an agreement about the Belles. But I am still your mother, and I have to say this. And, as I was saying, *on this particular topic*, I do have much more experience, so I need you to listen to me. When you find a man who sees you like…" She paused to add a two-handed spokesperson gesture toward the cart before adding, "*This*. You do not let him go."

"Thank you for that sage advice," she answered dutifully, even as she silently shouted, *How do I do that? How do I not let him go?* "I will consider it carefully."

"Thank you."

That was when another aspect of Flora's pronouncement dawned on her. "What do you mean we *had* an agreement about the Belles?"

"I want you to reconsider performing."

"No," she answered simply.

"Will you tell me why?"

"No. It doesn't matter why. My answer is no."

"You are remarkably stubborn."

"Thank you, because it means I am never talked into doing something that I don't want to do. Is that what you wanted to talk to me about, the show?"

"No, actually, it's not. I came to ask for help."

"Violet?" Garrett opened the slider, stepped outside and called her name, even though he could see very well that she wasn't on the patio. He'd texted over an hour ago, but she hadn't answered. He headed around to the front of the house, where a set of stairs led to the covered porch. Scaling the steps, he paused to think and look around. The situation wouldn't be so baffling if it weren't for her pickup parked in the drive.

She was here somewhere. He'd already checked the entire house, been out to the barn, the shop, where the ranch's equipment was stored, and all around the grounds. He'd even paid Ferdinand a visit.

The only place he hadn't checked was the riding arena, but she didn't ride, so that was out. Despite that assurance, he found himself heading there. The building was basically a large rectangle. The bulk of the square footage consisted of a huge open space for indoor riding. But there were also stables, a restroom, a storage area and an office. He entered through the office door and immediately heard music. He followed the sound, which seemed to be coming from the arena.

Garrett liked to believe that it took a lot to surprise him, but the sight of Violet in the middle of the space managed to stop him in his tracks. What in the world? She was…juggling, he realized as he absorbed the sight. The music and his distance from the action muffled his whispered exclamation, because she wasn't just juggling. She was standing on the back of a roping dummy, tossing, weaving and catching what looked like flaming bowling pins. Mesmerized, all he could do was watch. She hadn't turned on all the overhead lights, so the fire appeared very bright, threading around her in swirls and leaving vibrant trails. As she varied the height of her tosses, it was almost as if she were on fire.

Then he realized that she was also slowly and steadily spinning on the narrow space that made up the fake cow's back. He couldn't say how long he stared, but he was conscious of the music, the change of songs. When the torches eventually started dimming, she caught them one by one, hopped from the dummy's back and extinguished them.

Clapping loudly, he walked toward her.

She spun around to face him, looking both startled and maybe a little embarrassed.

"Garrett, hi." Her tone was completely casual, like he hadn't just found her playing with fire. "I thought you were working late."

"I did."

"You did? Is it late? Sometimes I lose track of time out here."

"It is late. I made dinner. You do this often?"

"Yeah. It's sort of my stress reliever."

"Juggling fire relieves stress?"

"What, you don't agree? Have you ever juggled fire?"

He chuckled and then kissed her. "That was amazing. You're like a professional juggler."

"Thanks. It's just for fun."

"Does this also explain how you're a cornhole prodigy?"

"You heard, huh?"

"It's all everyone was talking about at work today. They called it an upset when you beat Logan, but beating Darius puts you on a whole nother level. You're in the semifinals."

"The juggling skills probably help." She tipped her head back and forth in this cute side-to-side manner. "But my sisters and I used to play cornhole when we weren't practicing our stunts. Iris is good, too. We were unbeatable as a team. I've always been good with my hands, anything that involves fine motor skills. Unless we were throwing knives. Willow is next-level at knife-throwing."

"But not so great with a bow?"

"No, she's excellent with a bow. I'm not sure what happened that night."

"Huh. I need to meet these sisters of yours."

"Do you juggle?"

"Uh, no. I always wanted to learn."

"I'll teach you. You can shout at me in Spanish while I teach you the moves."

"No *fuego*," he said.

"What?"

"No *fuego*," he repeated. "It means 'no fire.' I want to make sure you understand that phrase before we start these lessons."

She tipped her head back and laughed. "Noted."

"Do you want to have brunch with my brother and his girlfriend this weekend?"

"I'd love to, but I can't. I told my mom I'd help her with this horse thing."

"What horse thing?"

"A volunteer program to help at-risk kids. It's an all-day thing out at the Tangled Y Ranch."

"Oh. That sounds awesome. I'll help, too." He'd been trying to figure out how to spend more time with Flora. He needed to get a read on her before she and Uncle Trent got any more serious.

"Really? Are you sure? I know you're looking forward to seeing your brother."

"Yes, I'm positive. I want to help. Cade's been traveling a lot lately doing these training sessions. He'll be back in the area again soon."

"Okay. Well, that's great. She'll be happy to have the extra hands."

"So…" Current circumstances collided with one of their earlier conversations. "You didn't use to juggle while riding, did you?"

"Yep. Juggling was my trick."

"So, you still juggle, but you don't ride?"

"Correct."

"Why?"

"Garrett, we've talked about the riding thing."

"Not really," he pointed out. "You've said you don't want to talk about it. That's not the same as actually talking about it."

Scowling, she inhaled deeply and let her cheeks fill with air. Then she puffed a loud exhalation. "That's a valid point."

"Thank you. I do have one occasionally."

That made her laugh again, which caused his

heart to skitter some quick beats. He loved how he could tease her and appreciated how open she was to his opinions. He wished he could just ask her about Flora. He trusted her, but the truth was, he hadn't known her that long. He'd trusted Alex once, too, and he'd known him since childhood. He needed to be careful and not let his feelings override his common sense.

"I can't," she said.

"Sure you can. Talking is one of the many things you excel at, along with juggling."

"No, I mean, I *can't* ride."

It took a few seconds, but finally, he got it. "You're afraid."

"That one," she confessed, and the sadness in her voice made his heart hurt. "To the point of terror. The accident… Seeing my sister, my beautiful, fearless twin, get shot with an arrow and almost die. And then when I couldn't see her in the hospital. I don't know. It just did something to me. I haven't been able to get back on a horse since."

"Violet, it's probably like a form of post-traumatic stress. Did you get any counseling?"

"Sure." She nodded but didn't quite make eye contact. "It was very helpful in sorting out the problem. My logical brain understands the cause, but my body won't cooperate. And, like my sometimes-wise mother says about horses, if you don't have confidence in them, why should they put their confidence in you?"

"This is why you refuse to participate in the reunion show?"

"Yes," she admitted. "Mostly. But there are other factors."

Factors that she'd undoubtedly made more important in her mind than they needed to be in an effort to offset the real reason. He wanted to read Flora Blackwell the riot act for the number she'd done on her daughter. On all of her daughters, from what he'd gathered.

"Flora knows nothing about this, does she?"

"Ha! No! Can you imagine how ashamed she would be to know her daughter is terrified of riding? It's easier to just let her believe that I'm stubborn. I wasn't good at it anyway."

"Is that the other factor you referred to?"

"Yes. It's embarrassing, but I just wasn't as quick or sure on a horse as my sisters. I tried, Garrett. I did. Aunt Dandy helped me, and I was getting better. A few months before she died, she gave me this special saddle. We were working on this act where we juggled together. You know how two jugglers toss the objects back and forth?"

"Yeah," he said simply, hoping she'd keep talking.

"We were practicing secretly—not an easy feat with Flora and four sisters around, as I'm sure you can imagine. But then she… Dandy had an aneurysm and died." She paused to snap her fingers. "And just like that, everything went downhill from there. I never got to perform with the saddle. After our breakup, I gave it to my sister Iris. She was always brave. She'd earned it. She *deserved* it."

"Violet, that is simply not possible."

"What do you mean? Which part?"

"If you could juggle flaming sticks while standing on the back of a moving horse, you were—you still are—an exceptional equestrian, not to mention an incredibly brave soul."

CHAPTER THIRTEEN

AFTER AN EXCEPTIONALLY hectic morning, Violet was getting ready to meet Garrett for lunch when her office phone rang. She could see the call was from Adam, and knowing she could make it quick, she picked up.

"Hey, Adam."

"Violet. Oh, good. I'm glad I caught you. Can I get ten copies of that new per diem form?"

"Sure. I'll print them for you right now. I'm on my way out, so I'll drop them by." Adam's office was only a few doors away.

The printer malfunction should have been her first clue. True to his word, Garrett had been waging a systematic campaign to make her laugh at work. Subtle attempts at first, but she couldn't help thinking these were just hints of the depth of his pranking ability. Like he was easing her into it. There'd been nothing for the last day and a half, and she'd been walking on eggshells, waiting for his next try. These facts should also have dawned on her. But his timing was also strategic, designed to allay suspicion. Not only had her morning been packed, he'd invited her to lunch at a popular new restaurant she'd been dying to try. Somehow, he'd gotten a reservation, and he knew her well enough by now to know that she despised being late. All of this had her perfectly preoccupied so he could more easily carry out his nefarious objective. Unfortunately, none of this occurred to her at the moment.

Now focused on the printing issue, she tried a couple of different troubleshooting methods to no avail. With the clock ticking in her mind, she gave up and navigated to the task manager, where she switched to the main printer, which was located right outside her door in reception. This space served as the common area where all the offices on that floor were accessed, and a large break room was at one end.

Frustrated, she called Adam. "Printer won't work. Can I get back to you after lunch?"

"Oh, shoot," he said. "I really need them now because I'm headed over to the refinery for a lunch meeting, and I told the guys I'd bring them."

Ugh. "Okay, well, I can try to—"

"What about a copy?" he suggested. "I'll just use the copy machine. I'm on a call, but then I'll come over and grab the original form and do it myself."

She glanced at the clock. No time to wait for him to finish a call. "No, I can do it," she said. "That's a good idea. I'm on my way out, so I'll do it right now. See you in a minute."

Form in hand, she headed out the door to the enormous freestanding copier. The thing was old but reliable. After opening the cover, she lined up the form and pressed the green button. The machine whirred to life and quickly produced her copy. But when she removed the paper from the printer to ensure she'd lined it up correctly, she immediately noticed something amiss. There was a paper clip in the middle of the form. Apparently, in her haste to get this done, she hadn't noticed the object on the screen. She opened the top again, then lifted the form to remove the paper clip, but there was nothing there—no paper clip, nothing but smooth glass. Somehow, she must have brushed it off without noticing.

She put the form back in place and hit the copy button again.

Adam exited his office, file folder in hand, and strode toward her. "Thank you so much, Violet."

She pulled the paper from the tray, only to discover the paper clip was there again. "Look at this," she muttered and handed the paper to Adam. "What is happening? What is that?"

"Um, a paper clip? Looks like a paper clip on the copier screen thing."

"I know," she said. "But there's not. There's nothing there. Look." She lifted the top.

Adam carefully removed the original and studied the surface. "Yeah, I don't see it."

"That's what I'm saying. Rhea?" she called out to the receptionist. "Have you made any copies today?"

"Uh, no. What's going on?"

Violet turned toward her and explained. Rhea joined them, asking questions and seeming perplexed.

"Let me look at this thing," Adam muttered, then fiddled with the paper tray, sliding it out and back into place.

"Nothing there now," he said, placing the original form back on the surface. He lowered the top and then pushed the button. The copier produced his paper, and he removed it from the tray. "It's definitely gone."

"Let me see." She looked at the nice, clean form. "Good." Shaking her head, she commented, "Weird."

"For sure," Adam agreed and then made another clean copy. Frowning a little, he nodded, looked over the paper and said, "Looks good. I guess I need, uh…eight more."

"Eight," she repeated. With exaggerated movements, she tapped the number eight on the keypad and then pushed the green copy button.

The copies whooshed out. He removed the stack and studied the top sheet. "Um, Violet, what did you do? There's a paper clip on this one." Continu-

ing to shuffle through, he said, "And this one...
There's a paper clip on all of these."

Frustration welled inside of her. "That's impossible!"

"Let me try again." He pressed the copy button, and it spit out a single sheet.

Violet snatched it from the tray. No paper clip.
"No way! What is happening?" With a frustrated
groan, she lifted the top again. "How is this possible?"

"I have no clue. But do you think *that's* a good
idea?"

"Yes," she said, attempting to pry open the next
layer of the machine. "There is obviously a paper
clip inside of here somewhere. It must have fallen
below this screen and...and it's only somehow
showing up on some copies or... I don't know!"
Pulling up the flashlight on her phone, she an-
gled it into the space she'd managed to create.
"I can't see anything. Rhea, can you get me a
screwdriver?"

"Sure," Rhea said and headed toward the supply room.

"A screwdriver?" Garrett asked from behind
them. "What's going on? Why are you assault-
ing the copy machine?"

When Violet turned to answer, she saw Bailey
and Alex had also arrived.

"This is so bizarre! A paper clip keeps showing up on my copies, but when Adam made copies, it didn't."

"A paper clip, huh?" Garrett said. "That is bizarre. And it's not on all the copies?"

Bailey stepped closer and said, "Let me see." She took the papers from Violet, and with Alex peering over her shoulder, she examined them for a few seconds. She looked at the copy machine, then at Garrett, and then placed a hand over her mouth as if to stifle a laugh.

Head shaking, she muttered, "Oh, Violet..."

Only then did it dawn on her.

"Oh, no, you did not!" She opened the paper tray and removed the top sheet, which already had a paper clip copied on it. "You did." He'd made the paper-clip copies beforehand and put them into the paper tray. Brilliant. And with Adam as his accomplice, he'd set her up so perfectly. How many times had they rehearsed this? How many times had they counted the sheets of paper so that she'd get the paper clip in her copies? That explained why Adam had "checked" the paper tray when her back was turned. She wanted to laugh. It was his best effort yet.

Instead, she sighed dramatically and faced a grinning Garrett. "Really?" she said. "I almost destroyed this very expensive copy machine. You think that's funny?"

"Yes," he said. "You're really not going to laugh?"

"No," she said. "It's not that good." It was, though.

They all knew she was lying. Adam, Alex, Bailey and Rhea were all chuckling now.

"Violet, you thought there was a paper clip *inside* the machine. Where did you think it was, and how would it show up on your copies?"

She bit the inside of her cheek to keep from smiling. "It was clever, sure, and elaborate, but you're going to have to do better." Even though she wasn't sure how much longer she could hold out. Not much longer if he was willing to go to these lengths. "Be better, Garrett," she joked.

Alex laughed hard at that.

"And you!" She pointed at Adam. "I expect more from you." She snatched the file folder from his hand and opened it. Inside were sheets of paper, both preprinted paper clips and blank sheets, which explained why he'd messed with the paper tray at one point, to make sure his copy came out "clean."

"He bribed me!" Adam said, holding both hands up in the surrender position. "Two rounds at Maddie Hills. Do you know how expensive the green fee is there?"

"Really? A couple of golf games is all it took? Pathetic is what you are," she teased, "letting him draw you into his evil web. What's next, Adam? Are you going to dress up like a clown if he offers you dinner and drinks?"

"Garrett? Adam?" Trent called from the doorway of his office. "Can I talk to you guys for a second?"

Garrett waved and answered, "Sure, Uncle Trent." Then he winked at Violet. "I'll be right back. Then we're going to lunch. Our reservation is a little later than I told you."

With a playful glare, she said, "So, we actually do have a reservation?"

"Violet, of course. I would never bait you with food and then not deliver."

Garrett followed Adam, who was already walking toward Trent's office.

"Well done," Bailey said, patting her shoulder after they'd gone. "I would not have been able to contain myself. That was good."

Alex chuckled and said, "I'm impressed, too. He's turning up the heat."

"I know!" she said, clenching her teeth and adding a frustrated groan. "Help! I don't know how much longer I can hold out."

"Yeah, I thought changing the ringtones was going to do it."

It nearly had. Garrett had somehow managed to change every office ringtone on the main floor. Not only had he changed them, he'd been extremely clever about the song choices. Adam, who considered himself an expert on men's fashion, got "Sharp Dressed Man" by ZZ Top. Darius, the office athlete, was assigned "Eye of the Tiger," and Trevor, the biggest playboy in all of McCoy Oilfield Services, got "Fancy Like." For hers, he'd chosen "Born to Be Wild." Not even Trent was spared, the entire building erupting in laughter when "Bad to the Bone" blared from his office.

"It was the desktop that almost got me." It had been his first official prank, so she'd been caught off guard. First thing in the morning, she'd booted up her computer and discovered that her new desktop photo was Garrett and his brother when they were kids dressed in homemade superhero costumes. They both sported capes made from bath towels and, for some reason, had oversize rubber boots on their feet. The best part was the leotards and tights, over which they'd donned their underwear. When Garrett had then strolled into her office similarly dressed, she'd nearly lost it.

"He's definitely upping his game," Bailey commented.

"Yeah, bringing other people into it is... I don't know, but I should have laid down some ground rules. Dang it! I'm going to lose eventually, and he knows it."

"That's it!" Alex cried. "You are going to lose."

"Thanks for the vote of confidence, Alex," she said dryly. "Although you sound oddly excited about it."

"I am." Grinning now, he stated, "Because you can't change the fact that you are going to lose, but what you can do is choose *how* you're going to lose."

Head shaking, she said, "I don't even know what that means."

After glancing over his shoulder toward Trent's office, he asked, "How do you feel about turning this around on him?"

CHAPTER FOURTEEN

WHEN GARRETT SHOWED up at the Tangled Y Ranch for his volunteer stint, he wasn't sure what he was expecting. But he could safely say what he wasn't, and that was the amount of people and horses milling around. In the distance, he thought he saw Big E holding court with a group of cowboys who were gathered around a corral. He parked next to his uncle's SUV, got out and meandered in the general direction of the crowd.

Near a huge red barn, under a sturdy white sun-shade, Flora Blackwell was talking to a group of teens. Even considering the early hour, she looked dazzling, if slightly overdressed. Rhinestones glittered on the bejeweled denim vest she wore over a white T-shirt. On her legs were snug riding pants tucked into patent leather knee-high boots with silver buckles. She wore a front pack with her tiny terrier tucked inside. The dog wore a sparkling gem-encrusted collar and tossed out a happy yip at the sight of Garrett.

Violet, who'd come early to help "set up," was nowhere to be seen. Flora gave him a friendly wave and informed him that Violet had his "assignment" at her "station," which was located outside the stables' main entrance on the other end of the barn.

He found her there, holding a tablet in one hand and a clipboard in the other. Not so different from how she often looked at work, he thought, except for her casual dress: a tank top tucked into denim jeans and well-worn hiking boots. A coiled length of rope hung over one shoulder.

He wanted to kiss her but refrained. He'd missed having coffee with her this morning and said that instead.

"Me, too."

"Also, you are gorgeous."

A playful glint lit her eyes as she smiled at him. He loved it when she looked at him as if he was the best thing she'd ever seen. It made his chest go warm and tight.

"Your mom told me to report here."

"Yeah, she's on a tear this morning."

"Was that your great-uncle over by the horses? And is my uncle here, too? I thought I saw his SUV."

"Oh, yes, Big E and Trent are both here. No able body has been spared. Where horses and kids are concerned, Flora is all business. And I mean that with a hyphen like it's all one word. Horses-and-kids," she repeated faster, running the words together. "For every troubled child in

the world, her answer is to put them on the back
of a horse. Girl from a broken home acting out?
Get her on a horse. Your son is what, he's *smoking*? Teach him to ride."

Garrett laughed.

"You think I'm joking, but I'm not. The kid
could be an aspiring gang member with a rap
sheet too thick for an industrial-sized stapler, and
Flora would say, 'Poor kid, obviously never had
a horse to keep him out of trouble.'"

Garrett secretly believed there was some truth
in the therapeutic aspect of riding but chose to
keep that to himself for now.

"What can I do?" he asked.

"You will be in corral number three with a shoplifting vandal named Cyrus. You are right next to
Flora, who happens to be working with Cyrus's
younger sister, Kelsey, a perpetually truant tagger.
And in case you're concerned that I'm divulging proprietary information about these minors, that's how
they introduced themselves on their get-to-know-me sheets." She held up a clipboard and chuckled.
"Cyrus will be riding a pretty bay mare called Misty.
You've been assigned to Durango, the tall, black
gelding. You're welcome. I chose him for you myself."

"And what am I doing exactly? Teaching him
how to ride?"

"Yep. These kids are all part of a new program based in Dallas. The point of the program is to take the kids out of the city and show them what's out here. They get to try a bunch of different activities—fishing, bicycling, backpacking, kayaking and now, thanks to Flora, horseback riding. The hope is that at least one of the activities will resonate with them, broaden their horizons, give them an outlet, et cetera."

"So, they've never ridden before?"

"Some have. Cyrus has, for sure. Again, he told me. They've all had a basic horse safety instruction class. Flora went to Dallas and did that last weekend. She wanted them to be able to get on a horse today. It's your job to evaluate Cyrus's skills, teach him accordingly, talk, bond—you know, and just spend time with him. When and if you think he's ready, you can go riding on one of the trails." She handed him what appeared to be a map.

"How long is this lesson?"

"Two hours. Then you get another kid and do it all over again. While this group is out riding, I'll be teaching the next bunch how to saddle a horse, proper form in the saddle and other basics. Then we switch. After your second lesson, we'll all gather for lunch at the chuck wagon."

"This sounds like quite an operation. Your mom is in charge of all of this?"

"Yep."

"How many volunteers?"

"Including you, she managed to round up seven volunteer instructors who'll be giving riding lessons to fifteen kids. She's going to take two of the more experienced riders together. Then there are another five support people like me, plus the lunch staff and a cleanup crew. Everyone has committed to three weeks of lessons."

"Wow."

"I know. All volunteers, too. She's been working her tail off putting this together. Her dream is to turn it into an ongoing thing and offer sessions on a regular basis all year round."

Garrett pondered the scope of this endeavor as he headed to his station. Impressive. What, he wondered cynically, was Flora getting out of this? He was sure the answer would reveal itself. In the meantime, he introduced himself to Cyrus and geared up for the day. He remembered the thrill of learning to ride himself and enjoyed sharing his knowledge. Luckily, Cyrus, the self-proclaimed sixteen-year-old troublemaker who reminded him of his brother, Cade, was enthusiastic, eager to learn, and seemed fascinated by the entire experience. Coupled with his confidence and natural athleticism, Garrett soon deemed him ready for a trail ride.

The timing couldn't have worked out better, intelwise. He and Cyrus ended up riding the trail with Flora and Kelsey. It didn't take him long to learn that Flora had her work cut out for her. As opposed to her brother, fourteen-year-old Kelsey seemed sullen, uncomfortable and eager to be anywhere but on the back of a horse.

"Kelsey, you are doing great," Flora told the teen. "Turn your legs inward just a smidge more. I know it feels funny at first. And remember, I want to be able to draw a line from your ear down through your shoulder, hip and all the way to the back of your heel."

Kelsey grunted and adjusted her body position.

"Do you have some spray paint in your saddlebag?" Flora asked. "I'll tag you with the line if it'll help you remember."

"Sweet!" Cyrus cried and then cracked up. Garrett couldn't help but chuckle, too.

A few seconds passed, and then Kelsey snickered. "That was actually pretty funny, Ms. Flora."

"Why don't you tell me what you like about tagging."

"Freedom," Kelsey answered immediately, a little defensively. "I like the freedom. I can do whatever I want. No adult is there telling me what I can and can't paint. No one is telling me to stay in the lines."

Good answer, Garrett thought, if a bit melodramatic. But she was a teenage girl, and it hadn't been all that long since Nikki had been one of those.

"And the thrill," Cyrus added. "She likes the adrenaline rush. That's why I used to steal."

"Well... Good," Flora said. "Freedom and thrills

are two of the top best things you get from riding a horse. Fortunately, it's rare to get arrested for riding."

Both kids smothered another laugh, and Garrett couldn't help but admire Flora's wit and direct style. Even though Violet was more subtle, they were traits her daughter had inherited. An observation that both surprised and troubled him because, up until now, he'd thought that Violet was nothing like Flora. Seeing her like this, he wondered about the three of her daughters who didn't speak to her.

Family dynamics were complicated, and clearly, he had much more to learn. For now, he focused on teaching Cyrus everything he could, because he had a good feeling about these two siblings. Cyrus spoke openly about how their dad had left when he was seven and Kelsey was five. In the blink of an eye, they'd been the children of a single mother without an income to provide for them. She'd had to work, scramble for childcare and go back to school to make ends meet. Similar to his story.

Once they hit the trail that wound along the river, Cyrus was riding comfortably on Misty. With Flora's gentle and creative instruction, he could see Kelsey visibly relaxing in the saddle and making a concerted effort to maintain her form. The scenery was breathtaking, and the kids eagerly drank it in. Kelsey spotted a red-tailed hawk. Garrett was impressed by her knowledge of birds, and she shared her dream of becoming a Texas conservation officer. Garrett told her about his brother, Cade, and asked if she'd like to shadow him sometime.

"Are you kidding me? Is that possible?"

Garrett assured her that it was.

Cyrus joked that he wanted to be a rodeo clown and then listened with rapt attention as Flora told him about both the excitement and danger involved in her daughter Maggie's job.

"Um, okay," he said when she'd finished. "Scratch the rodeo part. I'm going straight-up clown."

They all laughed at that. The kid was incredibly likable. Two hours passed quickly, and by the time they made it back to the barn, Garrett already felt an attachment to both of them. He assured Cyrus he'd be back next weekend.

The following session went well, too. Garrett's second student, Pierce, wasn't as enthusiastic or engaging as Cyrus, but he could see growth by the time the lesson was over. Pierce promised to return, too, and Garrett felt like that was the best outcome he could hope for.

At some point in the previous ride, the chuck wagon had arrived.

"Cool," he heard Cyrus say. "It's like a pioneer-style taco truck."

Garrett agreed, and they traded names of their favorite taco places. The sound of sizzling meat combined with a delicious combination of spices had his stomach growling with anticipation.

He discovered Violet by the drink station, scooping ice into tall paper cups.

"Hey," she said. "How'd it go?"

"Great!" After giving her a quick synopsis, he said, "Your mom is incredible. She's amazing with these kids and an excellent instructor, too. She has all these cool tricks and sayings. I thought I was a pretty good teacher, but she's next-level."

Violet gave him a tight smile. "Yes, she is good with kids, especially ones that aren't hers. I am also aware of her creative teaching methods. My sisters and I used to joke that she could teach a scarecrow to ride a horse."

"Of course," he said and chuckled. "Why am I telling you all of this?"

"No, I get it. It's fun to see her in action. Just be aware that she's probably using this whole thing as a ruse to scout for new talent. The Blackwell Belles 2.0. I can visualize the headlines now. 'From troubled teen to trick rider, Flora Blackwell uses horses to help kids triumph over adversity.'"

"I wouldn't have to scout for new talent if my own children would do their part."

They both turned to find Flora and Big E standing behind them. The statement had come from Flora. She fisted her hands, placed them on her denim hips and scowled at Violet. Once again snuggled into her front pack, Zinni let out an unsettling howl-growl sound.

"That's canine moral support right there," Big E commented wryly.

Or, Garrett silently speculated, it might be a dog with a canker sore; how in the world could you tell?

"Big E, hi. Sorry, Mom, I was just joking."

"I know," Flora said and chuckled. Moving to stand next to Violet, she used one hip to nudge her daughter. "I'm joking, too. Sort of. Admit it, Vi. This kind of makes you want to get in the saddle again, huh? Very satisfying to see these kids riding. Don't you agree, Garrett?"

"Uh, yes, ma'am, I enjoyed every minute," Garrett answered truthfully, even as he somehow felt like he was betraying Violet.

"See?"

"Mom, we agreed—"

"I know, I know…" Flora puffed out a good-natured sigh and said with feigned drama, "I need to stop dreaming about performing with all my girls one last time before I die."

"I know what that's like, Flora," Big E chimed in with no small measure of theatrical flair. "To dream about reuniting your family. I had to pull out all the stops to make my grandsons see the light. Faked my own disappearance. And Grandma Denny… I almost lost my sister, and she almost lost her ranch before those other stubborn grandkids of hers rallied round and saved the day."

Violet had told him about Big E's well-intentioned

meddling with her cousins. This was different. Violet and her sisters had very good reasons for their estrangement, as did Violet for not wanting to perform. Garrett knew Violet wasn't about to fall in line. He understood about her not wanting to perform, although secretly, he had his doubts about her not wanting to ride.

"Well done!" Violet gushed with no small amount of sarcasm and then clapped her hands. "Did you two thespians rehearse this beforehand? Because if that was all ad-lib, you need to take a whole new type of show on the road."

Big E chuckled. "I think she got the message, Flora."

"We tried," Flora agreed. "Good effort, too. I liked that bit about Grandma Denny. Nice touch."

"We'll keep trying. And thanks. I'm no slouch when it comes to doing what's necessary to help our youth. And that includes our Blackwell youth." He winked at Violet and picked up the ice scoop. "You two go fix your plates. We've got this."

"CAN YOU BELIEVE the nerve of those two?" Violet asked Garrett later that evening when they were back at Penny Bottom Ranch. They'd visited Ferdinand, mucked out stalls, then stabled and fed the horses. It had been a long day, and they were both exhausted. "Trying to *guilt* me into performing."

Garrett chuckled. "That was quite a performance. Big E is something else, isn't he? He's like eightysomething and out there in the heat teaching kids to ride. Impressive. The man has the stamina of someone decades younger."

"I agree," she said. "And I know he means well with this family stuff, but I don't get why it's so important to him. I love my grandma Denny. It's not like I'm estranged from her—or him, for that matter. He's awesome, too, and welcome in my home anytime. Plus, I'm still talking to both of my parents! Why are they so focused on me?"

"I'll tell you why. Flora thinks I'll be easy to convince. Once she gets a couple of us in line, the rest will topple like dominoes. I'll hand it to her—it's a good strategy. When I was younger, I would have caved. Ha! I'm almost glad I can't ride anymore."

Head bowed, hands tucked into his pockets, Garrett remained quiet as they walked toward the house.

"Say something," she urged. "Do you think I'm wrong?"

He reached over and took her hand. "No, Violet, there's no wrong here. I'm going to be honest, though, because I know you value honesty and because I do have an opinion. I think I understand where he's coming from. I don't have much family, which is why it's important to me to keep what family I do have. But maybe there's another element to all of this."

"What's that?"

"Riding. Horses. You need to ride again. Imagine if we could ride together. How much fun we could have."

"Are you kidding me?" She stopped and extricated her hand from his. "Not you, too."

"I understand you not wanting to do the show, and that's fine. But I think your mom has a point about riding. You saw what happened with those kids today. In just a couple of hours, a light came on inside of them. That's what horses can do for people. I mean, your mom is not wrong. I'm not saying it's going to be life-changing for every one of those kids. But if it changes even one life, and I believe it will change more than that, it's worth it. You had that light—you've said so yourself— and I know you miss it."

"My mom is not wrong? Did you just say that to me?"

"Yes, but what I meant is that she's… I think she's trying to help you."

Muttering under her breath, she shook her head and looked away. "I cannot believe this. You've fallen under her spell."

"What? No, there's no spell." A mystery, yes. At this point, the woman was a downright enigma. The more he got to know her, the more confused he became.

"Now that I think about it, you talk about her a lot. You've asked me a lot of questions."

"Well…" Oh, no, had she figured it out? How was he going to explain this now? *Hey, Violet, I started out with the intention of spying on your mother because I think she might be after Trent's money, but now I'm not sure, and somewhere along the line, I fell in love with you.* "Uh…" Glancing away, he swallowed and said, "I'm trying to get to know you, and your family is a part of you, right?"

She gasped. "Oh. My… I don't believe this. Flora put you up to this, didn't she? Did she ask you to talk to me? To try and convince me to perform?"

Garrett was caught off guard by the suggestion, and when he didn't immediately respond, Violet went on, "What did she promise you? Because I can guarantee you, Garrett, no matter what you saw today, that woman is not who you think she is. I can't believe she would stoop this low. I—"

"No! Violet, she did not ask me to talk to you. Listen, I—"

"Listen? No, I will not *listen*. I am done listening to people try and talk me into things I don't want to do. I…" Lifting her chin, she proceeded to slowly enunciate each subsequent word. "Won't. Do. It. Anymore. Period."

"Okay, but—"

"I shared my fear with you because I thought you would understand. I thought you wanted to get to know *me*. I thought you would accept *me*. I don't want to be fixed. I don't *need* to be fixed. I don't need you to fix…the thing that isn't wrong." She paused to inhale a deep breath before adding in a calmer tone, "There is nothing wrong with me."

"Violet, I know there's nothing *wrong* with you. And I'm not trying to fix you—I'm trying to help."

Violet turned back toward the barn.

"Can we talk about this?"

"No, no more talking. I'm done." She stormed off. "I'm going to go see Ferdinand. He's lived this, too. He understands. And then I'm going to bed. I have to go in early, so I'll see you at the office tomorrow."

CHAPTER FIFTEEN

VIOLET WONDERED IF that counted as their first fight. Did it count if they hadn't even defined their relationship? What were they even doing? They hadn't discussed whether they were exclusive, much less if they had a future. In her introspective fog, she realized how much she'd told him about herself, her family, the Belles, her mother. A flush of heat blasted through her. She felt like the poster girl for one of those "What Not to Do" dating articles—don't talk about yourself too much! And then, to add humiliation on top of embarrassment, she'd accused him of being callous with her and her feelings. She didn't believe it, but the episode brought an issue to light that she couldn't ignore: she'd overreacted about the riding thing.

She owed him an apology. Several, perhaps. If she ever got the chance, that was. She wouldn't be surprised if he never wanted to talk to her again. Maybe that would be a good thing.

The morning meeting with Trent brought her

a much-needed jolt back to reality. Until noon, her boss would be in subsequent meetings, which gave Violet time to check the badging paperwork. Their strategy had paid off. Every single worker, with one exception, had checked in and completed, if not all, then most of their paperwork. She stared at the name of the employee who hadn't logged in: Alex Bauer.

Huh. Why would Alex not have filled out his paperwork? Dread flooded through her. They needed him on this job. Did this have something to do with her, or more likely, with Garrett? Things seemed okay between her and Alex. They'd remained friends and even texted over the weekend. He wouldn't quit without telling her, would he?

She sent him a text and then tapped the call icon when a knock sounded, followed by Bailey opening her office door. Her friend stepped inside with two brown bags from their favorite lunch truck in hand.

"Hope you don't have plans with your cowboy oilman."

"I do not. He's at the refinery doing some training." *Most likely because I lost my temper, fell down a rabbit hole and probably drove him away forever*, she added silently, not quite ready to talk about it yet. No answer from Alex, so she placed her phone on the desk and said, "You are an angel and my best friend."

"I am? I mean, I know I'm an angel, obviously."

She joked and gestured at herself. "But I'm your best friend?"

"Yes, of course. You know that." Violet peered at her closely. "Do you not know that?"

"I do now, and I suspected. But frankly, I'm relieved to hear you say it, because how awkward when I ask you to be in my wedding, but you don't reciprocate."

"Bailey, will you be my maid of honor for the wedding of my dreams, which will likely never occur?"

"Yes, Violet, I will. If you'll also agree to be the maid of honor in my fantasy wedding."

"I'd be honored."

They shared a laugh.

Bailey settled in the chair opposite Violet and said, "And now that those niceties are behind us, let's talk about your strategy for your next match."

She'd completely forgotten about the cornhole tournament. The finals were coming up. But first, she needed to find Alex. He hadn't responded.

"Okay, um, how's this… I am the winner, winner, and then I claim my chicken dinner. The end."

Bailey grinned. "Well, my friend, that is a sound plan, except I think you might have some actual competition for your final match."

"Yeah? Who is it?"

"Alex."

"Have you seen him?" she asked excitedly.

"Yes. On Friday, I watched him annihilate Adam. I don't want to psych you out or anything, but he's *very* good. And, no pressure, but I have two steak dinners, a pedicure and lattes for a week riding on your victory."

"No, I mean, have you seen Alex here at work today?"

"Oh. Um, yeah, sort of. I saw him this morning at the coffee place across the street."

"Thank goodness."

"What's going on?"

"He didn't show up for badging, and I was afraid he'd quit."

"Why would he quit before the job even started? I've heard he's making crazy money."

"That's what I intend to find out."

HOURS LATER, Alex still hadn't answered his phone or returned her text. On the off chance that he'd realized his paperwork oversight, Violet headed downstairs to the conference room. The badging stations were still there and operable, but Alex was nowhere to be seen. Exiting the elevator, she headed that way, only to hear the telltale *thunk, thunk* coming from the large conference room where the cornhole tournament was being held. Inside, she was surprised to discover the man she'd been seeking.

"Alex, hi! I've been looking for you."

"Hey, Violet." He lowered the beanbag in his hand.

"It doesn't matter how much you practice," she teased, walking farther into the room and letting the door swing shut behind her. "I'm still going to beat you."

"Wow," he said with a grin. "Who knew Violet Blackwell was so good at talking smack?"

"No, it's fact. Doing you a favor, saving you time. Are you ignoring my calls?"

"Sort of," he admitted. "But not just you. Everyone."

"I see. Does the reason have to do with why you haven't filled out your paperwork for this job?"

"Yep."

"What's up?"

"I, uh…I'm not sure if I'm going to stick around."

Violet was only a few feet from him now. "Is everything okay?"

"No, not really."

"Do you…do you want to talk about it?"

"I really don't want to put you in an awkward position with Garrett."

"Alex, I would never betray your confidence. We were friends first. You were one of the only people around here who ever tried to get to know me. Besides, Garrett and I had a…disagreement. I don't even know if things are going to work out with us."

"Do you want to talk about that?"

"No. It's a complicated issue that has to do with my family. People think I need to be fixed, but I'm not broken."

"You are most definitely not broken, Violet."

Alex's gaze wandered over her face for a few seconds, but she didn't feel romance. She felt affection and concern. "Do you want me to punch him?"

"What? No!" She laughed. "What is it with you two?"

"Did he say something about punching me?"

Violet cringed a little. "He may have."

Alex smiled but it seemed sad. "It's this thing we've always said—and done—since childhood. When one of us needs an attitude adjustment, we punch each other in the shoulder. It used to be a form of affection, I guess. Now it's…" He sighed. "I don't know how everything got so messed up. Well, yes, I do know. It's Nikki's fault." He sighed and muttered under his breath.

"I just don't know how to undo it, and because Garrett is giving me the cold shoulder, most of the oilfield guys are following suit. I hate to admit this, but I don't know if I can be an effective leader on this job."

Violet didn't doubt the truth of his words. She knew now how carefully Garrett had fostered relationships within the ranks. Being the boss's nephew didn't hurt either. It wasn't okay for him to use those relationships at another employee's expense. She asked a few more questions until she was satisfied she had a handle on the situation and the repercussions of Garrett's behavior.

"I'll take care of it," she assured him.

He sighed and looked at the ceiling. "I can't believe it's come to this."

"Tell me what happened."

"I just did."

"No, I mean, tell me about Nikki."

"Oh. I don't... I'm not sure that's a good idea."

"Why are you protecting her?"

"I'm not protecting her, Violet. I'm protecting Garrett."

"Well, we're on the same page, then, aren't we? I'd like to have the information so that I can protect him, too. And you, as well, Alex."

He glanced skyward for a few seconds and then looked at her and nodded. "Okay. I can't believe I'm doing this, but I'm desperate, so I'll tell you what I know."

WHERE IN THE world could Alex be? Frustrated beyond words, Garrett stalked across the refinery grounds toward his pickup. Despite the state of their relationship, his ex-friend had always been a good worker. One of the best. It wasn't like him to blow off something so important. But because he had, Garrett had to spend twice the time doing training on this particular machine because he and Alex were the only two currently certified to run it.

To be fair, a good share of his irritation was impatience. He wanted to see Violet. He needed to apologize. If she truly never wanted to ride again, fine. She could pedal around on that silly bike of hers all she wanted. Even though he knew he was right about this, he'd let it go. He just hoped she forgave him; everything else didn't matter.

A quick check of the time told him she could be either on her way home or still at work. "Your powers of deduction are remarkable, McCoy," he muttered to his irritable self.

Fearing that she wouldn't answer a call or respond to a message, he dialed the office and asked for her.

"Hey, Garrett," Rhea answered. "I think she's gone. Did you try her cell?"

"I'll do that," he lied. Good. He'd rather have this conversation at home, face-to-face. He used the drive to practice his speech.

Once he arrived, a quick check of the house told him she wasn't inside. The second place he looked he hit pay dirt.

"Hey," he said, approaching the fence where she was positioned as she often was on the top rail, her body turned inward toward the field. Ferdinand was cozied up to her side. Horses grazed in the distance. How could she not see that she was a cowgirl at heart?

"Hi," she said, and her tentative smile gave him hope. "How was your day?"

"Long. Alex didn't show up for work, so I had to meet with his crew and do his job. Have you heard from him?"

"Yeah, I have. We...worked things out. He'll be there tomorrow, but we need to talk."

Jealousy twisted his gut. *We need to talk?* Everyone knew what that meant. One disagreement, and she was going back to Alex?

"Okay." He ground out the word, intending to grovel. Unless she told him that she wanted Alex instead. If he heard that, he was going to pack his stuff and go home.

"You need to stop treating him like a pariah."

"Excuse me?"

"You need to show Alex the respect he deserves. Garrett, I know you have personal issues, but you need to keep them out of the refinery. He's excellent at his job. He has a crew to run, but you're making things impossible for him."

Oh! This was about work. Relief rushed through him, and he barely managed to suppress a smile. "I haven't done *anything* to the guy. I've barely said two words to him since he's been here."

"That's the point, and you know it. All the refinery people are devoted to you, and they follow your lead. You've been giving him the cold shoulder. Worse, I heard from two other sources who say you're borderline hostile but careful not to cross a line."

"So, what? He ran to you and tattled that I'm not being nice enough?"

"No, *I found him* when he didn't complete his paperwork. Rather than talk to Trent about your behavior, he was going to quit. And before you say anything else, I'm telling you all of this because it's not only an efficiency issue, it's a safety concern. If the employees won't listen to their crew chief, how can he keep them safe?"

Garrett felt his stomach twist. She was right. How could he have been so shortsighted? He needed to get a grip on his anger toward Alex and accept his mistake. It was difficult to own, but finally, he nodded. "You're right. That was beyond stupid. It won't happen again."

"I don't need to remind you how much we need him on this job. How much your uncle needs him."

"No, you don't. I get it. I was completely in the wrong. I underestimated the influence I have on the employees."

"Thank you." With a nod, she turned back toward Ferdinand.

"Can I talk now?"

"Sure."

"Will you please get down and come over here so I'm not speaking to your back?"

With the athletic grace he admired and had become so familiar with, she twisted around and jumped from the fence.

He moved closer. "Violet, I am so, *so* sorry. I was also completely in the wrong where you and I are concerned. I never should have pressured you into trying to ride again. I only did it because I love you, and I want the best for you. Going forward, I can't promise that I won't mention it again, because I still believe it. But I'll try—"

"WHOA UP THERE," Violet said, emotion squeezing her lungs so that she could barely breathe, much less stand. She reached out and took hold of his shoulders. "You love me?"

He reached up and placed his hands over hers. "Yes, I love you. Obviously."

"No, not obvious! Not to me. How long have you known?"

"Uh, let's see… For sure, since you left me that note with the tiny heart."

"What note?"

"After I moved in, that Tuesday, before you left for work that morning, you wrote me a note, and you signed it with this tiny heart and a *V*. I read it, and I just knew… I said it to myself right then—I tiny-heart you, too, Violet." He placed one of her hands on his chest, right over his heart.

"Me, too," she said as tears gathered in her eyes. "I tiny-heart you, too. So much." She sniffled. "I thought you were going to break up with me."

"Break up with you?" Garrett gathered her in his arms, wrapping her up and holding on, and she pretty much never wanted him to let her go. "Why in the world would I do that?"

"Because I'm bossy and stubborn."

"Traits of yours which I was already *very* familiar with."

She laughed and hugged him tighter. Hugs had been missing from her life for way too long. Tears, too, probably because it felt almost good to let them fall.

"I freaked out on you."

"You didn't freak out. You shared your feelings with me about a sensitive topic. I don't ever want you *not* to do that. It just tells me how passionate you are and how much you feel. As I started to say before, I'll be careful about mentioning it in the future."

"You give the best hugs. Has anyone ever told you that?"

"No," he said, and she could feel him smile into her hair. "No one has ever told me that. I don't give them out much, actually. But I love hearing that from you, and you can have one whenever you want."

"Whenever I want?" she repeated. "What is the time limit on that?"

"Forever."

Forever? That was exactly how long Violet wanted this moment to last. But unfortunately, it couldn't. They needed to eat, and her nose was running, and bugs were starting to find them. Plus, she had that other issue to discuss with him. Reluctantly, she let go. Sniffling and tugging on her shirt to swipe at her tears, she said, "I'm sorry. I'm a mess."

Keeping hold of her shoulders, he leaned away and let his gaze travel over her. Expression solemn, he nodded gravely and said, "Yeah, little bit. Let's save the selfies for another day, shall we?"

She laughed again.

Chuckling, he drew her in for another quick hug. This time he kissed her, too, and then said, "I'm kidding. You know that, right? You are gorgeous."

"I do, and I love you for making me laugh. And I love you for many other reasons, too. One of which is your honesty. So, please don't stop being honest with me, even if I don't like it."

"Okay, but are you going to do that trick where you try on a hideous outfit and ask how you look just to see what I'll say?"

"No, I would never set you up on purpose. I'm talking about the whole riding thing."

"I told you I won't—"

"No. Nope. You were right."

"I was?"

"Maybe. Despite your reassurance, which I adore, I was too defensive about it. I can see now how my defensiveness was due to fear. For years, I've been telling myself I don't care about riding anymore. Using Flora as an excuse, like I'm not riding just because she wants me to! I can do—or not do—whatever I want. What I didn't acknowledge was how much I do want to ride, because that would mean admitting how scared I am."

"You do?" he asked, trying not to let too much excitement into his tone. "You want to ride again?"

"I think so. Except, as time has gone by, it's gotten worse. I've developed a full-blown fear of it."

"No, you haven't." Taking her hand again, he gave her fingers a gentle squeeze and explained, "I've been watching you. You're not *afraid* of horses. Last weekend, I saw you showing those kids how to saddle and handle a horse. I've seen you here inside their stalls, brushing them and fussing with their teeth, hooves, ears. Putting drops in Jewel's eyes. You do *everything*, and you do it so well. To Flora Blackwell standards, I'd be willing to bet. You've been caring for the horses here for what, over a year now?"

"Yes."

"I can help you, Violet. I'm a great teacher. Even your mom said so."

"Also true, and you're presenting a very Blackwell-level argument. But I already know how to ride. That's not the issue. The problem is that I am *terrified*."

"I know. You are scared to get in the saddle. That part, I believe." He brought her hand up to his lips and kissed her knuckles. "I want to help you get over that. I *know* I can help you."

Violet felt herself waffle because, deep down, she knew she needed to conquer this. The fear was eating away at her. The other day in the arena, he'd called her brave. She'd been kicking the compliment around inside her head ever since. The very idea that Garrett McCoy would call her brave, that he believed in her, was overwhelming in all the right ways. The fact that he loved her just took it all to another level.

She nodded. "Okay."

"What do you mean, okay? You'll ride?"

"I'll try."

"Seriously? Just like that?"

"If twelve years of fear and arguing with Flora, then having a fight with you, the man I adore, and me crying and pouring my heart out to you, and more arguing with Flora, and all the while dodging Big E, is your version of 'just like that,' then sure, just like that. To me, it feels like it's taken a while to get here."

He was smiling and shaking his head in that way he did when she said something surprising. "Do you know how precious you are to me, how utterly adorable?"

"I'm happy to hear it. I always knew I was precious. I'm so grateful to *finally* be appreciated for my preciousness. That's way better than being able to ride a horse."

He kissed her, undoubtedly to silence her silly nervous rambling, and then said, "I've given this a lot of thought, and I'd like you to ride Cadence. She's an exceptional horse, lively and spirited but not easily spooked. Flora picked a good one there."

"Okay."

Hand in hand, they started walking toward the

barn. With a gentle squeeze of her fingers, he asked, "You're sure you're okay starting on Cadence?"

She shrugged a shoulder. "I trust you. If you think she's the horse for me, then let's do it. Flora has been spotting excellent horses her entire life."

"Huh. I thought…"

"You thought I wouldn't want to ride her because she's Flora's?"

"Are you aware of this habit of yours where you talk about your mother and call her Flora instead of Mom?"

"What? I do…" She'd been about to say "not," but she absolutely did. "…that. Don't I? I do. I'm sort of aware of it, yes."

"Yeah, I mean, I get it. It's a way to keep some emotional distance. You're the only one of you five girls who has maintained a relationship with her all these years. You're the one she goes to when she needs something, and that can't be easy. The woman is a force of nature. You were bound to develop some coping mechanisms."

"That's incredibly apt. You may have missed your calling as a therapist."

"I didn't miss my calling. Like Flora, I believe wholeheartedly in horse therapy. I just didn't want to admit it to you too soon." He stopped in front of Cadence's stall. "We'll do as much as you're comfortable with today, okay?"

Violet agreed and opened the stall door. The

mare really was a beautiful animal. A quarter horse, Flora's favorite breed, she was a gorgeous deep brownish black in color with a white star on her forehead and four white socks. A good size, too, Violet had already noticed, for trick riding. Not too tall, muscular and well proportioned, but still lean enough to be nimble.

Violet stroked her sleek fur and felt a mix of fear and anticipation. "What about you, Cadence? What are you up for today?"

The horse pressed her muzzle close to Violet's side and nudged her arm with a soft whicker.

Garrett chuckled. "That's another thing I like about her. She enjoys moving. How about we saddle her up and take a walk?"

CHAPTER SIXTEEN

VIOLET DIDN'T RIDE that day or the next. Each evening, after work, she'd saddle Cadence, and the three of them would walk. She and Garrett talked about their respective days at work, planned meals, told tales of their childhoods and discussed life. Cadence exhibited endless patience and seemed content to be included in their adventures.

On the third day, Violet knew she was ready. They were in the arena: her, Cadence and Garrett. She liked how he hadn't pushed her and appreciated how he didn't ask if she was sure or if she was nervous or any other of the million questions he could have asked. He was just there, his quiet confidence boosting hers.

She wouldn't say it was like riding a bike, but once she put her foot in the stirrup, swung her leg over and committed to Cadence, she was a goner. Allowing herself one deep breath to calm her runaway pulse, she then executed a gentle squeeze with her legs, and the horse began to walk.

"How's it feel?" Garrett asked from where he stood, leaning against the rails, beaming at her.

It felt like...

Freedom.

"Amazing," she said. "My heart is still racing, but some of it's in a good way."

"You look beautiful. Like you've been riding forever."

"I feel beautiful." She smiled at him. "I've missed this. So much. I can't remember ever not knowing how to ride. I feel...happy."

"Good. Me, too."

"I can only imagine how happy my body is going to be after a twelve-year break from riding, though."

He laughed. "Yeah, take it slow...ish."

He was true to his word. Two days later, they went on their first trail ride. Despite her stiff muscles, Violet was on cloud nine. Everything Garrett said about Cadence was true; the horse was equine perfection. She was already in love, which created a problem she hadn't anticipated, a conundrum that had her preoccupied on the ride back.

They were approaching the stables when Garrett said, "Hey, someone is standing outside the barn. Are you expecting anyone?"

"No, but that looks like... Dad!" Violet dismounted and threw her arms around her father. "Hi! What are you doing here?"

"Hey, you." Barlow hugged her tight. "I'm visiting my sweet daughter, whom I haven't seen in way too long."

She laughed and let go. "Yeah, sure. You just saw me last month at the family reunion."

"We didn't exactly get any quality time together, though, did we?"

"True." They'd both been preoccupied with Blackwell family drama, the experience different for each of them.

"Violet, I am overjoyed to see you riding again. Does your mother know?"

"Not yet, and if you could maybe not tell her for the time being, that would be helpful."

"You're worried she'll pressure you to do the reunion performance?"

"Yes," Violet said and felt her heart clench with love. Her kindhearted dad was also insightful. "She's already doing that, but I have no problem saying no. I'm just not ready to let her know that she was right about the riding part."

"I understand."

"Thank you, Dad. I appreciate it." She turned to smile at Garrett. "Dad, this is Garrett McCoy. Garrett, my dad, Barlow Blackwell."

They shook hands, exchanged some small talk, and then Garrett said, "Violet, I'll take care of the horses and meet you guys inside if you'd like."

"That would be great. Thank you." She took Barlow's elbow and steered him toward the house. "Speaking of the reunion, did you know your uncle is in town? Grandma was going to come with him, but Levi and Summer just had their baby. Do you want to stay here at the ranch?"

"I did hear about Big E. Maggie told me. And no, I rented a place in Flame for a few nights. One of those vacation rentals that are all the rage these days. Even downloaded the app."

"Why didn't you tell me you were coming for a visit? You could have stayed here."

"I wasn't sure I could follow through with it until I got here."

Violet nodded, understanding slowly seeping into her. At the bottom of the porch now, she stopped and faced him. Her dad was a striking man, fit and trim, with thick brown hair, only recently growing flecks of gray. But now she could see that his handsome face looked drawn and tired, and the twinkle in his hazel-brown eyes had dimmed. Aside from his kindness, she loved his sense of humor the most. When he wasn't laughing, he usually wore a smile so bright it made you want to smile, too. Right now, neither laughter nor smiles were in evidence. It didn't take a genius to read between the lines, only a daughter who knew her father very well.

"You're here to see Mom."

"Maybe." Barlow sighed. "I'm still not sure I can go through with it."

"What's going on, Dad?"

"Oh, honey, I think I may have made a huge mistake."

"What do you mean?" Violet asked, even though she knew he meant the divorce.

"I still love her."

"Dad, she…" Violet wanted to say that Flora didn't love him back, but she knew that wasn't true. A part of her wanted to tell her dad to run, to stay away, to find someone who would love him the way he deserved to be loved.

But.

Flora Blackwell was a complex person. One of those enviable people who'd found their "thing" the very first time they'd tried it and never looked back. She lit up every time she told the story about how her earliest memory was from the back of a horse. And not just on the back of a horse, but a *horse* in a *parade* while she wore a sparkly *costume*. Performing on horseback was her calling, no doubt about that.

Could she help it that she loved her animals at the expense of everything important in her life? She'd made them her life, her career, and she'd never pretended otherwise. There was value in that. Was it really so much different from how devoted Violet was to her job?

That was when it hit her: she had more in common with her mother than she'd ever realized. More than she wanted, maybe, but she'd ponder that revelation later. Because this situation needed her full attention. Her dad deserved to be happy, too.

"Dad, let's go inside and talk about this."

Violet knew she needed to be careful. She didn't want to influence her father, and yet she couldn't help but have an opinion. Maybe she could make him see that he'd done the right thing.

After she got him settled on the sofa with a cold glass of sweet tea, she asked, "Dad, why did you file for a separation if you weren't sure you wanted one?"

"I hoped it would scare her. I wanted her to change. Not *change*. I don't want her to change, but I'd like to feel like I am more important to her."

"I understand. All of us girls wanted that growing up, except maybe Willow." Although, lately, with the memory of the accident waiting around every curve in the pathway of her thoughts, Violet couldn't help but wonder if Willow resented her place in the family, too. If she'd gotten too much attention, felt too much pressure.

Barlow's response gave credence to that thought. "Your baby sister didn't have it easy either."

"I think I'm beginning to understand that, too. But let's talk about you, Dad. What do you want to do about Mom? Do you want me to talk to her for you?" Violet hoped not. Because, frankly, she wasn't sure she could, in good conscience, encourage Flora to go back to her dad. Although, she was beginning to accept that it wasn't so much that he deserved better as he deserved different. The problem was that she had no idea what that should look like—for either of her parents.

GARRETT LIT THE GRILL. Violet brought him a beer. On the other side of the patio, Uncle Trent and Flora were seated at a table beneath an umbrella shade. They didn't need it, though, as the evening was balmy as the sun slowly floated onto the horizon. The sky was streaked in shades of orange, purple and red. Nothing like a Texas sunset, and this evening's was shaping up to be quite a show.

Violet had already served drinks. Zinni lounged on the ottoman at their feet, gnawing on a tiny chew bone. Despite the reason for the dinner, Garrett couldn't help but enjoy this pleasant slice of domesticity. It wasn't difficult to imagine a life like this with Violet by his side. He was so proud of her for conquering her fear.

"I'm super nervous," she whispered, lingering by his side. "What if she says no?"

"We'll make her an offer she can't refuse." Garrett was nervous, too, but wouldn't let Violet know. It had been his idea to invite Flora and Trent over for dinner and his idea to make her the offer. He'd put on an optimistic front for Violet but still had no idea how to read the woman. Flora Blackwell remained an enigma. The fact that her husband had shown up and seemed to want to reconcile added another layer to his dilemma. How much of his uncle's relationship with her was Garrett's business, anyway?

"Pretty sure I don't have the kind of money she could get for Cadence. And Trent bought her as a gift. Maybe she won't want to sell for that reason."

"All you can do is ask." And perform in her show. That was what Garrett was most afraid of, that Flora would use this as a chip to coerce Violet to perform. He was all for that, but only if she was ready. He would not go along with Flora pushing her into performing. His desire to protect Violet was unlike anything he'd ever felt before.

"Okay, you're right. I won't know unless I try. I have to try. Here goes."

"Are you sure you want to do this before we eat?"

"Yes, because she'll know something is up. She'll see that I'm nervous. She's already been giving me looks."

He didn't doubt that. For all of Flora's dramatics, she seemed very in tune with her daughter's moods. It was a point in her favor. "Okay, I'm going to wait on the steaks, then. Let's do this."

They settled around the table, and after a round of pleasant conversation and several minutes admiring the last of the sunset, Violet got down to business.

"Mom, I'd like to purchase Cadence from you."

Flora leaned back in her chair and tipped her head. "Is that so?"

"Yes. I've started riding again."

"Have you, now?" she said, her smile a match for the brightness of the now-retired sun. Zinni hopped over to her lap. For once, the dog remained silent, her gaze bouncing from Flora to Violet and back again.

"Garrett has been helping me with some, um, technical issues that were bothering me, and I—"

"Violet, I know that you were afraid. I know that's why you haven't ridden all these years."

"You… What? How did you know?"

Flora sighed and scratched Zinni's ears. "Honestly, Zinni, sometimes I think that my own daughters believe that their mother cannot understand the simplest things." To Violet, she said, "I've spent more of my life with horses than I have people. You think I can't see fear?"

"After Maggie and Willow's accident, I lost—"

"It actually started before that."

"What?"

"Your fear. It started when Aunt Dandy died. I blame myself for letting it get so out of hand. I was too preoccupied with my own grief to do anything about it. I kept telling myself I'd deal with it later. You and Aunt Dandy were so close. I know her death was hard for you, too. I kept telling myself I was giving you space and time to heal. Too much of both, it turned out."

Garrett had to give Flora credit for owning it all.

"Anyway, by the time Maggie managed to get shot by Willow—"

"Mom, please don't say it like that, as if Maggie did it on purpose."

"You're right. I'm sorry. When the *accident* happened, I was in panic mode. I'll confess that I'd pinned too much hope on Willow. Maybe I put too much pressure on her? I don't know, but she seemed to thrive on it. Regardless, the very thing I feared would happen to her happened to you instead. *You* ended up with the yips."

The dreaded yips: anxiety that plagued an athlete to the point where they couldn't function. Garrett could imagine that, for Flora, it was hands down the worst thing that could happen to a performer. Worse even than being thrown from a horse or struck with an arrow.

Violet nodded. "Better me than Willow, I guess."

"No, Violet! That is nonsense. I never wanted any of you to get it."

"But you always paid so much more attention to my sisters, especially Willow, which is fine. I get it. She was the most beautiful, the most talented, the *most*."

"All my girls are talented. Yes, J.R. had a special act, and Willow had that edge, that all-consuming *desire* to be the best. But a lot of that is just plain old confidence. The kind that comes with a passion for performing, the love of adulation, which you never had. For you, it was about executing every trick perfectly, and you never could. *That* was your problem."

"Gee, thanks, Mom," Violet said dryly. "I appreciate the recap of my shortcomings."

"No, listen, Violet! No one could live up to your own standards. You thought I was hard on you? Take a look at how hard you were, you are, on yourself. If you really think about it, a perfect performance isn't flawless. There's no such thing. A good performer just makes it appear that way. Your sisters understood this, but you… You never quite got it. Aunt Dandelion was working on that with you when she died."

"You knew about that?"

She talked to her dog again, "Zinni, are you hearing this? Further evidence of the blatant disrespect I have to contend with."

Violet looked at Garrett and rolled her eyes. "Mom, can you focus here?"

"Yes, of course I knew! You actually believe that you and Aunt Dandy could practice a fire stunt without me knowing about it?" She pointed a finger at herself. "Me? The woman who knows *everything* that goes on with my horses. The controlling dictator who knew every step and every move of every routine, both animal and human."

"When you put it that way, it does seem pretty unrealistic."

Flora smiled gently. "Aunt Dandy and I came up with a similar act when we were young, without the fire. When you turned out to be as good at juggling as she was, it just seemed a natural route for you. Aunt Dandy was so excited that you'd inherited her skills, Vi!"

Garrett wondered how different Violet's trajectory would have been if Flora had shared some of this information in the past. But, by her own admission, Violet wouldn't discuss it. Stubborn, like her mother.

"I'd hoped that the better you got, the more it would build your confidence."

Violet smiled. "You know what, Mom? It worked. It just took a lot longer than you thought it would. I'm riding again, and I am confident."

"Oh, honey, I can't tell you how happy that makes me."

"Good. Me, too."

"Now I have a confession to make."

"Okay?"

"Trent didn't buy Cadence for me."

"What do you mean?"

"I bought her for you."

"What?" She looked at Trent, who smiled and nodded.

"It's true," he said. "Your mother asked me to go along with it, so I did."

Flora explained, "As you know, I've wanted you to start riding again for a long time. I just didn't know how to make it happen. When I saw Cadence, when I rode her, I knew I'd found the horse for you."

"Wow, Mom. I...I don't know what to say."

"You don't need to say anything. It all worked out beautifully, even better than I anticipated. I was going to try and encourage you to ride her, but I guess your fella did that for me, huh?" She winked at Garrett.

"Oh, no," he said. "Violet did it all on her own. I just supplied the moral support. She's very talented, Flora, and Cadence is an exceptional horse."

Flora beamed. "Thank you, Garrett. That means a lot, coming from you."

"But, Mom, I know you are struggling financially. Let me buy her from you at a profit."

"Absolutely not! I'm no one's charity case, Violet, not even my daughter's."

"She won't let me help her either," Trent chimed in. "She won't even let me pay for her attorney."

Interesting. Garrett had assumed that when Trent said he was getting her an attorney, he was paying. Apparently not. Come to think of it, he hadn't seen much evidence of his uncle spoiling her beyond the occasional dinner or evening out.

"Pfft." Flora waved a hand through the air. "I'll have a little money after the divorce is final. In the meantime, I'm getting by just fine. Do you know how good it feels that I finally did something right where you're concerned?"

"Mom, I am overwhelmed. I love that horse. I feel…" Tears welled in her eyes.

Garrett was getting ready to put an arm around her when Flora put Zinni down, went to Violet and wrapped her arms around her. Violet stood and hugged her tight. "Thank you," she whispered against her mom's shoulder.

"You're welcome, Violet. Thank you for being the one who never gave up on me."

"You're welcome, and you've got Maggie now, too."

"We're working on it, that's for sure. She's talking to me, so that feels like progress. And she's working on her act, too. At least we'll have some of our Belles back for the performance."

Uh-oh, he thought.

Violet pulled away. "Mom, just because I'm riding again doesn't mean I'm going to perform."

"Violet, you have to perform. In order to completely conquer the yips, that's how it works. You know that."

"I don't believe that," she argued gently. "Riding has never been about performing for me. But I'll be there to support you, and Maggie, and any of my other sisters who choose to participate."

And then Flora shocked the heck out of him by patting Violet on the shoulder and saying, "If that's honestly how you feel, then I'm just going to savor this moment. As much as I'd like you to perform, as much as I believe it would be best for you, *this* is what I truly wanted. My Violet back on a horse."

CHAPTER SEVENTEEN

"HOW ARE YOU FEELING?" Bailey asked Violet. "Are you loose? Did you warm up? Do you need some protein?"

Violet laughed. "Bailey, calm down. I'm good."

"Look at Alex. He doesn't seem nervous at all."

"Why would he be? I'm not nervous either. It's just a game."

Although, it did appear that the entire office staff and most of the refinery workers had shown up for the final match of the cornhole tournament. The conference room was packed.

Bailey went wide-eyed and looked at Garrett, who was standing next to her with an amused smile on his face. "Just a game, she says." She threw up her arms. "I can't talk to her. Can you help me out here?"

"Can you at least pretend to be concerned?" he asked Violet. "For your friend's sake?"

"No can do. First rule of unnecessarily competitive backyard gaming—do not give your opponent any edge whatsoever. Trust me, I grew up with four cutthroat competitors-slash-sisters. They could smell weakness a mile away."

Adam was serving as the match's facilitator, with Darius, Hank and a welder named Tina, whom Violet adored, acting as "judges." The final match was different from the other rounds in that it would be a best out of three games event. To win a game, you had to be the first player to reach twenty-one points. Cancellation scoring made things more exciting, and house rules dictated that you had to win by two points.

The competition started with a coin toss to see who would throw first. Alex won the honors and got off to an early lead. But after he left three beanbags on the board, Violet knocked them all off, two with one slider, and then airmailed her last shot. It was still close, with her winning by a slim margin of twenty-one to eighteen.

During the second game, things got tense, with the score remaining close after each round. They were tied at fifteen. It was Alex's turn, and he'd just knocked one of Violet's two remaining beanbags off the board when the conference room doors banged open, causing him to pause midway through his windup.

Heads turned as a woman charged inside. A man wearing a sheepish expression followed at a slower pace.

"Time!" Adam shouted before addressing the

newcomers. "Hey, did you not see the sign on the door?"

"Sorry," the young man said. "I told her to wait."

"Who is that woman?" Bailey said.

Violet was struck with an uncomfortable feeling of foreboding. She turned to watch Alex, and by the time Garrett answered, her suspicion was confirmed.

"That's my sister, Nikki."

Violet walked straight to Alex.

"What is she doing here?" he asked.

"I have no idea. He didn't mention it to me. I would have told you. I hope you know that. Judging from the look on his face, I don't think Garrett knew she was coming."

"I don't want to be here."

"I don't want *her* here. Should we call it a draw?"

He almost smiled. "I think that would be a little obvious, don't you?"

"Do you want me to fake an injury?" she asked.

He did smile at that. "A cornhole injury?"

"Would you rather I injured you? I think I could take you out with one of these beanbags."

He laughed. "It's shocking to me how tempting that offer is, but let's just finish this thing."

"Now I'm going to feel bad when I win."

"Thank you for making me laugh. I wouldn't have thought it was possible."

Violet nodded, grateful she'd at least managed to convince him to stay, and resumed her place.

"Hold on," Garrett called out, stepping forward. He started to ask, "Cade, what are you doing—"

The crowd shushed him. Cade winced a little and waved a hand as if to apologize before he and Nikki melted into the crowd.

The game continued, and Violet was impressed with Alex's ability to fake it. He won the second game, and later, Violet would have to convince him she didn't give him the victory. The third match was the closest, but Violet ultimately pulled it off with a final score of twenty-five to twenty-three.

Bailey was over-the-top excited. Alex was gracious and adorable in defeat. In a move that Flora would approve of, Violet retrieved three beanbags and did a quick juggling act. Then she caught them one at a time before tossing them across the court and depositing all three into the hole. The crowd went wild.

She bowed and then hugged Alex, who whispered in her ear, "If he ever messes up, I'm swooping in."

"Deal," she said before letting him go. They were mobbed by the crowd. Violet wryly commented to Bailey that she felt as if she'd scored the winning goal in the World Cup.

Once the cheers and congratulations died down a bit, Garrett introduced her to his family.

"Nice to meet you," Nikki said with a fake smile and no eye contact.

Strike two, Violet thought, as she'd tried to remove Alex's version of events from the equation but found that she couldn't. Nikki's dismissal and patronizing personality only cemented Violet's opinion.

"I'm starving, Garrett. Can we go eat?" Nikki asked.

Cade, on the other hand, she liked instantly. Taller and even broader in the shoulders than Garrett, they had the same raven-black hair and matching curve to their eyebrows. Cade's brown eyes were a lighter shade, more like Trent's. He had an easy, engaging smile and the cutest dimples, which he turned on her in full force.

"Ah, the lovely Violet, at last," he said, taking her hand. "I have heard the nicest things about you."

Nikki frowned. "Why would you *hear* things about her?"

Scowling, Garrett removed his brother's hand from hers and replaced it with his own. "Stop pawing at her."

"You're right. How rude." Grinning, he held out his arms and waggled his fingers. "I should hug her instead."

"Violet," Garrett said, "please ignore my obnoxious brother."

Violet laughed while Cade wrapped an arm around her shoulders and squeezed. "It is very, *very* nice to meet you, Violet."

Garrett scowled at his brother, but she could tell he didn't mean it. Adorable.

Nikki huffed. "Excuse me, what is happening?"

To Nikki, he said, "Violet and I are dating."

"Oh." That earned her a look, something close to an assessing smirk. "You're *that* Violet."

"I am."

"That juggling thing was cute."

Cute? I'd like to see you do it. She hoped her look conveyed the sentiment. "Thank you," she said, allowing a bit of frost to seep into her tone. It seemed completely lost on Nikki.

"Before we go anywhere, will one of you please tell me what you guys are doing here?" Garrett asked.

"We wanted to surprise you!" Nikki gushed.

Head shaking, Cade said, "No, Nikki wanted to surprise you. I wanted to call you like a normal person would do."

"Cade." Nikki said his name like an admonishment. She might as well have stomped her foot, too.

"Where is Remi?" Garrett asked before his brother could respond.

"She's with my friend Kate. Remi loves her."

Cade explained, "I'm in Dallas this weekend for a training thing. The guy who was supposed to do it got sick, and they needed someone, so I volunteered. When Nikki heard I was coming, she hatched this scheme."

"It's hardly a scheme, Cade," Nikki said with an eye roll. To Garrett, she said, "I know the big company picnic is tomorrow, so I thought I'd come and be your date. But apparently, you already have a date."

"Yep, I do," he said, grinning at Violet. She couldn't help but feel a sense of satisfaction when he entwined their fingers. It wasn't as if they'd been keeping their relationship a secret, but this was certainly the first time they'd put it on display. It felt good.

VIOLET HAD ENOUGH last-minute party details to contend with when she got home that she didn't approach Garrett with the difficult topic of Nikki. Thankfully, Nikki and Cade were staying at a hotel in Dallas, and she wouldn't have to see Nikki again until the party.

She wasn't sure how much longer she could keep Alex's secret. He hadn't asked her not to say anything, but she didn't know what her role should be. He'd warned her that where his stepsister was concerned, Garrett could not see clearly. Alex had added plenty of examples and revealed other information about the woman that was concerning.

Saturday morning came early, and with it, party setup. Violet decided to put the situation out of her mind until she and Garrett had some time alone, preferably postparty.

A good call because, oh, what a party it was.

Violet could not have been more pleased with the way it all came together. Early afternoon saw the arrival of the grill masters that were Maple Boss, and by the time guests began arriving, the smoky barbecue aroma of brisket, ribs and chicken permeated the air. Potato salad, beans, brussels sprouts, roasted corn on the cob and skillet-style corn bread rounded out the menu. She'd also hired Pie Face, one of her favorite dessert bars, who'd come stocked with peach cobbler, pecan pie and chocolate Texas sheet cake with vanilla bean ice cream.

The event planner called the decorations "harvest chic," and Violet decided she'd never seen more festive autumn adornment. Chrysanthemums in orange, yellow, white and gold were arranged with cornstalks and greenery. Pumpkins and colorful squash were incorporated into the centerpieces and placed on the checkered tablecloths. Hay bales and weathered barn-board benches provided seating. Strings of vintage Edison-style lights stretched from the barn to the tents and all around the perimeter, casting a soft glow over the entire area. Bailey commented that it felt like a harvest-time fairy tale, and Violet decided that was the best compliment she could have received.

DJ Dax and Vonnie arrived on schedule and set up their sound system on the edge of the dance floor, a beautiful parquet rectangular-shaped slab that had been expertly assembled that morning. Adam and Darius recruited a team of office staff to put up cornhole, badminton and volleyball courts. People started arriving around two and were greeted with an assortment of drinks and appetizers while DJ Dax's "pre-func playlist" provided an upbeat vibe.

At four o'clock, the bar opened for happy hour. Violet was relieved to see people mingling, having fun and putting all the courts to use. Soon, the office staff challenged the refinery workers to a game of volleyball.

She'd just finished making the rounds, triple-checking that all the vendors had what they needed, when Bailey found her.

"Hey, it's going great already. However, I do not care for that sister of Garrett's. Talk about an attention hound."

"Join the crowd," Violet commented dryly, easily spotting Garrett in the sea of guests. Nikki and Cade were visiting with him and Trent.

"She totally made a play for Logan on the volleyball court."

"Oh, Bailey, I am so sorry."

"Don't worry. He handled it like a champ, my champ. He told her he wasn't interested in her, and even if he were, he would never go for a chick who would make a play for another woman's man right in front of her. Not classy." Bailey laughed.

"His words, not mine. He literally looked right at her and said that, *not classy.*"

"That's awesome."

"It was. I think he might be a keeper."

DJ Dax came on the microphone and announced that dinner was now being served buffet style. "So, queue on up to the chuck wagon and get those vittles while they're hot!" Then he warned everyone to limber up because the dancing would start soon after.

"Can't wait for this food, Violet. It's incredible. When I suggested you throw a party, this isn't exactly what I had in mind."

"Yeah?"

Chuckling, Bailey nudged her with one shoulder. "In typical Violet Blackwell fashion, it's about one million times better."

"Thanks, Bailey."

Violet hoped everyone else agreed with her. Soon, she began to relax, as the feedback was nothing but positive. She was riding high and hungry when she finally decided to find Garrett. They'd agreed to eat together once she was satisfied everything was going smoothly. Dinner was winding down; most people had already visited the dessert bar at least once. DJ Dax had just turned up the volume, and Vonnie was inviting everyone onto the dance floor to learn the "jiggy shake," whatever that might be.

Violet couldn't imagine how the evening could

get any better. Spotting Garrett, she made her way through the crowd, and even though he was chatting with Nikki, Violet vowed to be warm and welcoming.

"So, THAT'S HER," Nikki said to Garrett. "She's pretty, I'll give her that. Wow, I hope I look that good when I'm her age."

"Who?" Garrett said, half listening while scanning the crowd for Violet. He was so nervous he could barely think straight. What if she said no? Was this even a good idea? Maybe it was too soon? No, he knew what he felt, and he was confident she did, too.

"That's Flora, right? Trent's girlfriend, the woman who is trying to steal his money. Brown hair, blue dress, cute little dog in her arms. Heading out onto the dance floor right now with Trent."

"Yes, but—" Garrett started to correct her, to tell her that he'd made a mistake. He was now convinced that Flora didn't care about Trent's money. She liked attention, sure, but accolades and horses meant way more to her than dollar signs. If Trent wanted to marry Flora, it didn't seem like the bad idea it once had. In fact, he'd give his blessing. His uncle might have his work cut out for him convincing her to stay in Flame, but that was his problem.

Nikki kept talking. "Sounds like Flora has already got her hooks in deep."

"What do you mean?"

"I overheard Cade and Trent talking about a proposal."

Garrett smiled. "Yeah, that part is true. And now that you're here, you should probably know about it, too. I—"

"Where is the daughter?"

"Who?"

"The daughter. Violet, right? The woman you're supposedly dating but in reality you are using to find out about the gold-digging mother. Has she figured this all out yet?"

"No," Garrett answered tentatively. He'd completely forgotten about the conversation he'd had with Nikki that day Alex had arrived and interrupted him and Violet. "Nikki—"

"Yes, *she* has," Violet interrupted smoothly. "She's figured it all out. Don't worry, Nikki. There will be no proposal. My mother isn't going to marry Trent. She's already married to my father."

"Violet," Garrett said, his stomach falling and hitting the hard-packed dirt as he raced to replay the conversation in his head. "How much did you hear?"

"I've heard enough."

"Good," Nikki said, looking smug and satisfied. "I think this charade has gone on long enough."

"I agree," Violet said, nodding sagely. "Let's

all be honest, shall we? When are you going to tell Garrett the truth about Alex?"

Nikki gasped. "That is none of your business."

"It is my business. Alex is my friend. And if you don't tell Garrett, I will."

"How would you…? It's my word against his."

"Is it, though? Or is it your word against science? Plus, one of your friend's words, too, who you've apparently confided in and recently stabbed in the back. Denise, I think her name is, and she's been singing like a canary to Alex."

"How dare you?"

"How dare *you*?" she returned calmly. "You think you can ruin someone else's life to cover up your own mistake? The way you're headed, you're probably going to do damage to multiple lives before you're through. But I won't let you do this to Alex."

To Garrett, Violet said, "If you don't believe what Alex has to say, you might want to call this Denise person. Your sister is a liar."

And then she walked away.

VIOLET WAS REMINDED of one specific time when she'd been knocked off a horse, not thrown, *swept*. She and Maggie had been trail riding and having a ball. She'd been goofing around and carelessly turned in the saddle to make a silly face at her sister when her horse rode under a low-hanging tree branch. Like the motion from a giant broom, she'd been swept off the back of her horse. It had hurt, sure, but what she remembered the most was the way the wind had been knocked clean out of her. She'd panicked trying to breathe, and it had seemed like hours before her lungs would cooperate. This sensation might be worse, however, because at least the pain from the fall had eventually subsided. The pain she felt now seemed to be getting worse.

Stopping by the side of the barn, she reached out a hand for balance, placed the other on her breastbone over her lungs and tried to catch her breath. Was she having a panic attack? She'd had one on the day of Maggie and Willow's accident. She never thought she'd ever experience another awful moment like that.

It was that sensation, the knowledge, that for one split second, the earth had stopped spinning. Maybe no one else could feel it, but you knew once it started moving again, your world would never be the same. At this point, she wasn't even sure she wanted it to.

Later, she'd be proud of herself for holding it together so well. She'd recognize the strength she'd gained by working for Trent, by getting back on that horse, so to speak, and yes, being raised by Flora Blackwell. Even Garrett's deception would leave her stronger. That which didn't kill you and all that.

But now, lungs engaging, body cooperating, she moved and tried to think. How much longer did she need to stay at this party? She didn't care that it was technically her house. As soon as she could get away, she was out of here.

"Violet, there you are, sweetheart." Flora hustled over. "Can you hold Zinni? Trent wants to dance again, but it's tough with a dog between us." She let out a giggle.

Violet opened her mouth, only to discover that words wouldn't form.

"Violet? Honey, what's wrong? You look like... You're pale. Are you feeling okay?"

"Tired."

"Well, no wonder. You've outdone yourself with this party. Everything turned out perfectly. It's like some sort of Hollywood event."

"Thanks. That means a lot." She mustered a weak smile.

Gaze narrowing shrewdly, Flora lifted a hand to feel her forehead.

"Really, Mom?" she said, even though the gesture was kind of endearing. Until Garrett, she'd gotten used to not having anyone to care for her, to look out for her. She could see now how she'd eaten up every crumb of his contrived attention. The shock was wearing off, hurt and humiliation seeping in to take its place. Tears gathered in her eyes. How could that all have been a lie?

Because he was not only a liar, he was a mean-spirited liar. She'd known that about him, hadn't she? And yet she'd fallen for every word. She'd been incredibly and embarrassingly naive. He and Nikki were probably having a good laugh right now. What a fool. No, she couldn't think about that right now. She'd tend to her wounds after she was gone. And before she could leave, she needed to take care of some business.

"I think you need to lie down."

"Me, too."

"Can Garrett escort you to the house?"

"No. I can do that myself. It's not that far. But first, I need to ask you something."

"Okay, shoot."

"Do you want to marry Trent?"

"Marry him! Violet, I'm still married to your father. At least I think I am. I haven't heard from him in days. Trent is a delightful man and a very dear friend. But even if your father and I do get a divorce, I will never get married again. It's too… difficult. For me, anyway. I want that for you, though, honey. You're the marrying kind. You'll be a wonderful partner and mother."

"Mom… I'm pretty sure that Dad wants you back."

It was Flora's turn to go pale. Violet reached out and took Zinni, then walked her mom sideways and back, tugging her down to sit on a nearby bench. She sat beside her.

"How do you know?" her mom asked.

"He came to see me."

"When? Where? Here, in Flame? Why didn't

he come and see me? I've been waiting for him to come to me."

"Yeah, I see that now. The same way I've been waiting for Maggie to come and see me. But why should they be the ones?"

"Because!"

"Because?" Violet repeated and waited.

"Because…" Violet could see her mom searching for words, and after a few long seconds, she nodded. "Hmm. I think I see your point. I've been…selfish."

"Yeah," she agreed. "You have."

"Gee, Violet, thank you for consoling me."

She chuckled. "It's okay, Mom. I've been selfish, too, and I didn't realize it. You know the good part about all of this mutual selfishness?"

"Well, yes, for me, I do. It's been you. It's the healing in our relationship. It's seeing you get back on that horse, and I mean that metaphorically, too. You've also found a wonderful man. You're finally living again, Violet, and that makes me happier than anything, even the riding."

She winced. The words were physically painful, a jar to her already flayed heart.

"Mom, I need to tell you something. But there's something I need to do first. Can you wait here for me?"

CHAPTER EIGHTEEN

"Nikki, what have you done?" Garrett gaped at his stepsister and tried to understand. Like a horror film, the ramifications of her actions kept unfolding before him. He wanted to scoop up the words and stuff them back inside her.

"What?" She belted out a laugh. "You're welcome. I did you a favor. It's nice to do something for you for a change."

"No, you did not do me a favor. You…" What was he going to do? "Ruined everything."

"Come on, Garrett. It was time to cut her loose, and you know it." Nikki smoothed her long blond hair over one shoulder. "She's a complication you do not need."

"Why would you think you get to decide who is in my life?"

"You don't really care about her, do you?"

"I do." Garrett nodded slowly. "Not that it's any of your business." He'd never cared about a woman this much, not even close. He was in love. That felt like a miracle in itself. But now the absolute worst had happened: she'd walked away. And he knew she wasn't coming back. Not when she believed he was only using her.

Even worse, he couldn't blame her. Because he *had* been using her, hadn't he? But it had become so much more than that, to the point where Flora and her intentions had become, if not unimportant, then certainly not foremost in his mind. And he was positive now that Flora didn't have an ulterior motive, so that had become a moot point. But how could he explain? That might be doable; it was her forgiveness that felt impossible. He didn't think he could if the situation was reversed and he was in her shoes. Betrayal was the worst, and he knew that better than anyone, didn't he? Evidence of which was standing before him, looking smug in her conviction that she'd helped him.

Panic bolted through his bloodstream, sending his pulse racing. His chest hurt. Vague concerns of a heart attack or stroke surfaced in his mind, but Nikki quickly reminded him of the true cause.

"Of course it's my business! Garrett, I'm your family! *Me!* And Cade. We're the Three Musketeers. That's what you used to tell me when I was little, remember? We are all the family we need. And now we have Remi."

He studied her, carefully thinking about the meaning behind her words. "No, Nikki, *we* don't have Remi. *You* have Remi. You and her father, who should be helping you raise your child." He purposely didn't say Alex this time. Violet's comments left him plagued with doubt.

"Don't say that! I need you. We need you. We don't need Alex. I hate him. He doesn't—" She stopped and huffed out a breath of frustration before calming herself. "Garrett, listen, you're the one who loves Remi. We'll raise her together."

That was when it hit him. How could he have not seen this? This was what Nikki did. It was what she'd done with Alex. Somehow, she'd turned him into the bad guy. No matter what had really happened between them, and he was now convinced it couldn't have been as Nikki claimed, she'd purposely driven a wedge between Garrett and Alex. Alex saw her for who she was, and when he tried to tell Garrett, he refused to listen. Garrett had always seen Nikki's shortcomings as his fault and did his best to make up for them—and make excuses for her. When in reality, he was rapidly realizing that he'd made a terrible mistake by not getting his sister to face up to the consequences of her actions.

"Nikki, this isn't right. You have to admit whatever it is you've done and accept what's happened as a result. Time to grow up and be a grown-up, not just for your sake but for Remi's. Alex isn't her dad, is he? Who is Remi's father, Nikki?"

In his pocket, his phone chimed. He pulled it out to discover a text from Cade:

Hey, having kind of a crisis here. Can you meet me by the barn?

He let out a frustrated sigh. "I have to go talk to Cade. Get ready to go. We're leaving before you do any more damage to my life."

VIOLET FOUND TRENT standing near the DJ, looking both anxious and excited. Under different circumstances, it would be endearing. Then again, under different circumstances, she would be excited, too.

"Violet, there you are! I'm just about ready to say a few words and make an announcement. I need you out there with me—and Garrett, too. Now, if only my wayward nephew would get here. Do you know where he is?"

Yes, she did. She'd asked Bailey to find a way to distract Garrett so she could have a few minutes alone with her boss. She'd suggested enlisting Cade's help and could only assume Bailey had been successful.

"Trent, I can't let you do this."

"Do what, Violet? What's wrong?"

"I can't let you make this announcement. As much as I want this for myself, I have to stop you."

"How do you know?"

"I overheard…some stuff. That doesn't matter right now. The point is, I can't let you go through with it."

"Of course you can. I've given this a lot of thought. Garrett and I have discussed it. There is no one better."

"I know you love my mom, and as much as I would love for you to be my stepfather, I can't let you propose. She's not right for you. She's…" Violet didn't know how to say exactly what needed to be said. "Flora is wonderful in many ways. But she doesn't love you like she should."

Trent seemed more confused than devastated. Violet knew he was probably in shock. She hated hurting him like this.

"What's going on?" a breathless Garrett asked, jogging up to them. How could he have gotten here so quickly? He looked from her to Trent. "Are we still making this announcement?"

"No," Violet answered. "There will be no proposal."

"Um, I'm not sure what's going on…" Trent trailed off, shaking his head. "Violet is telling me all the reasons why I can't marry her mother."

"What?" Garrett stepped forward and tried to take her hand. She pulled away. "Oh," he said simply, and then, "Violet, listen to me. You don't need to do this. I know that your mom isn't after my uncle for his money. I knew that—"

"Stop." Violet tensed, squeezing her eyes shut in a futile effort to ward off the searing pain in her heart. "It's not about that, Garrett. This isn't about you. Or us." She faced Trent, and it devastated her to see his baffled expression. But she had to get through this.

"Trent, I believe that Flora wants to change, to settle down. I know she cares about you. I think she thought that if she moved here, it would give her a fresh start. That is partially my fault. Over the last twelve years, I put the idea in her head. I never liked the traveling that we did when I was a kid. It contributed to my unhappiness, and she now feels some guilt about that." And possibly some other guilt, too, that wasn't relevant to this topic but might help her family reunite. Violet held on to that idea, used it to keep herself from falling apart.

She went on, "She likes the way my life looks here in Flame." *Especially the way it was when I had Garrett, but, of course, none of that was real.* "I know now that she's proud of what I've accomplished, but the truth is, she's not being honest with herself. She has her own issues to deal with, and I don't think she's capable of settling down— not in this dramatic a fashion, anyway. And she's definitely not ready to get married again."

Violet was beginning to think that maybe Flora could compromise and slow down a little, but she knew her mother would never be happy staying in one place forever.

Trent scrubbed one hand across his cheek. "Violet, I don't even know where to begin. I'm not sure how wires got so crossed tonight."

She shook her head. "It doesn't matter. Trent, in light of everything that's happened here, please consider this my two weeks' notice. Garrett can fill you in however he likes, but the bottom line is that I cannot work in the dishonest and hostile environment that he's created. As a result, I won't be coming back into the office. I'll do everything I can remotely to turn over whatever in-person tasks I can to Rhea and the rest of the staff until you can replace me."

"What?" He nearly shrieked the word. "Violet, no! You can't quit. You are irreplaceable. That's part of what I wanted to…" Trent's face was now a mix of panic and outright concern as his gaze darted back and forth between her and his nephew. Eyes narrowing, his focus finally landed on Garrett. "Garrett, what is happening? What did you do?"

But Garrett was too busy watching her. "Violet, please, this isn't how it appears. Nikki shouldn't have said what she did."

"Shouldn't have said it, or shouldn't have lied?"

He sighed. "It's complicated."

She scoffed. "No, it's not. Did you or did you not get close to me in order to spy on Flora because you thought she was after Trent's money?"

"Yes, but only at the beginning."

"The beginning of what?"

"You did what?" Trent repeated, gawking with horror at Garrett.

"Violet, I need to talk to you. Let me explain."

"No. I—" *I don't want to hear any more of your lies.* "There's nothing to say. Congratulations, you got what you wanted. We're gone. I'm going. After tonight, my mom and I will both be out of your lives forever."

GARRETT ONLY REALIZED a few hours later that Violet meant that statement literally. At the time, he'd considered following her but thought that giving her a little time to calm down might work in his favor. Plus, he'd needed to calm down, too. He was so angry at Nikki that he could barely think straight. Sticking around to explain to Uncle Trent after the party wrapped up had felt like the right thing to do, too. Now he realized what a glaring miscalculation he'd made.

He'd given her a three-hour head start.

Thankfully, Cade had taken Nikki and left. Despite his strategy, his anger toward her hadn't cooled. Inside the house, pacing in the kitchen, Garrett called Violet again, for the fifth time, his agitation growing as he listened to the same message: "The person you are calling is unavailable." Multiple texts were showing sent but not delivered.

"I don't understand how she cannot be available," he muttered to himself.

"She blocked your number, buddy."

Garrett looked up to find Alex standing in the doorway.

"How do you know?"

"She told me she was going to."

"When did you talk to her?"

"Earlier, hours ago. I saw her crying. She was walking toward the parking area, so I stopped to see if she was okay."

That was when it dawned on Garrett how odd it was for Alex to be here. Eighteen months ago, Alex walking into his house wouldn't have fazed him. Heck, he'd always had a key. Seeing him here now felt comfortable. Old habits died hard. Despite everything, he missed his friend. Another person who probably wouldn't forgive him.

"What are you doing here?"

"Violet asked me to tell you not to bother contacting her or trying to find her, because you won't."

"She may have blocked my number, but I'll find her."

"I don't know." Alex shook his head sadly. "She reminded me about how her family used to travel around with that show. They have a lot of friends, connections, tons of places to hide out."

"She doesn't need to hide out! This was all a misunderstanding."

"Was it?"

"Yes!"

"So, you're saying you didn't use her to find out if Flora was after Trent's money."

Garrett looked away, trying to find the words to explain how quickly it had evolved into more than that, so much more. "Yes, but… I fell in love with her."

"Why didn't you tell her?"

"Not that it's any of your business, but I have told her—repeatedly. I was going to propose tonight." He removed the ring from his pocket and placed it on the countertop.

"Not the love part. I mean, when were you going to tell her about using her?"

"I wasn't usi—" He stopped short of denying it, because he had done that, hadn't he? He'd used her. How could he have been so thoughtless? "I just need to explain."

"I'm afraid that ship has sailed. You should have explained a long time ago. Violet *trusted* you. Do you know how valuable that is to her? I'm sorry, Garrett, but I don't think you'll get another chance. I don't even think you'll get the opportunity to explain." Then he turned around, but before he left the room, he faced Garrett once more to add, "Now it's your turn to see how that feels."

The words hit hard, crashing into his heart. Alex was right. He'd lost his best friend, and now he'd lost the woman he loved. A woman like Violet only came along once in a lifetime, and he'd blown it. He didn't deserve another chance.

"WHERE ARE WE GOING?" a despondent Violet asked Flora from her spot at the little dining nook in the back of Big E's motor home. "Did you tell me already?"

Zinni, bless her, was napping on Violet's lap. As if sensing her sadness, the little dog hadn't left her side. She was so out of it that she could barely remember how she'd gotten here. The evening's events kept flashing in her mind like scenes from some sort of evil slideshow. The horrible Nikki, news of Garrett's betrayal, talking to Flora, waylaying Trent's proposal, quitting her job, blindly heading to the parking area to meet her mom. Alex stopping her. His concern was extremely sweet but somehow only made her feel worse.

After telling Flora what had happened, she didn't say a word, nor did she hesitate. Wrapping one arm around Violet's shoulders, she escorted her to her pickup, opened the passenger seat, buckled her in and placed Zinni on her lap. Then she'd climbed into the driver's side, started the vehicle and driven them to the house. With the high degree of speed and efficiency polished through years of practice, Flora had packed two suitcases and a duffel full of Violet's essentials. Back in the pickup, they'd driven for...a while, eventually meeting Big E at a truck stop where they'd left the pickup and climbed inside his motor home.

"The Gustafsons' ranch," Flora answered. "Do you remember them?"

"Of course. I love Brooke, and Mary Sue, and

Bill. Is Brooke still in Arizona?" Brooke was the same age as Iris, a talented equestrian and champion barrel racer.

"Unfortunately, they aren't home right now. They are in Arizona visiting Brooke, who just had baby number six. Can you believe I have five daughters around her age and only one grandchild? She has one daughter and six grandchildren."

That hurt, too, because lately, Violet had been daydreaming about little kids with black hair and impossibly dark eyes. Just another reminder of what an absolute fool she'd been.

When she made no comment, Flora apparently realized her teasing had fallen flat. She patted Violet's hand and said, "Mary Sue said to make ourselves at home in the guesthouse. We'll help with their horses. It'll be good for all of us."

"That sounds nice," Violet said, because it did, even the part about the Gustafsons being away. The thought of socializing felt like too much. Then another thought occurred to her. How was she going to get Ferdinand and Cadence? Maybe Alex could help. She'd text him as soon as she could find the energy to dig her phone out of her bag. Had she remembered her phone?

"My phone…"

"I got it, honey. It's in the bedroom," Flora said.

"Ferdinand," she whispered, and she could feel fresh tears trailing down her cheeks. He'd be anxious when she didn't greet him in the morning. She couldn't even be sure Garrett would be there for him. Did he even like Ferdinand? Had that been an act, too? She didn't know who he was anymore.

"He'll be okay." Flora reached over and covered Violet's hand with hers. "Big E and I have arranged for him and Cadence to be delivered tomorrow."

Relief flooded through her.

"Don't worry, kiddo," Big E called from his spot in the driver's seat. "It'll be done tomorrow while Garrett the ferret is off on a wild-goose chase that I've arranged."

"Thank you, Big E. Oh, Mom, I can't tell you how relieved I am."

"Don't you worry, honey. For once, I've got *your* back."

"Why don't you go get some shut-eye in the bedroom?" Big E suggested. "By the time you wake up, we'll be halfway to Colorado."

With Zinni in her arms, Violet scooted out of her seat and gladly took him up on that suggestion.

CHAPTER NINETEEN

IT WAS EARLY one morning when, a week later, Violet found her parents sitting side by side in matching Adirondack chairs on the deck of the Gustafsons' guesthouse. Colorado's early fall felt not only cooler but different from Texas's. The air was crisp and thin but also refreshing. The sun shone brightly in the sky but without the intensity of Texas's rays. Frost glinted off the grass like billions of tiny gems, and the mugs they held emitted tendrils of coffee-scented steam.

"Mom, I need to ask a favor."

"Anything."

"Okay, don't say *anything*, because what if I was asking you to walk the runway without makeup or travel across the entire country in Big E's motor home?"

"I would do either of those things for you."

"If she was dead," Barlow muttered, not quite under his breath.

"Barlow!" Flora admonished, but her lips were twitching with a smile. Her dad had shown up the day after they'd arrived at the Gustafsons' ranch. Violet had never doubted her dad's affection and devotion, but the sight of him driving up with a trailer that held Ferdinand and Cadence had been her undoing. Without a word, he'd climbed out of his pickup and walked straight to her. His hug had driven her to tears and he'd silently held her while she cried.

Her parents loved her, and Violet now knew, without a single doubt, that they loved each other. These solitary days had been good for them all.

"Ha. Good one, Dad!" It felt good to laugh, even if she still couldn't quite feel the same joy.

"Seriously, honey, what do you need?" Flora asked.

"Can you…? I want to do the trick, and I need someone who can juggle."

"Yes! I'd love to. I was *almost* as good as Dandy anyway."

"Great," Violet said, noting how *not* surprised Flora was by this news. Although, she couldn't really blame her. Violet had spent nearly every waking hour either riding or juggling. She didn't need an expert, or Garrett, to tell her that riding had become her outlet.

Flora stood and transferred Zinni onto Barlow's lap. The dog circled a few times before curling into a tight ball of fur. "I just need to change my shirt. This one is too flowy for juggling."

"I didn't mean we had to start right now."

"Sure we do! No time like the present." Violet smiled at the familiar words of her youth. Nice, how the old sayings no longer filled her with dread. "Besides, I don't want you changing your mind. We have a lot of work to do."

"Mom, this doesn't mean I'm going to perform in the show. I just want to prove to myself that I can do it, and I want to do it for Aunt Dandy."

"Oh, I know that," she said and waved a breezy, unconvincing hand. "I just meant that it's going to take a bit of practice to get the trick down."

Violet and Barlow exchanged knowing smiles; Flora would never give up. But now Violet had to admit there was a bit of comfort in that.

FOR THE FIRST two minutes, Garrett ignored the pounding on the door. The pounding in his head hurt too much. During the following two minutes, he put a pillow over his head and shouted, "Go away."

He wasn't so out of it that he was unaware that he couldn't be heard—he just didn't care. Another twelve-hour shift without enough sleep had wiped him out, and yet he still couldn't relax. The noise continued with a stubborn persistence that had him thinking of Big E. Was it possible?

He removed the pillow and sat up. Big E might have news about Violet. Gambling on this off chance, he shuffled to the door and opened it, only to be disappointed.

"Alex, what are you doing here?"

"I'm here to talk to you."

"No, thanks." Garrett moved to close the door but his friend reached out to stop him. "Alex, I know we need to talk, but I can't right now."

"It wasn't an offer, McCoy. We're talking whether you want to or not. I won't leave, and you know I mean it."

Not only did Garrett know well the degree of Alex's stubbornness, he didn't have the energy to fight. He made a shooing motion toward the chairs on the porch. Alex walked toward them. He followed.

Garrett slumped in his seat as Alex silently studied him for a long moment. "You look great," he finally commented in a wry tone. "Like you've been out on the range for a week or so without coffee, bathing water or a change of clothes."

"What do you want?" Garrett snapped.

"Rumor going around is that you're the reason Violet quit. The office is in chaos, not that you'd know. Half the refinery workers are threatening to jump ship and head to Peachtree."

Garrett scowled. "I didn't force her to quit." She wouldn't even listen to him, so how was he supposed to explain? Phone calls and messages were pointless. As for her whereabouts, Alex was right; he couldn't find her.

Initially, he'd held on to the hope that Ferdinand would bring them together. The day after the picnic, an anonymous phone call to Jorge had quashed that potential. Someone had called and said at least a dozen head of Penny Bottom cattle were loose on the county road bordering the ranch. While he was off searching for "lost" cattle that turned out not to be lost at all, he'd returned to the ranch and discovered both Ferdinand and Cadence had disappeared. The day after that, Bailey had come over and packed the rest of Violet's things but claimed she had no idea where she was.

"I did my job." He'd reported to the refinery every shift but hadn't been to McCoy Tower since she'd quit. Not even to check in with his uncle or pick up his paycheck now that the job was done.

"I can't believe you let a woman like her get away."

"I didn't want her to go. She left."

"Why?"

"It's dumb. Embarrassing."

"That I can believe. Because you're not the brightest crayon in the box. You've always been pretty dense. I don't know why I was ever friends with you in the first place." Alex softened the harsh words with a grin.

Garrett grunted. It was the closest he'd come to a smile in days. "You're a jerk."

"I know. And you're—"

"The dull crayon. Yeah, I get it, and you're not wrong."

"This is why we're friends. Because we've always been honest with each other. That is—was—until your monster of a stepsister ruined it all. Well, I contributed, so that makes me a fool, too. One more thing we have in common."

Garrett inhaled and blew out a long breath. Maybe it was time for him to hear the truth. "What happened?"

"If you really want me to, I'll tell you everything. I'll do my best not to make excuses and try to explain it away. No pulling punches, no sugarcoating, just the way we've always been with each other."

"Okay."

"Nikki and I slept together once. It was right after Cara and I broke up. As you know, I was heartbroken." This Garrett did know. Cara was the love of Alex's life. They'd been together two years, and when she left him, he'd been... Well, he'd pretty much been much like Garrett was now.

"I'd worked my last fourteen-hour shift at the refinery in Fairmont and then driven seven hours straight to get home. I was exhausted. Completely out of it. When I got home, I found a woman in my bed. At first, I thought it was Cara."

"Nikki was in your bed?"

"Yep. I climbed in and kind of freaked when I realized it was her. She woke up and started crying and told me she had nowhere else to go. That you and she had a fight, and you kicked her out."

"I never kicked her out!" Although, he was beginning to believe he should have, a long time ago.

"I know. I mean, I know that now. It seemed strange at the time, very out of character for you. But she was… She can be… Never mind—no editorializing. She is beautiful, sounded convincing, and I was weak. The next morning, we agreed it was a mistake and that we'd never tell you. But then, a few weeks later, she shows up at my house and tells me she's pregnant."

"You never doubted the baby was yours?"

"Sure. I used protection, but nothing is one hundred percent. I had doubts, but I didn't think she'd lie, not about something like this."

"But she did."

"Yes. By the time Remi was born, I was even more suspicious for a couple of reasons. She wouldn't let me go to her doctor's appointments. I wanted to go, but she always had weird excuses. Then, when Remi was born 'early' and weighed eight pounds, it was pretty obvious. I confronted her. She confessed but promised she didn't want anything from me except time. Time to figure out how to tell the father. According to her ex-friend Denise, the father is married and older. That's all I know."

"Why did you go along with it?"

"I didn't want to. She begged me to give her some time. I said no, but she went ballistic."

"But still, Alex…"

Wincing a little, Alex cocked his head to one side and said, "Garrett, you've never really seen her clearly. Remember that time in high school when all those kids got caught drinking on the bus? Nikki and two other girls denied it, but everyone said they were lying. You didn't even question her bogus story. And how about the time she said she was going on a college visit and ended up at that music festival? You only caught on when she called you because she ran out of money."

That incident had made him suspicious, so he'd tracked her phone. Didn't change the fact that he'd let her off the hook, writing it off as normal teenage rebellion.

"Do I need to go on?"

"No." Mistakenly, in wanting to give Nikki the life, the love, she'd missed out on, he'd spoiled her. Which probably wouldn't have been so bad if he hadn't so naively trusted her, too. The revelation hit him like a ton of bricks. He genuinely felt like a fool—for that story and for the one he'd just heard, and who knew how many others? Was this how Violet had felt? She'd trusted him, and he'd deceived her.

"Alex, I'm so sorry. I'm the jerk."

"You're lucky I still love you, buddy."

"I am. But I don't understand why she did it. Why did she choose you?"

"Desperation, I think. And opportunity. She knew you wouldn't rest until she gave you a name.

I think she regretted that after she saw what it did to us, or at least I want to believe that."

Garrett nodded. "You know where Violet is, don't you?"

"Maybe. I mean, I can find out. If I tell you, you have to promise me three things."

"Let's hear it."

"Okay... One, we are going to wipe the slate clean and never again allow *anyone* to come between our friendship. Two, you are never going to hurt Violet again."

"Done and done. What's the third one?"

"You won't invite her to compete in the cornhole tournament next year."

"NIKKI, I WANT Remi to take a DNA test." Garrett had arrived at his house, the house where Nikki and Remi were staying, late the evening before. After barely sleeping, he'd gotten up early so he could catch her before she left for school. He'd already unpacked and repacked his bag and had no intention of staying any longer than it took to have this conversation. He was going to find Violet.

"Absolutely not!" She looked affronted from where she sat on the sofa, coffee mug in hand.

"Why?"

"I will not subject my baby to an unnecessary and invasive test."

"There's nothing invasive about swabbing her

cheek. I know Alex isn't the father. He told me everything."

Nikki went pale and plopped the mug down on the end table beside her. "He had no right to do that!"

"He had every right. He should have done it sooner."

She quickly changed her tack. Tears sprang to her eyes. He'd admire her acting skills if the subject weren't so serious. "Garrett, wait until you hear what he did."

"Enough, Nikki. You will not say Alex is responsible for something when he isn't. He told me what you did. A simple test will reveal the truth. If you don't agree, we'll get a court order."

"Fine," she huffed. All trace of tears vanished in an instant. "But just so you know, I wouldn't have taken anything from him. That's why I refused your offer to help me get child support. I just needed more time to…" Changing course yet again, she pleaded with him, "Garrett, it doesn't matter who Remi's father is. She has you. The best uncle ever."

"No." He sighed and shook his head. "Yes, she does have me, but, Nikki, it's not the same, and you know it."

"It can be. You don't have to be related by blood to be family. That's what you always told me."

"And I still believe that. As angry as I am with you, you will always be my sister, and Remi is my niece. But, someday, hopefully, I'm going to have children of my own to support."

Those words cut deep. He'd been dreaming about having those kids with Violet, having a family. He'd never imagined any other woman as the mother of his children.

"Garrett, if this is about money, you know that I'm going to make good money once I'm a nurse."

"I'm not going to lie—it is partially about money. I have sacrificed a lot for you and for Remi. I'm not saying I regret it, but it's not fair for me to give up my own dreams in the process."

"So, you're kicking us out?"

"We'll circle back to that." How could she not see the issue here? "This is about way more than money. Whoever the father is, Nikki, he has a right to know. Remi has a right to know. You and me and Cade, of all people, know how much kids need both parents." It was possible they wouldn't be in this mess if Nikki had had a proper mother or a more responsible dad. "Besides, what happens when you find a man that you want to share your life with? What will you tell Remi then?"

"Fine," she said.

"Fine…?"

"Fine, I'll tell you who her dad is."

"Good. No more lies."

"I just want you to know that this is going to be *really* hard on me."

"Harder than it was on Alex?"

Nikki ignored the comment, and Garrett hoped he was finally getting through to her. "It's Jeffrey Hammond."

"Your friend Betsy's husband, Jeffrey?"

She nodded. "He's a nursing instructor."

"Oh, Nikki." This was worse than he'd imagined.

"How am I supposed to tell her? I'm going to have to switch schools because everyone is going to find out. I'll be a…a pariah."

"Does he know?"

"No. I mean, he probably suspects. But the fact he hasn't asked says a lot."

Garrett agreed. "Well, I suggest you start by telling him and seeing how he wants to handle it. The best thing would probably be to test Remi first to confirm."

"It's his. There's no doubt."

"How can there be no doubt?"

"I've already done the test."

More lies. He didn't even know what to say.

"Betsy is going to hate me."

"Undoubtedly. But Jeffrey is responsible, too. And it doesn't matter what the fallout is for either one of you—do you understand that? The only innocent people here are Remi and Betsy. And Alex, who you selfishly used. The damage you did to him and to our friendship is… I'm not even sure what the extent of that will be long-term."

Shockingly, Nikki remained silent. Once again, tears pooled in her eyes, but he refused to be moved.

"You owe Alex a huge apology."

"I know. Do you think he'll talk to me?"

"Probably not, but you need to say the words anyway. If he won't take your call, then write him a letter or an email, whatever it takes." He folded his arms.

"Are you going to marry that Violet woman?"

"If she'll have me."

"Why wouldn't she? Because of what I said?"

"No, Nikki. I mean, that didn't help, but I messed up, too. You're not the only one who makes mistakes. But when you make a mistake, the only thing you can do is apologize and try to make it right."

CHAPTER TWENTY

VIOLET EXTINGUISHED HER TORCHES, lowered onto the saddle and bent low over Cadence's neck to give her some encouraging words and a pat. Only then did she realize she had company. Garrett and Trent were standing behind the rail. Her heart seemed to stall in her chest. Only to ramp up, it seemed, so it could then beat extra hard.

She shouldn't have been surprised that they found her. And she supposed she wasn't. The part that shocked her was that they'd wanted to. Hadn't she suffered enough?

Unemployed, humiliated, displaced, living with her parents in temporary quarters? Still, she'd harbored a silent fear that Trent would sue her for...something. She felt terrible about the way she'd left. He had to be angry. He had a gazillion dollars and all the attorneys that money could buy who sat around and dreamed up reasons to sue. But she didn't live by fear anymore, did she?

No, she did not, as evidenced by her nearly flawless practice. Best to get this confrontation over with. Cadence, who always seemed to know exactly what she wanted at the exact instant she wanted it, proudly trotted over to them.

"Wow, Violet," Trent said with no small measure of reverence. "Garrett told me what you can do, but I think you have to see it for yourself."

"Thank you, Trent. It's a lot of fun. My hard work is paying off. And Garrett's, too," she added graciously—and truthfully, because she wouldn't be here if it weren't for him. She also wouldn't be heartbroken, she wanted to add, but why make things more awkward than they already were?

"No, Violet," Garrett said. "This is all you."

She smiled tightly.

Trent's smile felt warm and genuine. "It's wonderful to see you, Violet. Do you have a few minutes to talk?"

"Sure, of course. I just need to take Cadence back to the barn." Nervous tension tightened her entire body. Cadence executed a little side step, alerted to her stress. What could they possibly need to discuss with her? If he really were suing her, wouldn't she just receive a summons? She hadn't yet applied for any other jobs. Trent had to know that she'd never disclose any proprietary information.

"I'll do it," Flora offered, walking over to join them. "Great practice, Vi. Hello, Trent," she said, and then, in a tone that could be aptly described as ice-encrusted, "Garrett."

To his credit, Garrett ignored her disdain. "Flora, lovely to see you. You're looking well."

"You're not. You look like—"

"Mom, thank you so much," Violet interrupted on a dismount.

Flora entered the arena through the gate, took hold of Cadence's reins and walked with her and out the other side. Violet easily scaled the barrier and joined the men. She had to admit that her mom was right; Garrett didn't look great. Still handsome, but his face was thin and drawn, and the usual spark in his eyes had dimmed. He looked tired, she decided, like she felt.

She pointed to Flora's "office," a group of plastic chairs set off to one side. "We can sit over there."

Trent started off by saying, "Violet, what you did—"

"Trent, I'm so sorry. I know I ruined the party. I ruined..." *Everything*, she added silently.

"You didn't ruin a thing. You gave me exactly what I wanted. It was the party of the year. No one but us knew what happened. The only thing I didn't get was my announcement."

"I promise I did it for the right reasons."

"I know that, and, Violet, I'm the one who owes you a thank-you. Actually, I don't even know how to tell you how much I appreciate what you did. You ended my relationship with your mother at the expense of yourself. You did it to save me from making the biggest mistake of my life."

"Yes, I did." Trent deserved the truth, so she added, "I was also thinking about my parents."

"Of course, and that's admirable, too. The part I don't understand is why you quit your job."

"Didn't Garrett tell you what happened?"

"You mean, how he was watching out for me, too? Just like you were, like you've always done. I agree that using you to get information about your mother was not the smartest idea he's had, but you didn't put a foot wrong, unlike my dear nephew."

Garrett raised a hand. "Yeah, sitting right here, Uncle."

"I wouldn't say it if you weren't," he teased.

The bantering, the love between these two, reawakened the ache in her wounded soul. She missed Trent. She missed her job, Bailey, her co-workers, Penny Bottom Ranch. *Home.* The only place she'd ever found that had earned that distinction in her heart.

She didn't include Garrett because the man she fell in love with wasn't real. In fact, she needed them to get on with this, whatever *this* was, so she could get over all this "missing" and this heartache once and for all.

Trent went on, "The two people I love the most in the world love each other, and I'm the reason they're not together. How do you think that makes me feel?"

"He doesn't love me, Trent."

"Aha! So, you're saying you do love him despite his colossal mistake?"

"Again," Garrett said. "Still sitting here."

Heat flamed in her cheeks. "I…I thought I did. But it doesn't matter now."

"Well, the thing is, Violet, it does kind of matter. To me, anyway. And to Garrett, too, which is why he's here with me."

"I don't understand."

"I know, but you will. That night at the party, I wasn't going to propose to your mother."

"You weren't?" Confusion knitted her brow as it clouded her brain.

"No, ma'am. My announcement was all about the new ownership and management structure of McCoy Oilfield Services."

"I see."

Garrett must have decided to take over after all. That would be a good thing. It hurt her heart a little, though, because she knew it wasn't really what he wanted. "I… Um, wow. I'm sorry I spoiled that for you, too."

"I'm not." Trent grinned. "I'm here to make that announcement now. Violet, I want you to take over McCoy Oilfield Services."

"Excuse me?" Surely, she hadn't heard that right.

"Ultimately, I want to give McCoy Oilfield Services to you, Garrett and Cade. Garrett and Cade's shares will make up fifty-one percent, and yours will be forty-nine." He held up a hand as if to ward off any interruptions. Little did he know, Violet was in shock, rendered incapable of speaking, much less interrupting. "I know you're thinking that the boys will overrule you at every turn. But I don't believe that's the case. Despite my giving them a hard time, they're both levelheaded when it comes to business.

"Besides, you'll also have a board who has a say over certain aspects of the business, and I'll be involved, too, for a while. We'll go over all of that later with the attorneys. The important point is that you will be the CEO, so it's really your show to manage." He winked, letting Violet know he used the metaphor on purpose.

"And if I decline?" Because how could she possibly accept?

"If you decline, the company goes public."

"Then Garrett and Cade would get the cash?"

Trent smiled his approval at Garrett. "See how smart she is?"

"I'm aware," Garrett said, and this time he couldn't hold back a grin.

"No, they wouldn't. The money would go into a trust for a bunch of charities. For this deal to work, I'd like you to run the company for five years. If, after five years, you don't want to do it anymore, a new plan will be implemented."

"I don't… Why would you do this?"

"Because you love it as much as I do. You're the right person for the job. Violet, you help me run the place already. More than help—you're instrumental. You've only been gone a week, and I'm lost. The office staff is ready to mutiny. I'm afraid Rhea and Caleb are both going to quit. Even the oilfield employees are asking where you are."

She suspected he was being dramatic, but she couldn't help but smile.

"Violet, as you very well know, I don't have any kids of my own, but if I did, if I could handpick one, you'd be it. You are the child of my dreams. The one I want to follow in my footsteps."

"Um, she's the *child* of your dreams or the *daughter* of your dreams?"

Trent guffawed. "You heard me, nephew. Don't get your nose out of joint. You have your strengths, too. Like ranching and… Well, I'm sure there's other stuff," he joked. "Now, I'm going to visit with Flora and leave you two to discuss…" He gestured between them. "This." He pointed a finger at Garrett. "Don't mess this up."

"Thank you, Uncle, for that boost of confidence," Garrett answered dryly. "I'll do my best."

GARRETT HAD NEVER been so nervous in his life. Not even the night of the party, when he was about to propose, had put him at this level. He wanted Violet back so much that it was all he could think about. He couldn't sleep. He'd lost weight. He could barely function. If there was even a sliver of a chance, he had to try.

"Violet…" he said and then paused to just drink in the sight because what if this was the last time?

"Garrett?"

Nodding, he swallowed around the nervous knot in his throat. He inhaled a shaky breath and then released it. "You look beautiful."

"Thank you."

"I am so sorry that I hurt you."

Expression somber, her only response was one of her slow blinks.

"I am so sorry that I used you, that I ever thought getting close to you to investigate your mother would be okay. I didn't really grasp what I was doing until it didn't matter anymore."

"I don't know what that means. How could getting close to someone to find out about their mother's intentions *not* matter?"

"Because I fell in love with you. Violet, I think I was always *intrigued* by you. Uncle Trent once said that I was always talking to you." He chuckled. "Looking back, I can see that he was right. I did seek you out. It was sort of like a little kid poking a beehive."

"Oh, you just had to make a Buzzkill reference there, didn't you?"

Garrett was watching her, and the way her mouth curled at the corners gave him the tiniest slice of hope. At least maybe they could be friends.

He laughed. "See? That's… You challenge me. You make me think. No one I've ever dated or been attracted to has ever been a match for me in that way… You make me *feel* things I've never felt before.

"I admit that I agreed to live at Penny Bottom Ranch with you because I figured it would be a way to find out what Flora was up to with my uncle. Or at least that's what I told myself. I've thought about this a lot, and I'm not sure you'll believe me, but I would have said yes anyway. I wanted to be around you. I wanted to get to know you.

"I realize I don't deserve a second chance, but I want one. I want that more than I've ever wanted anything in my life. So, I guess, I'm asking for one. Violet, will you give me another chance?"

VIOLET'S HEART WAS beating like a drum inside her chest. Interesting how the cause was completely different now. Terrifying how desperately she wanted to believe him, how she had to bite her lip from blurting out a big fat yes!

Instead, she nodded and calmly replied, "I've given this situation a lot of thought, too, and there are some things I want to say."

He nodded.

"There's a part of me that likes what you did. I mean, if I take myself out of the equation, I can respect that you were trying to protect your uncle. The problem was that it made me feel less than."

"I know. I get that, but I never meant for that to be the case."

"I believe you."

"You do?"

"Yes. It's taken me a while to get here, but I can see now that my family issues, my Blackwell Belles insecurities, played a part. I've spent my life trying to prove myself *to myself.* It seems so simple now to just appreciate who I am and what I've accomplished. You know, to see those things. Why is it so difficult to see yourself clearly?"

"Everyone else appreciates who you are, Violet. Especially now that you've let them see you. No one is as smart and capable and skilled as you are. I know you think Uncle Trent was exaggerating about how missed you are at the office, but he's not. Logan came up to me the other day, just out of the blue, and told me what you did for him, how you got him a raise that he very much deserves. He was all choked up. Almost everyone has a story about you, and now that you're gone and the place is a mess, you've become a legend. You are more than missed. You are revered."

Violet felt tears gathering in her eyes.

"But you know what? I don't care about that."

"What?" Had she heard that right?

"I don't care what other people think or feel. Because *no one* could ever miss you more than I do. Violet. Your wit slays me, your thoughtfulness overwhelms me and your beauty mesmerizes me. You've shown me who I am, how much I can care about someone else. I am lost without you."

Wow. She took a few seconds to lean into his words, to allow the meaning to settle around her heart like a warm, soft blanket before looking at him and answering, "Okay."

"Okay? What does that mean?"

"You said you wanted a second chance. I'm saying okay."

"Really? Just like that?"

"Yes, just like that."

Garrett stood and reached out a hand. She took it, and he gave it a gentle tug, urging her to her feet. His gaze searched her face like he was waiting for her to change her mind.

He whispered, "Did I mention how much I love your generosity and your willingness to forgive?"

"No, but speaking of forgiveness, I don't think I can forgive your sister for what she did to Alex."

"You don't have to. I've taken care of that. Or at least I've called her out on her lies and deception. She's making it right, or as right as it can be."

"Yeah?"

"Yes. She's confessed everything. Remi's father is one of Nikki's professors at the university, a married professor. His wife is a friend—*was* a friend of hers. She's gotten herself into quite a jam, but for once, I'm not bailing her out. From now on, she'll be renting my house, and everything else will be spelled out in the future. No assumptions. No taking advantage."

That all sounded satisfactory. She had more questions, but she'd settle for that for now. "Where are you going to live?"

"I'm buying Penny Bottom Ranch."

"What? Wow. That's…"

"Expensive? Yes, I know. Even with the family discount."

She chuckled. "I was going to say 'amazing.'"

"Well, now, I'm hoping that my future wife will be the CEO of an oil company and help me run the ranch."

"Help you pay for it, you mean?" she teased.

"That, too."

"Speaking of…" Narrowing her gaze, she twirled a finger at him and said, "All of this better not be because you're trying to influence any decisions I make as future CEO of McCoy Oilfield Services."

Garrett smiled, and Violet saw the spark return in his eyes. "Uncle Trent is going to flip."

"I can't believe he's doing this. What if things don't work out between us?"

"Pfft. That's impossible. Even if they didn't work out between us, he's already admitted that you're the child he never had but always wanted."

"What if I'm a terrible CEO? Never mind—I'm going to be a brilliant CEO."

That made him laugh. "Yes, you are. Better than I would be."

"True. But you're an excellent cowboy and a highly skilled oilfield worker."

"Thank you."

"I've got an idea about another area where you might excel, something I might be willing to give you a shot at."

"I hope it's the same thing I've been thinking."

"Let's see…" Then she smiled and said, "Garrett."

At the exact same time that he said, "Violet."

And together, they asked, "Will you marry me?"

CHAPTER TWENTY-ONE

"HERE YOU ARE!" Violet threw open the doors of the small conference room where Garrett was conducting a meeting. She made a show of pushing her cart, loaded with a ridiculous amount of extra stuff that she didn't need, into the room. She hoped it all didn't topple over before she got through this. The place was packed with refinery workers, office staff and eight men and women who he believed were members of the new board of directors. They were all watching him with rapt attention. This stunt was starting off great, she thought.

Garrett looked at her, a quizzical expression on his face. "Hey, Violet. What's up?"

"Work!" she barked. And lied. "I need you to get started on these forms ASAP."

He frowned. "Okay, sure. But can it wait a few minutes?"

"No."

"I'm sorry?"

"No, it cannot wait." Plucking a random stack

of papers from the cart, she pointed and said, "Forms."

"I'm in the middle of an orientation meeting with some employees and our new board."

"I don't care what you're in the middle of, McCoy. This isn't one of your dog and pony shows." She almost cringed at that line. Alex had thrown it in, and it was funny when they were practicing, but now it felt like it could be over-the-top. She didn't want to tip him off too early. "In case you've forgotten, I am the COO of this organization, and I need these forms filled out. Now."

"Yeah, I get that. But I have people here who—"

She scoffed. "These people can wait. I can't. Let's roll," Violet said and then began stacking reams of paper in front of him, one after another. It was all she could do not to laugh at the look on his face. His expression was straight-up mortified, which was what she, Alex and Bailey had been going for. They'd spent a lot of time pulling this prank together.

Thankfully, he seemed so focused on the situation and the sheer amount of paper now piled in front of him that it didn't occur to him to question her further.

Garrett looked up and into the face of one of the "board members," who was actually Bailey's neighbor, Chris. Chris owned a doggy day care and grooming business.

"You heard your COO," Chris said with a straight

face and a future career on the stage. "Her word is gold around here. You'd best get on with it. We'll wait."

GARRETT GLANCED AT VIOLET, who was now busy on a tablet doing who knew what. He couldn't help but wonder what had gotten into her. It wasn't like her to throw her authority around, not like this. He wanted to ask if she was okay, but the expression on her face told him she meant business. What could possibly be so important to interrupt a meeting like this?

"Uh, well, if you will all excuse me for a minute or so, I guess I'll take a look here..."

He plucked the top sheet of paper from a stack next to him.

"Not that one," Violet snapped.

"What?"

She huffed an impatient breath. "Not *that* stack. The one closest to you."

"Oh-kay," he drawled and then followed her instructions. Several seconds passed as he tried to make sense of what he was seeing. *What the heck?*

When he looked up, she said, "Are you ready?"

"I thought you said I needed to fill out a form. This is a math test."

"Yes, I told you that we would be instituting new testing for oilfield workers. That's you."

"Times tables?"

"*Timed* times tables," she repeated, and that was when he realized that she was now holding another object in her hand.

"Is that a stopwatch?" he asked.

"Yes." Holding it aloft, thumb poised, she pressed the side, and it made a clicking sound as she said, "Go!"

There were only ten problems, and he finished quickly. When he looked up, the entire room seemed to be staring at him.

"How'd I do?"

"We'll see. Pick up the next paper," a now-smiling Violet ordered, albeit much more gently.

He did. This one said: *Who's laughing now, McCoy?*

From the other side of the table, Alex guffawed. One hand went up in a signal of surrender, and he said, "It's over. I blew it, Violet. I can't do it anymore." He tipped his head back and lost it.

Laughter broke out all around the room, and that was when Garrett realized he'd been had.

He groaned and shook his head. "Are you *kidding* me?"

Alex was now laughing uncontrollably so that he could barely get the words out. "Dude, she had you take a math test in front of the—" he paused to add air quotes around the word "—*board*, and you just... You did it."

Logan chimed in, "And then he asked how he did?"

More laughs all around.

Garrett looked around the table. "None of you are new board members, are you?"

Chris lifted a hand. "Bailey's neighbor."

"Bartender at Seventy-Six Pub," the man beside him said.

"I'm Rhea's cousin," an older woman offered from the other side of the table. "We've met, and I was afraid you might recognize me."

And on it went, all around the table.

He totally deserved this. He'd spent the preceding days making jokes, pulling out every *antic* in his repertoire, trying to make Violet laugh at work. She'd remained resolute.

Garrett looked over at Violet, who was also laughing too hard to speak. Head shaking, she shrugged and made a garbled attempt at an apology. "I'm…s…ss…sorry." She pointed at Alex. "It was his idea. You know how I've been on pins and needles trying not to laugh at your jokes and stories here at work. Alex had this idea of putting it back on you and just getting it over with, and I…" Composing her features, she lifted the math test and spoke in an overly serious tone. "You got a hundred percent on your test, if that helps at all?"

A mixture of love and admiration had his heart clenching tightly in his chest. The ordeal was worth every embarrassing second because his beautiful fiancée was not just laughing. She was laughing at work.

"You." He pointed a finger at Alex. "You know what my paybacks are like."

"Bring it," Alex said, still chuckling. "It's difficult to be afraid of you right now. You get that, right?"

"And you." He spun his chair so that he was facing Violet. He tried glaring at her, but he couldn't keep it up. Finally, he sprang from his seat, rushed toward her and wrapped her in a tight hug. Chuckling, he whispered, "Well played, Blackwell. Well played."

"So," GARRETT SAID the next Saturday, shifting in the saddle to look at her. "Before we get there, I need to tell you something."

"Yeah?" Violet was riding Cadence, and Garrett was on Henna, and they were headed to the creek for a swim. She'd been looking forward to it all week, but stuff kept getting in the way.

"With all the mega-gifting that's gone on, what with you getting a horse, us getting a company, buying this ranch, I'm afraid my gift isn't going to measure up."

"You got me a gift?"

"I did. Well, I built you something. Had it built, technically, but now that I'm about to show you what it is, I'm all nervous and second-guessing myself."

"Garrett McCoy nervous? That is not a thing."

He laughed. "It is absolutely a thing. The first time I kissed you, I was shaking."

"Huh." She smiled.

"You think that's funny."

"A little because I was worried that you'd notice how nervous I was and be like, this fine woman is an inexperienced dork. I no longer care for her and will discard her forthwith."

"Forthwith?"

"Aye. Be off with you, fair maiden, for I now go to make merriment and mirth with my oilfield brethren. But first, I will purchase expensive tarts for all, near and yonder!"

He laughed. "Chattering to myself in this fourteenth-century lexicon is something you think *I* revert to when I'm feeling nervous?"

"Apparently."

"It's official. You are a dork. But a totally lovable one."

"It's time you learned the truth," she joked. "I can't hide it any longer."

"Lucky for you, I love you anyway. Bonus— I'm no longer worried about my corny gift."

"Good. I love you, too. And just the fact that you went to the trouble of having something *built* for me has me feeling all melty inside."

He went uncharacteristically quiet as they approached the creek. She immediately spotted the tall wooden structure on the far side of the swimming hole. It was shaped like an upside-down L, and the crisscrossing planks reminded her of a bridge or a railroad trestle. Was it a diving board? No, it seemed too tall, and there was no place to stand. And wait… There was a cable or something strung from the end of the L to the base of the tower.

"Is that a *rope*?"

"Yep."

"You're not going to hang me, are you? For my bad jokes?"

"Violet!"

She chuckled. "Well, I don't know!"

"Yes, you do."

It dawned on her then, and she gasped. "I do! I do know. It's a swing. Garrett, you built me a swing? This is why you've kept me away from here."

"I did. And it is. I actually built the swing part myself." The way he was smiling at her made her melted insides turn molten. She reined Cadence close to Henna and then stood in the saddle.

"Are you ready?" she said, climbing so that she was standing on Cadence's back. "I'm heading your way."

He held out his arms. In one smooth motion, she spun and dropped onto the saddle in front of him. He cradled her as she wrapped her arms around his neck.

"That was a swoon," she joked. "Swooning has made a comeback in popular culture these days."

"I like it," he commented dryly. "Right in keeping with my medieval thing."

"I think Big E and Flora would approve of that type of dramatic gesture, don't you?"

"One million percent." He squeezed her a little tighter. "Especially with how you incorporated it into a ride. Can't believe how far you've come."

Once she'd gotten a handle on her fear, it really had all come back to her and then some. Every day, she seemed to get braver, and she and Flora's juggling act was as close to perfect as it was going to get. Sheer stubbornness prevented her from admitting that Flora might be right; she might need to perform the trick before she was truly satisfied. The stubbornness was crumbling in the face of her longing.

"Garrett," she whispered into his neck. "Thank you for the swing. I am…speechless. I have no words. No, that's not true. I have so many words and feels that I don't know where to start." Tears gathered in her eyes. "The way you love me, it's… I never even imagined how it would feel to be loved like this."

He held her. Emotion swirled between them. "Me either," he finally said, and Violet felt the truth of his words. Then he whispered, "You want to try it out?"

"Heck, yeah." She dismounted easily and headed

for the pool house. They'd been keeping swimming gear and towels there for these regular jaunts. She changed quickly and discovered that Garrett had been even quicker. He waited outside on the deck.

"You go first," he said. "There's a pocket on the stand. The rope is tucked into it."

"Okay!"

Once she got around to the base, she freed the rope and discovered a slat of thick plastic had been secured as a seat near the bottom, and a solid knot was tied several feet up from there. You could sit and swing or hold on to the knot and just drop into the water. Brilliant.

She was trying to decide which option to choose when a piece of twine looped around the upper knot caught her eye. Reaching up, she discovered a small pouch hanging from the rope. Loosening the knot, she freed the bundle and heard Garrett moving behind her.

"What is this?" she asked, her pulse now mimicking a runaway horse.

"Open it."

She did. It was a ring: gold, simple, with a single pear-shaped diamond. Perfect. "Garrett."

"This is the ring I was going to give you on the night of the party."

"I didn't know you bought a ring. It's beautiful."

"Of course I bought a ring. I couldn't ask you to marry me without a ring."

She gave him a dreamy smile. "It's nice that we asked each other, I think."

"I agree. Violet, I've never met anyone like you. Every day, I wake up, and I can't believe you like me. I am so very grateful that you do." He took the ring from her palm and slipped it on her finger.

She smiled. "That's not all that surprising, seeing as how I *didn't* like you for about three years."

With a confident grin, he said, "Yes, you did." He gave her a quick kiss. "Pretty sure you liked me a little, Buzzkill."

"Maybe. A very little," she conceded and then kissed him. "But I like you so much better now that you're not so unpleasant, McCoy."

EPILOGUE

"I'LL DO IT," Violet announced the next morning to an audience of two. Three if you counted Zinni. Flora and Big E both looked at her expectantly from their comfy chairs on the porch at Penny Bottom Ranch, where they were sipping tall glasses of sweet tea. She felt good about the words.

"You will?" Flora said. "I assume you're talking about the Belle reunion performance."

"Yes, but I have conditions."

With a dramatic sigh, Flora glanced out toward the horizon. "Not you, too." Then she looked at Big E. "Why don't my children want to perform for my sake, to pay homage to the childhood they were lucky enough to have, or simply for the glorious sake of performing? Why all the drama?"

Violet rolled her eyes.

Big E winked at her and said, "We're all wired a little differently, aren't we? I didn't understand why my grandsons didn't want to save their ranch just for the sake of their heritage and posterity."

"Maybe because posterity doesn't pay today's bills?" Violet quipped.

"Oh, listen to little Miss CEO over here." Flora pitched a finger in her direction, but Violet could hear the pride in her tone.

"Not CEO quite yet, Mom, but soon." Her official title was COO, and she was loving training under Trent. She already dreaded his leaving, and because he hadn't decided when that would be, she hoped they had a long time piloting the McCoy Oilfield Services ship together.

"Hey, if Maggie wants Ferdinand, she can have him. She and I will work out the custody arrangement. But if I'm going to perform in the show, I want to ride with my saddle."

"The one that Aunt Dandelion gave you, the one that Iris has."

"Yes."

Flora looked grim but said, "I can understand that."

Violet had thought her mother would argue, and she was prepared to lay out her case. Iris had built her RV remodeling business around that saddle. Not that she used it, per se, but it was a part of her professional identity. Violet felt bad asking for it, but she felt worse without it. She needed to close this circle.

"You can?" she asked.

"Of course," her mom replied.

"Will you do the trick with me?"

"I'd be honored." The training had been good for Flora, too. Violet enjoyed watching her mom's strength and agility return. The twinkle in her eyes seemed to be gaining brightness, too.

"I didn't believe you when you said I wouldn't totally get over this until I performed again. I thought you meant my fear, but you meant something more, didn't you?"

"I did. You can never really know that you've perfected a stunt without an audience."

"I get that now, and I'm not afraid to do it. I *want* to do it. I just need to do it with my saddle. For so long, that saddle felt like a symbol of my failure, but now... Now it feels like redemption."

Big E chimed in, "Well said, kiddo." Then he looked at Flora and slapped his palms on his knees. "You ready to head out?"

"Sure thing." Flora set Zinni on the porch and stood. "You know, I can't believe I'm going to say this, but that RV is kinda growing on me. What do you say, Zinni? You want to go for a ride?" Zinni trotted from her to Big E and back again, making a weird huffing sound like a tiny gorilla.

"You're leaving now? Where are you going?" Violet asked.

Big E wrapped an arm around her shoulders. "To visit your sister Iris. We're going to go get you a saddle."

FROM THE PASSENGER SEAT, Flora stared at Big E. He could feel her gaze on him and imagined the wheels in her mind spinning along in time with the RV's.

He let a long moment pass before glancing in her direction. "Flora, I can see there's something you want to say, so go ahead and spit it out."

"You have a plan about how we're going to convince Iris to hand over her saddle? The saddle that inspired the name of her business, Saddle-Up? The saddle that means more to her than…probably anything on this earth other than Cosmo."

Big E had learned from tracking Iris's social media that Cosmo was her dog, a fine specimen of a border collie. Smart, well-behaved, and quite a ham for the camera. He was a nice addition to her marketing efforts.

"The apple didn't fall far from the tree there, did it?" He added a chuckle in an attempt to lighten her mood.

It didn't work.

"I don't know," Flora said and shrugged. Zinni, who'd been napping on her lap, lifted her head as if to join the conversation. "Unfortunately, I don't know much about my daughter Iris."

"What?" At the age of eighty-six, there wasn't much that surprised Big E. This flash of vulnerability from Flora caught him off guard.

"She's… It's interesting because, as a child, Iris was probably the easiest. She'd do anything I asked. Unlike some of her sisters, she rarely argued about what trick to do or which outfit to wear or even when she had to practice. But after the Belles' breakup, she was…different."

"Different how?"

"Rebellious? Stubborn?" she offered, thinking out loud. "I don't know. She barely speaks to me. She's civil but guarded."

"I see," Big E said, reading between the lines and drawing on the history he'd already learned: Flora had taken Iris for granted. Although he certainly wasn't going to say that. She needed to reach that conclusion herself, which might be a tad more difficult than her issues with Maggie and Violet. Admitting this maternal shortcoming to Iris would be a challenge. That stubborn trait she'd mentioned seemed to have been passed on to several of her girls.

"There is *no way* she's going to give up that saddle."

"We'll see," he answered.

"What do you have up your sleeve?"

"Don't underestimate the power of family," he said and winked at her.

"I don't know about that," she returned dryly. "It seems as if I've spent the last decade over-estimating the love a daughter has for her mother. I was one for five for many years, and only that thanks to Violet's giant heart, which she inherited from her father."

Big E chuckled. "No one ever said parenting was easy."

Pushing her chin forward, she squinted out the windshield, then craned her neck to read a passing road sign. "Where are we going?"

"Piston Hills, Texas."

Despite her traveling so much, it hadn't been difficult to pinpoint Iris's current location. She posted the progress of every RV restoration job on her social media. For weeks now, Big E had been following right along. Pride didn't even begin to describe what he felt for his great-niece. The woman had inherited her Grandmother Denny's business sense, his spatial ability and her mother's knack for performing. That last observation was not something he intended to share with Iris. At least not initially. It was a conclusion he planned to help his great-niece realize in a sort of more natural evolution.

He was looking forward to getting to know her in the process.

"That's what I thought. You missed the turn-off."

"We're picking up Denny at the airport."

"Of course we are," Flora stated flatly. "That's a good idea, actually. Maybe her grandmother has some ideas about how to convince Iris to part with her most prized possession."

"Stop fretting about the saddle. I have it handled."

Two sisters in, and Big E knew how this branch of the family operated, even if they couldn't see the complicated dynamics themselves. All he had to do was figure out what Iris wanted *more* than the saddle. And despite Flora's claim, Big E was confident that such a thing existed.

"You just concentrate on mending the fence separating you and your daughter. I'll take care of the rest."

* * * * *

Don't miss the next installment
of The Blackwell Belles,
A Cowgirl on His Doorstep,
coming next month from
author Anna J. Stewart and
Harlequin Heartwarming
at www.Harlequin.com!